The
Delusionist

The Delusionist

DON CALAME

CANDLEWICK PRESS

Copyright © 2021 by Don Calame

First edition 2021

Library of Congress Catalog Card Number pending
ISBN 978-0-7636-9689-4

21 22 23 24 25 26 LBM 10 9 8 7 6 5 4 3 2 1

Printed in Melrose Park, IL, USA

This book was typeset in Minion.

Candlewick Press
99 Dover Street
Somerville, Massachusetts 02144

www.candlewick.com

MIX
From responsible
sources
FSC® C103098

To my brother, Robert, who sawed me in
half, made me levitate, and showed me how
to perform my very first magic trick.

and

To Kaylan, my magician of an editor, who has performed
some very *real* magic on my manuscripts over all these
years. Your pen is mightier than a wand. Thank you!

1

"LADIES AND GENTLEMEN! BOYS AND GIRLS!" PERRY strides onstage, beaming like a game show host, his arms wide, as though he's embracing the entire school auditorium. Which he would, if he could. He's that kind of guy. "Welcome to the wonderful world of mystery and magic."

I scuttle after Perry, trying not to trip on the electrical cords that lead to the gleaming silver-and-black drill press looming at center stage. I take my place beside a long table where Perry has set our duffel bag full of props.

"I am Perry Larsson." Perry gestures to himself. "*This*"—he thrusts a palm out toward me—"is my silent partner in illusion, Quinn Purcell. And together we are *Quinn and Perry*."

The theater erupts in applause. We have become a talent show favorite here at Fernwood High. It's the only reason I'm not completely invisible when I walk down the halls.

Well, that and the fact that I'm usually walking with Perry.

I can't pinpoint the exact moment it happened, but somewhere around twelve Perry became ridiculously handsome, spellbindingly charming, and—maybe most unbearable of all—impossibly good at anything he does. It doesn't seem fair that someone could just wake up and suddenly be amazing at everything—sports, theater, music, girls, poker, video games, dancing, beatboxing, finger whistling—but that's what happened to my best friend.

One day we're both just a couple of bean-thin dorks with greasy hair, squeaking voices, and uncontrollable wangs, and the next day I'm still that very same scrawny dork but now, somehow, Perry is four inches taller and the proud owner of a voice as deep as the ocean, flowing blond locks straight out of a comic book, dimples that seem to have increased in adorableness, eyes that somehow have become an even more bottomless blue, and an unnatural ease in the world that makes everyone want to be around him.

I will give him credit, though. Perry has never forgotten where he came from. He still loves sci-fi, continues to belong to the Video Game Club, and has remained a dedicated magician. Perhaps most inconceivable of all, no matter how many popular-people parties he gets invited to, no matter how many cheerleaders he dates or how many winning touchdowns he scores, Perry continues to be best friends with me.

I would like to think I'd have done the same if the roles were reversed. But I can't say for sure. I'm weak-willed. So he has that over me as well.

Onstage, I shift a bit so that I'm not *literally* standing in Perry's shadow—the symbolism a little too on the nose—and give a quick bow, grateful I don't have to speak. We've tried the act where Perry and I dialogue a bit. Bantering back and forth. But once you've heard Perry's smooth radio baritone, my reedy sneaker screech is like a dark pube poking from a pillowy mound of whipped cream.

"Tonight, my friends," Perry says, conspiratorially whispering to a crowd of four hundred, "*tonight* you are going to witness a true Quinn and Perry original. Something we have never attempted before in front of a live audience."

Perry sweeps around the stage like we're the headliner and not just one of two dozen acts performing in tonight's talent show. He lets the thunderous ovation continue longer than he has to.

"Now, if you've been to previous shows," Perry says, pacing the stage like a rock star, "you've seen us read minds, summon the dead, make billiard balls float in the air, and change the paint color on a bicycle right before your eyes." He stops center stage, directly in front of the drill press, and addresses the audience with laser-focused seriousness. "But this evening is different. This evening has an air of danger about it. *Real* danger that could result in *real* death."

I clear my throat, standing stock-still, trying to keep my heart from leaping out of my chest. Normally I can rein in my nerves. Get through a performance without passing out or, you know, throwing up all over myself.

But Perry's not kidding. This act *is* very much a life-and-death situation.

My life.

Or my death.

"You see behind me an industrial-strength drill press," Perry says, stepping aside and pointing at the menacing machine. "Many of you may have used a similar one in shop class to drill holes in wood, plastic, even steel. This one happens to be my father's. A Delta 18-900L, eighteen-inch laser drill press. Fully functioning. Nothing has been tinkered with in any way. My father can attest to this. In fact, he would kill me if I tampered with it at all."

"I wouldn't kill you," Perry's dad hollers from somewhere at the back of the theater. "I would stop *just* short of that."

This gets a nice big laugh from the crowd. Because, you know, child abuse.

"Always the jokester," Perry says. "For more of my father's humorous take on life, or if you'd just like to see some of the lovely homemade pine hallway tables he has for sale, you can check him out @realrockylarsson on Twitter and rockylarssonwoodworks on Instagram."

The crowd hoots and applauds.

"So, my father has confirmed that I haven't tampered with his drill." Perry taps his lip. "But then, why would you trust someone I'd so shamelessly give a plug to? No. I think we need an impartial volunteer from the audience to come up here and run this powerful press through its paces. Just to be certain."

Instantly three-quarters of the hands in the audience shoot for the ceiling, everyone calling out to be chosen. If this were anyone other than Perry asking—*me*, for instance—all you'd get would be crickets and violently averted gazes.

"Can we have the lights turned up, please?" Perry asks.

A second later the auditorium is illuminated. Hundreds of faces staring up at us. Mom and Dad are out there somewhere. Probably oversharing and handing out business cards to their seat neighbors.

I drop my gaze to the stage. Having all those eyes on me makes me feel like I'm in front of a firing squad. A trickle of sweat dribbles down my left side and I have to suppress a shiver. I'm wondering now if we should have scaled this effect back a little.

"Hmm." Perry strokes his chin, carefully considering all of his choices. "Such a fine-looking crowd we have here tonight. Let's see. OK." He points to one of the middle rows. "How about the lovely lady right there?"

I glance out to see that he's pointing at his ex-girlfriend Gwen Wilson, who's excitedly wiggling her long, manicured fingers in the air like she's reaching for a ripe apple that's just out of reach. Gwen is that rare breed of beautiful girl who will actually acknowledge you outside of school. Everything about her—her smile, her big heart, her bouncy auburn hair, her sense of humor, her sunbeam eyelashes, her ridiculously sexy English accent—is an all-encompassing glow of happiness.

Why Perry ever let her go continues to be a mind boggler. I mean, sure, they're both young and have their whole lives ahead of them, but still, if you think that you've found your absolute perfect match at sixteen and *it's Gwen Wilson*, you don't throw it away because you're worried it's bad timing. You make it work.

Clearly I haven't gotten over their breakup yet. And listening to Perry talk about her all the time, neither has he.

"Give it up for Gwen Wilson, everyone." Perry applauds, and the entire audience follows suit. "A more perceptive, beautiful, fair-minded person you will never find."

Gwen hoists herself up as her current boyfriend, the very jacked

Carter Burns, blinks uncomfortably from the seat beside her. You've gotta feel bad for the guy. I mean, it's hard enough being best friends with the most handsome and charming guy on the planet. I can't imagine what it's like to follow him in the romance department. How do you not drive yourself insane with comparisons?

Particularly since Gwen and Perry have remained such good friends.

As Perry seems to have managed with every one of his exes.

Gwen bounds up the stairs to the stage, stumbling on the top step and catching herself before she does a face-plant in front of the whole school. She starts to laugh, which makes her snort, causing her to laugh even more.

"Nearly went arse over tit there," she says in her intoxicating British lilt. If Gwen were a telemarketer selling the air I already breathe, I would be a repeat customer. "Now we know why I quit ballet."

Gwen shoots me a smile and a mini wave as she passes. I smile back as I am engulfed in the trailing scent of her perfume. It's a mix of melons and grapefruit and flowers, and it's so heady that it nearly knocks me over. Gwen is so far out of my league that we might as well be different species. The fact that Perry—the kid who once helped me put on a Star Wars sock puppet show complete with Pixy Stix light sabers—actually kissed her makes me want to jam a fence picket into my skull.

But also, you know, I'm happy for him, too.

"Thank you for helping us out," Perry says, giving her a grateful head bow as she approaches.

"My pleasure," Gwen says. "Are you going to make me levitate like you did with Vivian at the Fall Frenzy?"

"Sorry, no soaring above the stage this evening, I'm afraid." Perry gestures at the towering power tool beside them. "Instead, we're just doing some ordinary, garden-variety skull drilling."

Gwen grimaces. "Not mine, I hope."

"No, no, no," Perry says. "Risk the life of one of our volunteers? I wouldn't dream of it. I just need your assistance in operating the machinery."

Gwen turns and looks at me, real concern shadowing her eyes. "Don't let him make you do anything you don't want to. You have a choice."

This is very sweet. I can imagine Gwen giving this same speech to her younger sister before the prom.

It's so much worse when beautiful people are also decent human beings. It makes it harder to muster the hate necessary to feel better about yourself.

I give Gwen a thumbs-up so she knows I'm fully on board with what's about to happen here.

Even though I'm a little less on board than I was yesterday.

"All right." Perry claps his hands together and glances around. "First, we're going to need something to use for a practice run." He takes hold of both of Gwen's hands, flipping them over and back again. "Do you happen to have anything made of steel with you? Perhaps a quarter-inch-thick disk?"

Gwen laughs. "Not that I'm aware of."

"OK, well, then do me a favor." Perry cups Gwen's hands together and holds them tight. "Let's try to have you manifest one. Do you think you can do that?"

I glance out to the audience and see the expression of anguish on Carter's face. I can almost hear his internal monologue. *Why is he touching her? Why is she blushing? Are his hands warmer than mine? Stronger? Less sweaty?*

Yes, Carter. Yes, they are.

Gwen laughs and shrugs. "I can try. What do I do?"

"It's simple," Perry says, shaking her clasped hands up and down. "You just need to concentrate. Think, *Steel disk. Steel disk. Steel disk.*" Perry gives one last, exaggerated shake, then releases Gwen's hands with a flourish and steps back. "Please show the audience what you've manifested."

Gwen slowly uncups her hands like she's cradling a baby bird, revealing a shiny, quarter-inch-thick steel disk lying in her palm. The crowd oohs and aahs as Gwen grabs the disk and holds it out, laughing giddily, like she really did just perform something miraculous. "Brilliant! A talent I did not know I possessed."

"Yes, well, I wouldn't try it at home." Perry plucks the disk from Gwen and shows it to the chuckling audience. "Solid, quarter-inch steel." He attempts to bend it, then places the piece of metal on the drill press table. "Now, if you would kindly slide these on." Perry materializes a pair of safety goggles out of thin air and gives them to Gwen.

She smiles and pulls on the lab goggles. Somehow—against all the laws of nature—they make her look even hotter.

"Excellent," Perry says. "Please place your hand on this handle here." He indicates the feed lever that lowers the drill.

Gwen steps forward and grabs hold of one of the spokes.

Perry turns to the audience. "You will now witness the sheer power of this professional, industrial-grade drill." He moves to the back of the machine and flicks a switch, and the machine hums to life. It's surprisingly quiet for a power tool. Which is why we've attached a microphone to the base to make it sound more menacing.

"OK, Gwen." Perry nods. "Give that bad boy a spin."

Gwen turns the feed lever, slowly lowering the drill. There's a high-pitched grinding sound as metal chews into metal, the bit boring a hole through the steel disk like it was made of cheese.

Gwen raises the handle and Perry shuts off the machine. He snatches up the steel disk and holds it out for everyone to see.

"Look at that," Perry says, peering through the hole. "Clear through. So then, if this drill can effortlessly carve a hole in a piece of quarter-inch steel"—he taps the disk—"imagine what kind of damage it could do to my partner's skull here." He points to me. Then he waggles his eyebrows and grins. "What do you say we go ahead and find out?"

Huge whoops of encouragement and raucous applause come from the audience.

Which, I have to say, doesn't do a lot for my self-esteem.

Not to mention my rapidly fraying nerves.

2

THE ONLY REASON PRINCIPAL RIDDALL IS LETTING US DO this "life-threatening" trick is that we diagrammed it out for her. Explained the whole thing: How it was just going to *look* like my head was being strapped to the worktable. How there was no way I could actually get hurt. How I was going to be well clear of the drill press before the drill came down.

Which, of course, were all colossal lies.

Truth be told, if we didn't get the timing and spacing exactly right, I would not live to see my seventeenth birthday. Which would be disappointing, to say the least. You know, still having never kissed an actual girl and all.

We practiced doing the trick the way we described it to Principal Riddall, but it ended up looking silly. We also tried using various false heads—a piñata, a pillow, a pumpkin—but it was never as convincing as when my real noggin was, in fact, strapped down to the drill press table.

Exactly how it is right now. My neck is clamped to the platform, my body is bound with rope, my hands are cuffed behind my back, and my ankles are shackled with leg irons. I've been completely sealed inside a laundry bag and have been rendered sightless by the four-inch-thick papier-mâché mask that's meant to be a barrier between my face and the drill bit.

I release the deep breath I've been holding for the last minute and feel the ropes that Gwen wrapped around my arms and thighs loosen and slide down my body, spilling around my feet.

"And now," Perry says, his voice filtering through the laundry sack, "the time has come for the final chapter in our little tale." I hear him flick a switch, listen to the drill motor whirring to life. I can feel a gentle purring vibration through my left cheek, like a dozen happy cats getting belly rubs.

"He's going to get out, though, right?" Gwen asks, a worried crack in her voice.

Perry laughs. "Of course he will. We're practiced magicians here. It's all an illusion. To tell you the truth, Quinn's pretty much out of the ropes and shackles already."

This is a very stupid thing we're doing. Perry tried to talk me out of it a half dozen times, but I assured him nothing could possibly go wrong.

Even though both of us know this isn't *exactly* true.

Four inches of paper and glue might seem like a nice-size shield, keeping my face a safe distance from the drill, but it really isn't. Not when you're dealing with a half-inch carbon-steel bit spinning at three thousand revolutions per minute and only the tiniest margin of error when it comes to the placement of my head.

But it's a Hail Mary pass. The Drill of Death is our last chance to get noticed by the Magic Society of America. If we don't receive an invitation to audition for their Masters of Magic Fantasy Camp after we submit our third—*and final*—tryout video, we are done. *Forever.* The camp—which has produced the likes of Richie Ronzo, Sakkaku, and Luna Moon—is for sixteen-year-old magicians only. "The perfect age to begin your apprenticeship," according to the camp's website. Which means that next year Perry and I will have aged out.

"I'm going to ask you to put on this blindfold," I hear Perry say to Gwen as I surreptitiously pigeon my feet to release the ankle shackles. "And these noise-canceling headphones. The blindfold is so you can't see the damage you're doing to Quinn's skull, and the headphones are so you can't hear his tortured screams."

The audience laughs.

Gwen doesn't.

"I can't really hurt him, though," Gwen says. "Even if I pull the lever. *Correct?*"

I twist to the side and wiggle my fingers behind my back, reaching toward the belt loop with the hidden handcuff key clipped to it. The handcuffs are a little too tight and the bracelets dig into my wrists.

"I suppose that depends on what you mean by *hurt*," Perry replies.

"As in *murder* him," Gwen says. "By drilling a hole in his head."

"Oh." Perry clears his throat. "Then yes. You could kill him. *Potentially.* But we're going to do everything we can to make sure that doesn't happen."

More chuckles from the audience.

"I don't know if I trust you," Gwen says.

Perry gasps. "*Gwen Wilson!* That really hurts. It does. I thought we were friends. If you can't trust your friends, who can you trust?"

Gwen exhales. "All right. But if I kill him, I will never forgive you."

Perry laughs. "Deal. Now—blindfold and headphones, please."

My fingers fumble at the belt loop, but the tiny key clip is caught on a thread or something. I give the metal clasp a tug. Then another. Finally I yank hard, snapping the thread and freeing the little handcuff key. Thank God. I don't know what the hell I'd do if I couldn't get the—

Oh, shit. I frantically pinch my fingertips together, then scrabble at my palms, the backs of my hands. Like the miniature key is just stuck to my skin and hasn't vanished altogether. Hasn't fallen to the bottom of the laundry bag, lost forever in a thick pile of flaccid ropes and gingham.

"When I tap your shoulder," I hear Perry say over the thumping of my heart, "you count to ten and then lower that drill. Do not stop for any reason. I will take full responsibility for whatever happens."

I have to shut this thing down. If I can't get the cuffs off, I can't trigger the neck clamp release, which means I am not getting out of this laundry sack. And if Perry was even an inch off when he strapped my head down—

"*Mmmmm!*" I groan through the mask. "*Mmm mm mmm-mmm!*"

"All righty, then. Here we go!" Perry bellows to the howls of the audience. "Why don't you all count along with Gwen? Starting . . . now!"

"*Mmm! Mmm! Mmm!*"

"One! Two! Three!" The audience counts in unison.

"*MMMM!*"

But my screams are muffled by the mask and the sack, and drowned out by the mic'd-up drill.

I shift and wriggle, summoning every ounce of strength I possess, trying to get my hands in front of me, but there's not enough room in this laundry sack to thread my legs back through my arms.

Supposedly Houdini was able to dislocate his shoulder in order to help with his escapes. That skill would come in very handy right about now.

"Four! Five! Six!"

This is bad. This is so bad. "*Mmmmmmm!*"

I try *one . . . last . . . contortion . . .* until . . . my body sags in exhaustion. I give up. It doesn't matter anymore, anyway. If I can't escape, then we are *not* getting invited to audition for the fantasy camp and so what's even the point of living?

"Seven! Eight! Nine!"

There is a collective scream as I hear the whir of the drill getting closer to my ear, feel the heat of it approaching.

"Ten!"

"*Omigod, don't do it!*" some lady shrieks from the crowd.

The audience is apoplectic. Shouting, screaming, crying.

But there's no stopping it now.

The Drill of Death is coming.

3

THIS IS WHAT THE AUDIENCE SEES: THE DRILL ENTERING
my head; a big bloom of red blood splattering the laundry bag, then
spilling in a crimson stream onto the stage; Perry freaking out and
screaming for the curtains to be drawn.

I know this because it's what we want them to see. It's what we
rehearsed. What we filmed on our phones over and over.

I can hear the pounding of feet as parents and teachers storm
the stage. We expected this. Hoped for it, really, because it adds to
the verisimilitude.

I have no clue what Mom and Dad are thinking at this moment,
having just witnessed their son being trepanned onstage. I told
them they might not want to come to this particular show because
it could upset them, but they insisted. They never miss a school performance, being theater nerds themselves.

Plus, "it's a twofer," my dad always says. A chance to see me
perform *and* an opportunity to chat up dozens of potential home
buyers. According to this logic, everything my parents do must be
"a twofer" because wherever they go, they end up handing out either

business cards or flyers for their latest musical spectacular at the Sage Hollow Dinner Theater. Sometimes both.

"Someone call an ambulance!" "Jesus Christ!" "How did this happen?" The shouts and cries come from every direction.

If I'd had more time—if I could have gotten out of the handcuffs without having to tear off several layers of skin—I'd have triggered the neck shackle release sooner, slipped out of the secret compartment in the laundry bag, and would now be bolting backstage, out into the hall, and up to the entrance of the auditorium, where I'd magically appear, unscathed.

But my timing was off, *obviously*, and I've barely managed to rip the handcuffs from my wrists, free myself from the neck clamp, and crawl out of the "blood"-stained laundry sack when Principal Riddall appears, her cell phone mashed to her ear, presumably calling 911.

"It's OK. It's OK," Perry whisper-shouts, waving her off. "It's part of the trick. Hang up, hang up. He's fine. See?"

I wince as Principal Riddall approaches. People often liken her to Michelle Obama, always smiling and waving at everyone. They wouldn't make that mistake today. She is neither smiling nor waving. In fact, Principal Riddall looks like she might hurl. Or tear us a new one. Possibly both.

My chest tightens, and there's an ache in the back of my throat.

"Stay back!" Mr. Zuzzolo, the school's twig-thin custodian, dashes onstage, brandishing his janitorial toolbox like it's Thor's hammer. "Give him some air—*Jesus-what-the*—" He reels back upon seeing me, skidding to a halt, his long, straggly hair whipping around his face like a greasy mop. "Oh, thank the fuck." Mr. Zuzzolo exhales, dropping his toolbox like the useless thing it is. He winces, his eyes darting toward Principal Riddall. "Pardon my German."

Gwen is standing off to the side, blindfold and headphones dangling from her hand, her eyes the size of coasters. "Blood. Dee. Hell."

"Very sorry, false alarm," Principal Riddall growls into her phone before clicking it off. Her jaw tightens and jumps. She lowers her gaze at us. "We need to have a little chat, the three of us. I'll see you both in my office. Seven thirty, Monday morning. Don't be late."

Principal Riddall shakes her head, turns around, and slumps off. Her posture is world-weary, like the very fact that she has to deal with so many idiots every day has completely worn her down.

Perry shoots me a *yikes* look, then shrugs because he knows he'll be able to charm his way out of this, no problem. If it's anything like last year's Sulfur Smoke Bomb Affair in chemistry class, Perry will not only get Principal Riddall to commute our sentences, he'll also have us heading up a brand-new committee on performance safety standards.

"Sorry, I messed up," I say, once the coast is clear. "I dropped the handcuff key."

"Doesn't matter," Perry says. "You want to know why?" He yanks the curtain aside, grabs my chafed-raw wrist, and pulls me out onto the proscenium.

There is a collective exhalation from the audience. Then big whoops of laughter and thunderous applause as the lights come up, the entire theater illuminated.

Perry raises my arm high in the air like I'm a boxing champion. "Drill of Death, ladies and gentlemen!"

Everyone leaps to their feet, including Mom and Dad, whose cheers—not surprisingly—can be heard above everyone else's.

"Take your bow, my friend," Perry says. "You did this."

We drop our arms and lower our heads.

The applause feels nice, for sure, but all I can think about is how the effect could have been so much better. When I first designed it, I was absolutely certain this performance was going to be the thing that got us the fantasy camp audition.

Now I'm not so sure.

4

"Door-to-mall service," Dad says, pulling up to the loading zone in his always-new-smelling Ford EcoSport.

"You guys meeting anyone here?" Mom asks. She twists around in the front passenger seat and smiles at Perry and me. "Friends? *Girls?*" She's trying to act all casual and indifferent, but it's not working. Not even a little.

"Magic shop," I say, unstrapping my seat belt. "Like always."

I need to get out of this car before this becomes a thing. You never know with Mom and Dad. There's always the chance they could break out in a show tune. Something from *Guys and Dolls*. Or worse, a song from the original musical they're staging in a few weeks. A show in which they've managed to incorporate many of the most tragic moments from my own miserable life. But, you know, set in Eurasia three hundred thousand years ago. It's basically *Romeo and Juliet*. With Neanderthals.

"Right," Mom says, nodding like she's going to drop the subject even though we all know she isn't. "I just figured that with your big talent show win Friday night, you might have . . . I don't know . . . gotten a few invitations."

This makes Perry laugh. He *can* laugh. He actually likes my obliviously oblivious parents. And they *love* them some Perry. I have no doubt they'd adopt him if the opportunity presented itself.

"We *did* get invited to a barbecue this afternoon," Perry says, glancing over at me. "At Gwen's place."

"Your ex-girlfriend?" Mom squees, like she and Perry are besties. "I love how you two are still close. It's so sweet. You were such a good couple. I still don't understand why you broke up."

Perry sighs and nods. "Yeah. It was hard, for sure. We really clicked. Too much, I think. I don't know. I'm still questioning it."

"Why don't you talk to her?" Mom says, all parental and supportive.

Perry shakes his head. "Nah. She's dating someone else now. It wouldn't be fair to him. We'll see how that plays out." He shrugs. "Besides, I'd rather take my time and figure some things out on my own before I say anything to her."

"Well, I think it shows great maturity," Dad says in his deep, man-of-wisdom voice. "Which is probably why you're both close enough that she still invites you to her parties."

"Speaking of which." Mom turns on me accusingly. "You didn't tell us you got invited to a barbecue."

"Uh . . . because . . . I'm not going?" I say, glaring at Perry. "As we previously discussed." I pull on the door handle, but the child locks are on. "Dad? The doors?"

"Why not?" Mom presses. "Barbecues are fun. All those interesting people. All those yard games."

"All that flaming meat," Dad adds. "It's very primal, *the barbecue*. I saw this documentary once where they explained how the smell of meat cooked over open flames increases testosterone production. I think. Don't quote me on that. It might not be true. But it sure sounds like it should be, right?"

I yank on the useless door handle like I'm being kidnapped.

"*You're going,*" Mom announces, then looks at Perry. "He's going to the party. Make him go to the party. He never goes to parties."

Clearly this is *not* about parties.

Perry throws his hands up. "He's always invited, Mrs. Purcell."

"I know he is," Mom coos, her face and shoulders going all soft. "You are *such* a good friend to our little Quinn. Glenn and I appreciate how nice you've always been to him."

"Hey," I say. "I'm right here. Also, not a rescue dog."

"Well, then, prove it," Dad says, his eyes defying me in the rear-view mirror.

"Prove what? That I'm here? Or that I'm not a rescue dog?"

"Go to the party," Dad insists. "Make your mother happy. She's on edge. Work has been very stressful. Trying to get our musical up and running has been very stressful. Don't be another stress on her."

I groan, long and guttural, dragging my hand down my face so hard I nearly sprain my nose. "OK, fine, I'll go," I say, relenting only so this can be over. "Can you please unlock the doors now?"

Dad smiles at me in the mirror and I hear the click of the locks.

"Oh, goody." Mom claps her hands like a cymbal monkey. "This is exciting. We can pick you up later and drive you. Where does Gwen live?"

"That's OK." I shove the door open and step out onto the sidewalk. "We'll take the bus."

"Oh, I see," Mom says, her words falling off a cliff. "All right. Fine. Sure."

"He's going to the party," Dad says, patting Mom's shoulder. "Let that be enough."

"Hey-hey, thanks for the lift, Purcells," Perry says, throwing his door open. "Love you guys."

"Love you, too," Mom and Dad sing in harmony.

Oh, good Christ.

Mom turns and calls out her window to me, "Love you, Quinn."

"Yeah-mm-hmm-OK," I mumble, giving a half-hearted wave from the sidewalk, glancing around to make sure no one I know is witnessing this.

Mom suddenly leans forward, gesturing me toward her. "Pssst. Quinn. Come here."

"What?" I take a cautious step forward as Perry rounds the back of the SUV.

"Do you have a condom?" she says, all matter-of-factly, like she didn't just ask me if I had a condom. Her eyes dart to the glove compartment. "I can give you one of your father's. Just in case you meet someone at the party?"

"It's a barbecue, Mom," I say. "Not a brothel."

"Yes, but you never know. Your father and I first got together in the basement broom closet of a—"

"Yup. Know the story. Wish I didn't. Thanks."

"The point *is*," she says, "you have to be ready for the unexpected. We've talked about this."

"What have we talked about?" Dad bellows, leaning over from the driver's seat just as Perry steps up beside me.

Mom sighs like this is harder for her than it is for me. Which it most definitely is not. "OK. All right. I didn't want to do this because you know how I hate comparing people, but . . ." She looks over at Perry, and my insides shrink up like hot cellophane. "I don't mean to embarrass you, Perry," Mom says to my best friend since kindergarten. "Can I ask you a personal question?"

"Please-don't-please-don't-please-don't," I mutter to the pavement.

"Do you carry condoms?"

"An Eagle Scout is always prepared, Mrs. Purcell," Perry says, without a hint of mortification. "Why? Do you guys need one?"

5

"WHY DO YOU ENCOURAGE THEM?" I SAY TO PERRY AS WE approach the frosted-glass door of William's Wizardry. "They're bad enough on their own."

"Are you kidding me?" Perry says, laughing. "Your parents are the best show not on Netflix. I love how they just say stuff. At least you never have to guess where they're coming from."

"I'd *prefer* to guess sometimes," I say, tucking the condom—the one I finally had to take from Mom just to shut her up—in my pants pocket. "Or *not* have to guess about some things because, oh, I don't know, maybe certain subjects *are never brought up.*"

Perry quickens his step, opens the door to the magic shop, and ushers me inside.

I have to start opening doors for people. I have to start being nicer to people in general. Even though I hate most of them. Everyone loves Perry because Perry loves everyone. Maybe I should take a page from his playbook and greet the world with a smile.

Ugh. I'm exhausted just thinking about it.

I step into the Wizardry and am immediately greeted by the familiar mildew stew that commands the air. It's a comforting mix of soggy cardboard, carpet mold, and cigarette smoke, and it tugs at my heart every time I come here.

The store is a tornado of books, DVDs, magic tricks, and novelties, stacked everywhere and on every surface. I love the wonderful mess of the place, with its promise of unexpected treasures under every pile. But I can see why William's Wizardry has never been a booming success. And why the Fernwood Mall management refuses to list the "filthy shithole out by the loading docks" on the mall directory.

Perry and I wend our way through the aisles. It's actually busy today. Usually it's just me and Perry and maybe one other magic nerd, but I count nearly a dozen other customers, at least.

A spiky-haired anime character paws through the costumes, trying on various capes and posing in the mirror. A very blinky, bespectacled girl spins the book rack, clearly looking for something specific. And at the center of the store, a couple of sagging hoodies are circling an oversize Houdini-inspired steel milk can. The dusty, dented, antique milk can that I will own one day. The cornerstone for a showstopping trick that I have yet to create. Houdini's escape is still a classic, but there's an updated version of it somewhere in the ethers that will drift down to my mind someday. I feel it every time I'm near this thing.

At the back counter, a handful of people watch someone—Isaac, the owner's stoner nephew and part-time employee, presumably—

performing some close-up magic. Card to Box, maybe. Or Scotch and Soda. Whatever trick is overstocked and on sale this week.

"Hey, hey," Ed says as we approach the cash register. "How are my two best customers?" He jams a cigarette between his thick, rubbery lips and grins, flashing a set of enormous, tobacco-stained horse teeth.

Everything about Ed is oversize. Huge hands, sagging earlobes, bullmastiff jowls. Even his gray hair is large. Puffed up and greased back in a sort of makeshift pompadour.

"We won the talent show, *again*," I say, waving our spoils—a fifty-dollar Fernwood Mall gift certificate, to be split between the two of us—in the air. "Not that it will get us an audition for the Magic Society's Fantasy Camp. But whatever."

"I love the optimism." Ed chuckles, his laugh quickly devolving into a phlegmy cough. "Pardon," he says, letting the unlit cigarette dangle off his lower lip. He pulls a handkerchief from his back pocket and spits something gelatinous into it. "If it's any consolation"—he drags his cow tongue across his teeth like a windshield wiper, then, without missing a beat, repositions the cigarette back between his lips—"I happen to know for a fact that they are *still* sending out invitations."

"Really?" Perry asks. "Where did you hear that? I thought you said you'd been expelled from the MSA."

"Indeed," Ed says, sliding a Zippo off the counter and finally lighting his cigarette. "And proud of it." He takes a long, deep drag and releases a giant plume of gray smoke. I can't believe he hasn't been shut down for smoking inside. Although if someone from the

Department of Health ever did show up at his door, Ed's smoking habit would probably be the least of their concerns. "However, my new intern, Dani—who has not yet offended the magical powers that be—just received her invitation to audition a few days ago."

Perry looks at me, arching an eyebrow. "That's good news."

"For *her*, yeah," I say, then turn on Ed. "Who is this *intern*, anyway? What happened to Isaac? I've been begging you for a job here for the last three years. You always say you can't afford it."

"I can't," Ed says. "Why do you think I let my perma-fried, laze-about nephew work here in the first place? He's cheap as chips." Ed lifts his massive chin toward the back of the store. "Dani just happened to show up on a day Isaac happened not to. Offered to work for free. Just to get experience." Perry and I turn our heads in sync, following Ed's gaze. "At first I thought, no way, no how. Even for an intern I'm probably going to have to file some bullshit paperwork. But there was something about her. I don't know. Blew my mind with a couple of tricks, smooth-talked me with some whoopdeedoodle about winning a Girl Scout cookie salesperson award, and suddenly I thought, what do I have to lose?" He grins. "Turns out, *nothing*. Girl's already sold more tricks in the last hour than I have all week. So, big win for me." He clears his throat into his fist. "And for her, too. Because . . . experience."

I watch as the people surrounding the back counter burst into applause, laughing and cheering at what they've just witnessed.

"Thank you," the intern calls out from beyond the gaggle of heads. "Thank you very much." Her voice is a little hoarse, like she's just getting over a cold. It's kind of sexy.

27

"Do another one!" a woman shouts from the crowd. "My daughter and I have never seen a female magician before."

"OK, OK," I hear the girl say. "I'll do one more for you and then I have to get some lunch. I've been working on this new effect for an upcoming act. I think it's pretty sparky, but you'll have to let me know what you think."

I haven't even seen her face, or watched her palm a single card, but I already know she's talented. I can hear it in her tone. A dead-calm confidence. And it pulls me toward her.

I don't know if the crowd parts to let us by, or if we just shove our way through the sweaty horde to the front, but somehow Perry and I are standing at the glass counter, two feet away from a girl who breaks my heart the second I lay eyes on her.

Dani is a vision of warm colors in her paisley genie pants, burnt-orange belly shirt, and large gaucho hat. My stomach lurches and I have to choke down an anxious retch. The fact that my first reaction to seeing a beautiful girl is nausea does not bode well for the propagation of the Purcell gene pool.

"This is a little card trick," she says, expertly shuffling a deck of cards on a green felt mat, "that was inspired by my great-grandmother Maria, who, when she was a child, absolutely loved going to the circus. This was quite some time ago. You know, when people could still be amazed by things."

Dani does a series of ridiculous cuts, spreads, and riffles without even looking down at her hands. *Of course* she received an invitation to audition for the fantasy camp. And *of course* Ed hired her.

Between her talent, her looks, and her confidence, she's a force of nature.

"That's ridiculous," I whisper to Perry. "Her dexterity is off the charts."

"No kidding," he says, the awe palpable in his voice.

"Grammie Maria told me a story once," Dani continues, turning and smiling at me, her eyes mesmerizingly green. "About this one time the circus came to her small town when she was eight years old."

My jaw hinges open. I can feel the air drying out my tongue. Everything around me disappears, the world tunneling until all I can see is this stunning, magical, elfin creature. Her hair, a golden apricot color, is long and curly and pulled to the side in a sort of unkempt ponytail.

I could watch her all day. Just like this. The two of us sharing a look.

"That circus had a sideshow magician," Dani says, still smiling at me. "And that magician showed Grammie Maria something impossible. Something I am now going to share with you."

She finally breaks our gaze and addresses the stack of cards in front of her. "This road-show magician seemed to possess an incredible power." Dani takes a card from the top of the deck and shows it to us. It's a two of hearts. "Transmogrification." She flicks the card with the middle finger of her other hand, and the card turns into a king of spades.

"Snap change," I whisper to Perry. "Super crisp."

The small crowd oohs and aahs. It's a pretty simple but impressive effect. If you didn't know the trick, you'd have no idea she did a double lift, then slid the king on top of the two with a quick snap of her fingers. So fast that your eyes can't pick up the switch.

"It seems that this mysterious stranger could transform one card"—Dani flicks the king, changing it into a five of diamonds—"into any card in the deck."

"Wait. How'd she do that?" Perry murmurs, his brow furrowed. "Triple lift?"

"No way," I say. "You can't snap three cards. She must have gone back to the deck."

"You, there." Dani points to a dark-haired girl with bright red-rimmed glasses who looks to be about ten. "With the super-cool gogs. Name a card. Quick. Without thinking."

"Um," the girl says, scrunching up her face, biting her lower lip. "Seven of clubs, I guess."

"Seven of clubs?" Dani says, winking at her. "That's a good card." She flicks the five of diamonds with her fingers and it immediately turns into the seven of clubs.

"Holy shit," I blurt, getting a withering look from the pale, mole-pocked woman beside me.

"Amazing," Perry says. "That's three changes. That's four cards. And how the heck did she force the seven of clubs?"

I shake my head. "No idea. The kid must be a plant."

"You," Dani says, pointing at me. "Mumbles. You can't seem to keep quiet. Make yourself useful. Name a card. Any card but the ace of spades."

I laugh, glancing around like I'm missing something, my cheeks burning. "Why not the ace of spades? If you can turn it into any card."

"OK, fine," Dani says, shrugging. "You want the ace of spades, then?"

"I didn't say—"

Before I can finish my sentence, Dani has turned the seven of clubs into the ace of spades. The crowd applauds even though this was a clear misdirection.

"I was going to say the jack of diamonds," I call out righteously, because people shouldn't be clapping for such a lazy trick. It's not the kind of thing they'll put up with at the MSA auditions. "But clearly you wanted me to pick the ace of spades, so good job."

"You think I *made* you pick the ace of spades?"

"I *didn't* pick the ace of spades," I say. "*You* picked it. And then just *said* that I picked it. I chose the jack of diamonds."

"Did you?" Dani says, staring straight into my soul. "Or am I so inside your head that I made you pick *that* card, too?" She grins at me, leans forward, and flicks the ace of spades on my nose, simultaneously turning the card into a jack of diamonds—

and securing my undying love for all of eternity.

6

"Hey," Perry says, swatting my arm as I stare out the bus window, seeing nothing but a world stained with my despair. "You OK? You seem upset or something."

I shake my head. "I'm fine."

This is a lie. I am anything but fine. I'm finding it hard to even perform basic human functions. Like breathing. And keeping my heart beating.

I've had crushes on girls before, but this is different. Dani's almost too perfect for me. Like someone read the up-to-now-useless Vision Board I've got hidden on my phone and is playing a joke on me. Because the odds of something like this happening—*to me*—are Powerball huge.

First of all, how often do you meet a girl our age who actually *admits* to loving magic? I can count the ones I've met on a single hand while wearing a mitten. There might well be armies of magic-obsessed females out there somewhere, but it's not like the magic community has exactly encouraged them to come out of hiding.

Which is a shame. Because if Dani's any indication, we're being deprived of some seriously killer talent.

But what makes this nearly improbable situation absolutely, completely impossible is the fact that this wonderful, beautiful, talented female magician actually seemed to be flirting with me over a card trick.

And I did nothing about it. *Nothing.* Just let her scurry off to lunch without so much as a "Hi, I'm Quinn."

The depth of my self-loathing cannot be measured.

"If it's about Gwen's barbecue," Perry says, "it's cool if you want to bail. I get it. Other people's parents and everything. I'll probably just make an appearance and skip out."

I sigh and press my forehead against the cold, finger-smudged window. "It's not about the barbecue." I can smell the harsh scent of Windex someone forgot to wipe off the glass. It's oddly pleasant.

Perry leans forward, trying to catch my gaze. "OK? So? If it's not the barbecue . . . ?"

"It's nothing. I just . . . I have a headache. I need to go home, take an Advil, and lie down for a while."

"Suit yourself," Perry says, exhaling as he leans back in his seat. "But if you need to talk about something, *anything at all*, I'm here."

Of course he is. He's always there. For me. For you. For everyone. It kind of makes you want to puke, his unconditional availability. No wonder everybody loves him. Including me.

I return my forehead to the window and start doing a little rhythmic, pulsing push, pressing my brow against the glass, again and again and again. I imagine that the harder I push, the more my skull spreads out and the more space I am making for my fevered, swollen brain.

"We still might get an invitation to audition, you know," Perry announces, like he's just put his finger on all my worries. "I mean, like Ed said, Dani just got hers a few days ago."

"Yeah," I say, feeling the window flex as I press even harder. What if the glass shattered and my whole head went through? It feels like this is what needs to happen. "Maybe."

"And even if we don't get an invite, whatever. It's not the end of the world. We'll do our own summer workshop. Book gigs all across Fernwood. Make some actual money so you can buy that milk can you've been lusting after." He waggles his eyebrows at me. "Huh? What do you think? Then you'll be *glad* we didn't get to audition."

"Sounds good." I sigh really long and loud and dramatically. "Anyway, I don't care about the stupid audition."

Perry jerks his head back. "OK, now I know you're lying. The 'stupid audition' is the only thing you've been talking about for the last nine months."

I groan. "It doesn't matter, OK?" I swallow the bitter taste at the back of my throat. "Forget it. You wouldn't understand."

"I might," he says. "If you actually stopped speaking in code."

"Yeah, well, *I* don't even understand," I say. "So I don't know how you would."

"Maybe if you just tell me what's on your—"

"It's the girl at the shop." The words spew from my lips, like pus from a popped pimple. "She got under my skin for some reason. I can't explain it."

"Under your skin?" Perry squints at me. "As in, you *like* her?"

I drag my hand all over my face, trying to clear the flulike fog that seems to have settled over me. "OK, so, this is going to sound completely ridiculous, but . . . you know how love at first sight is just a made-up thing that never happens in real life?" I suck in a shaky breath. "Well, it just happened. To me. And I don't know what to do about it."

"You don't know what to *do*?" Perry laughs. "We were right there. Why didn't you talk to her? Why'd you let her just wave goodbye and go off to lunch?"

"I don't know," I say, my skin feeling like it shrank in the wash. "I'm not you. I don't do . . . *you*. I can't just . . . talk to people."

"You talk to people all the time, Quinn. You talked to her when she was doing the trick. Why couldn't you talk to her after?"

I shake my head and look away. "I knew you wouldn't understand."

"Of course I understand. You're scared. I get scared. Remember when Gwen came to school last year, how hard it hit me when I first saw her? I avoided her almost the whole first day. But then . . . I just . . . went up to her and introduced myself. That's the thing. I take the leap *even though* I get scared. That's the only difference."

This makes me snort. "It's *not* the only difference. Not even close. You and I can take the very same leap and it's like you're a cat who always lands on his feet and I'm like . . . a cat without feet. Which is exactly why it's so frustrating to talk about this stuff with you." I feel my throat getting thick. "You're my best friend, and I'm happy that everything always works out for you, but . . . *everything always works out for you.*"

Perry scrunches up his face. "That's not true."

"Oh no? Name one thing in your life—*one* thing—that you *really* wanted that didn't turn out the way you wanted. Just *one* time you can remember desperately wanting something and being completely devastated with disappointment."

Perry shrugs like I've lobbed him a softball. "Easy. There are a ton of them. Gwen. For one. Not a day goes by I don't think about her. Wondering if we made a mistake breaking up."

I shake my head. "That doesn't count. Because the decision was mutual. And also, you wanted *both* things. To be with her. And not to be with her. You got one of them. And if you changed your mind, I'm sure you could have the other one."

"Not when she's going out with Carter."

I shoot Perry a you-can't-be-serious look.

"It's true," Perry says. "Carter's a pal. I'd never go behind a friend's back like that."

"You wouldn't have to," I say. "Do you not see how Gwen looks at you? One word from me about how you feel and she would drop Carter like a . . . hot crumpet, or whatever English people instantly dump when something better comes along."

"Don't you dare." Perry points at me. "I'm serious. If she breaks up with Carter on her own, fine. But it has to be her decision. That was the entire point of us splitting up. To find out for sure if what we had was as special as we thought it was."

I roll my eyes. "Yeah, I'm still trying to twist my brain around that one. You guys were perfect for each other and *that's* why you didn't want to be together?"

"You're not supposed to find your soul mate at sixteen, Quinn." Perry shakes his head like he's not so sure about this. "I mean, sure, everything was effortless between us. But that was the problem. It was *too* easy. *Too* comfortable. Like we were already a happily married couple. When her parents actually pointed it out, it kind of scared us. We were worried that if we never dated anyone else, we'd always have questions. And that would end up ruining our relationship. That's all. In a year or two, after we've both played the field a bit more . . . who knows? We'll have fewer questions."

"Oh yeah?" I say, staring at my best friend who, after three months, has yet to even step foot on the field. "How's that working out for you?"

Perry sighs and shrugs. "Every time I think about asking someone out, my brain just ticks off all the ways she isn't like Gwen. But I'll do it. Eventually. I will."

"Right. Sure. Keep telling yourself that." I exhale. "Anyway, *the point is,*" I say, bringing us back around to what the point actually is, "if you *wanted* to date Gwen again, you could have her back. As I said. Everything always works out for you."

"Not true," Perry argues. "What about the audition, the fantasy camp? I really wanted that, too. As much as you did. Because I love performing magic with you." He throws up a hand, the matter settled. "So there. Your theory is shot. Despite your rose-colored view of my life, I *don't* always get everything I want."

As if on cue, Perry's phone *pings* from the front pocket of his pants.

He laughs and looks at me. "All right. Very funny, Quinn. Nice timing."

I glare at him, because we both know what's just happened here.

Perry rolls his eyes. "Oh, come on. That's not the audition invitation. You're hilarious." He slides his phone out and swipes at the screen. "I bet you a million dollars that it's just some annoying spam—" His eyes dart back and forth as he reads. "Holy . . . cow." His hand goes to his mouth.

I stare at him, dead-eyed. "So, the invitation."

He looks at me, blinking in disbelief. "We did it, Quinn. We got it. An invitation to audition." Perry turns his phone toward me and I take it.

> The Magic Society of America is proud to invite *Perry Larsson* to audition for one of 50 coveted spots at the highly selective *Masters of Magic Summer Fantasy Camp*. One talented magician from each state will gain entry. Will you be your state's lucky winner?

My heart stops, my breath catching in my chest. *Perry Larsson.* That's all it says. Not *The magic team of Quinn Purcell and Perry Larsson*, the way we entered our videos online.

Just . . . *Perry Larsson.*

"Congratulations," I mutter, handing him back his phone.

"To you, too."

"That's your invitation," I say. "It doesn't mention my name."

Perry blows a lip fart. "Whatever. We entered together. I'm sure you'll get one. They probably just send them out separately."

"Sure. Probably. Maybe." I casually slide my phone from my pocket and check my own emails. "But maybe not."

"You'll get one," Perry insists. "And even if you don't, so what? We're a team. We're auditioning together, and if we win, we're going to that camp together. They don't get one of us without the other. This is good news, Quinn." He grabs my shoulder and gives me a shake. "This is congratulations to both of us."

I force a smile at him. I want to believe this. I really do.

But, you know, history.

7

I'M LYING ON MY BED, MY HANDS JAMMED BEHIND MY NECK, staring up at a long, swaying cobweb that trails from the ceiling. I've run out of things to distract myself from the parade of disappointments that have made up my day. Seems there's only so much Rocket League playing, card riffling, and porn watching a person can do before the real world stomps its feet and demands attention.

Normally I can laugh off my best friend's obscene good fortune, but the fact that I have yet to receive an invitation to audition—five hours and twenty-three minutes after Perry got his—and the fact that I might never receive one, is a dark, walnut-size pill to have to choke down. I mean, seriously. I designed the Drill of Death. I was the one who actually *performed* the magic. I don't understand. We *both* submitted the video. How is that even fair? How do they even justify that to themselves?

I suck in a deep, dispirited breath and exhale it toward the ceiling. A few seconds later, the fluffy, dangling cobweb starts to dance around. I pretend I'm moving the fluff with my mind. All of a sudden, I'm creating an effect. *Using my breath as an invisible propellant . . . making something out of balsa wood—A mug? A cell phone? Something the brain would clock as too heavy to be moved by simply breathing on it . . .*

This is how my brain works. Everything is a magic trick in the making.

I remember the exact moment when I knew that I wanted to be a professional magician. It was my eighth birthday. Mom and Dad took me to the Beltway Theater to see *The Three Magi: An Evening of Enchantment Featuring the Wonderful Wonder Phil, the Magnificent Marissa, and the Dazzling Lazlo.*

All three magicians were great that night, but it was Robert "the Dazzling" Lazlo who made me fall in love with the art of illusion. His final effect—the Monkey's Paw—was so absolutely mind-bending that, to this day, just thinking about it gives me chills. It's the closest thing I've ever seen to *real* magic in my life and the only effect that I've never been able to figure out how to do.

And believe me, I've tried. And tried. And tried.

Which was another reason I so desperately wanted to get into the fantasy camp. I thought for sure once I trained under some of the country's greatest magicians, I'd finally be able to crack the mystery to the Monkey's Paw.

Oh God, I have a screaming migraine. I suddenly realize my hands are clenching the back of my neck like a vise. I relax and my headache immediately eases. Clearly I'm not handling this well.

It's funny, ever since Perry emerged from his chrysalis as an all-enchanting, all-talented butterfly, performing magic was the one thing that still felt like mine. The one thing I was still better at. And the only time I ever felt seen when standing beside him.

And now he gets the only invitation to *my* dream.

I might have to kill him. I know it sounds awful, killing your best friend, but I don't see any other options. How can I be expected to spend the rest of my life watching him achieve everything I've ever wanted—without really having to try very hard to get it, no less—while I wallow in a bog of mediocrity, eating my envy and resentment until it grows into a giant envy-and-resentment tumor in my stomach, causing my entire torso to explode?

When you really think about it, it's just a simple case of survival.

Although, to be honest, even if I did snuff out Perry's wonderfully charmed life—which I won't, of course, because I love him too much—he would still find some way to turn his untimely demise into something positive. They'd probably name a park after him. The Perry Larsson Memorial Gardens. Where I'd sleep on a bench every night, right next to my shopping cart full of bottle returns.

So he wins again.

"I hate my life," I groan at the ceiling.

"Sorry, I didn't quite get that," my phone's AI calls out in her flat mid-Atlantic accent. *"Could you repeat it?"*

"I said I. Hate. My. Life."

"I'm sorry, Quinn Purcell. Human life can be a rocky road. Or so I've heard."

"You don't know the half of it," I mutter.

My virtual assistant doesn't respond. Maybe she's smarter than I give her credit for.

I feel around next to me for my phone and swipe the screen. Just in case my invitation came through in the last seven and a half minutes.

I already have six unread emails. Most of them will probably be from Tasty Bouquets. Oh, who am I kidding? *All of them* will be from Tasty Bouquets. They are aggressive marketers who don't seem to realize they were responsible for one of the more miserable days in my life.

You see, I mistakenly took Mom's advice last year and sent a secret-admirer Valentine "fruit-quet" to this girl at school who I had no business admiring from the start. It did not turn out well. First of all, what the hell is a girl supposed to do with a fifteen-pound basket of fruit at school? Second of all, fruit flies. And lastly, once the mystery sender was rooted out—and it didn't take long—I spent the rest of the day plucking cantaloupe wedges out of my underwear and finding chocolate-dipped pineapple stars squashed inside my textbooks.

Every time I get an email from them, it's another citrus-rubbed razor cut to my heart. I've tried unsubscribing, but they never listen. It almost feels like every time I click unsubscribe they sign me up with another account so I end up getting even more spam.

I scroll through my inbox.

TASTY BOUQUET: LEAVE HER SPEECHLESS . . . NOT PEACH-LESS.

TASTY BOUQUET: SHOW HER SHE'S ONE IN A MELON.

TASTY BOUQUET: HONEY DEW YOU WANT SOME FRUIT?

THE MAGIC SOCIETY OF AMERICA IS WRITING TO INFORM YOU . . .

TASTY BOUQUET: LET MOM KNOW HOW GRAPEFUL YOU ARE!

Wait, what?

I scroll back up and read the words again. My heart starts to gallop. The Magic Society of America is writing to inform me of . . . *what*? That I've been invited to audition for their fantasy camp? Or that I won't be receiving an invitation?

I hover my thumb over the email. I don't remember Perry's message starting like this. But then again, I don't remember looking at the subject line.

I click the email and wait for it to load. The wheel spins. The server's slow. It's only a matter of seconds before the message appears, but it feels like forever.

As the words wash over me, a sense of relief settles around my soul, like a cool cotton sheet on a hot summer's day.

My own invitation. Addressed to me, Quinn Purcell. My heart races, my chest full of soda bubbles. I did it. I can't believe it. It's almost too much to comprehend.

I scroll through the rest of the message, each subsequent boilerplate sentence making me happier and happier.

Until I reach the Guidelines and Requirements section.

And that's when my stomach opens its trapdoor.

8

"I DON'T KNOW HOW ELSE TO INTERPRET THE AUDITION rules," I say as Perry and I lumber down the hallway, lugging our monstrous backpacks like a couple of Himalayan Sherpas. The Monday morning reprimanding with Principal Riddall went as expected: Perry smiled sheepishly, took all the blame for the "obvious miscommunication," then somehow had *her* apologizing to *us* for getting so upset. It was a beautiful thing to watch. "They say we have to perform separately. Which is probably why they sent us individual invitations."

Perry screws up his face. "I didn't get that at all. They can't mean magic teams. That doesn't make sense."

"I don't know," I say, reading off my phone: "*Each performance shall last no longer than five minutes, including introduction, and shall consist of a single act onstage at a time, with no aid of assistants. Volunteers, as long as they are random and not confederates, are allowed if absolutely necessary.*"

Perry shrugs. "See? 'A single act.' We *are* a single act. A team. Quinn and Perry. We don't use assistants."

"You think that's what they mean?" I say.

"That's how I'm reading it," Perry says. "If they meant something else, they shouldn't have been so vague."

"It says no assistants except volunteers. To me that sounds like one single magician onstage at a time."

"And to me," Perry says, hoisting his backpack straps higher up on his shoulders, "we are a 'single act' performing onstage. I don't see where the problem is. We submitted our act as a team. We're going to perform as a team." He glances over at me. "Don't you think?"

"Yeah, of course, sure," I say, nodding. "That's what we should do. Absolutely. It's just . . . I don't know, maybe we should get more clarification. We worked so hard to get to this point. I'd rather not blow our only chance."

Auditioning separately would be a monumental risk. And not my first choice by any stretch. If we perform on our own, Perry could easily beat me. I might be the better magician, but he's the better showman. So it's whatever the judges respond to more at the time. Which, let's be honest, will probably be Perry.

Although . . . with magic . . . who knows? If I needed to pick one thing where I had the tiniest hope of besting him, it would be with magic. *And magic alone.* So no matter how queasy it makes me to think of having to compete against my best friend, I'd rather have *some* shot than no shot at all.

"Fine," Perry says. "I'll write them an email and explain the situation. It'll all work out, I promise. I'm pretty good at wording persuasive arguments."

"No, I'll do it," I say, trying to moisten my dry lips with my drier tongue. "You have enough on your plate. Besides, I'm the one worried about it. Plus, I know how to talk to magicians. They're a sensitive bunch. I'll write to them. Get it sorted."

"That's the attitude," Perry says, nodding and grinning, like the problem has already been solved. "Stop stressing. It's all going to work out. You'll see." He reaches over and grabs my shoulder. "You're a cat with newfound feet."

I'm glad someone's confidence is flying high. Because I don't think mine could sink much lower.

"Hey-hey, look who it is," Perry says, lifting his chin.

I follow his gaze and see a flash of gaucho hat, the flutter of a floral skirt, a splash of color in the gray hallway. My heart whiffles in my chest, a bird buffeted by an unexpected gust.

It's Dani.

Here.

At Fernwood High.

"Jesus Christ," I say, like I've just been caught with my pants around my ankles. "Do you think she moved here?"

"There's one way to find out," Perry says. He winks and smiles at me. "A familiar face is always nice when you don't know anyone." I watch Dani move down the hallway. She looks out of context in our high school. Like a butterfly flittering through a prison. She's scanning the numbers on the lockers and glancing down at her phone, deep frown lines furrowing her brow.

"She's trying to find her locker," I say, biting my lower lip.

"Uh-oh," Perry says. "OK. We better go save her before the wolves descend." He starts heading toward her.

I scuttle after him, whisper-cursing at his back, "Stop. No. Shit. Christ. Perry. Slow down. Let's talk about this."

Perry picks up his pace, knowing if he doesn't, I might try to tackle him.

Dani doesn't seem to notice us as we approach, just squints up at the locker numbers, then back at her phone. I wait for Perry to say something to her, but he just raises his eyebrows at me expectantly, then jabs me in the ribs with his elbow.

"Hello-hi-hey," I cough out. "I didn't . . . we didn't formally . . . we met you, kind of, sort of . . . at the magic shop? Yesterday. Sunday? This weekend. You were performing a card trick?" My voice pitches high at the end of my sentences, turning everything into a question.

Dani studies me like she's trying to place my face. Then she smiles, her green eyes practically glowing. "Oh yeah. Mumbles. Hey."

"You ran out so fast after your performance," I say, forcing the words past the stone in my throat. "Which was amazing, by the way. The effect? Seamless. Anyway, we didn't get a chance to, you know, introduce ourselves." I press my hand to my chest. "I'm Quinn and this is . . . uhhhh"—I gesture at my best friend since forever, completely blanking on his name—"my best friend?"

"Perry," he says, thrusting out a hand, which Dani shakes. "Lovely to meet you. Incredible trick. Really impressive, as Quinn said. We're magicians, too."

"I know." Dani continues to make her way down the row of lockers, Perry and me trailing behind her. "I saw the talent show

Friday. I wasn't officially a student yet, but they said I could go. Talk about impressive." She laughs. "The impaling? I did *not* see that coming. I should have, with that kind of setup. But you guys sold it really well."

"Oh." I feel my cheeks get hot. "You were there? You saw it? And you . . . thought it was good?"

She raises her eyebrows. "It got you your invites, didn't it?"

"Yeah, but—wait." I glance over at Perry, who looks as surprised as I am. "We *just* got them. How'd you find out?"

Dani shrugs. "I guess I just assumed," she says. "An incredible act like that? It would have been a crime if you didn't get an invitation for your performance. Even if you couldn't close it out like you wanted to."

Wait, *what*? How did she know we didn't—? Again, I check with Perry. Again, he looks surprised.

"Anyway." Dani sighs, returning her attention to the lockers. "What's the deal with these numbers? They aren't in any kind of order."

"Someone changed them around last year," I say, blinking up at one of the little riveted number plates, still baffled by how this girl can know so much about us. "As a joke. I guess."

"Great," she groans. "How am I supposed to find 234?"

"You're not," Perry says. "That was sort of the point. It took a really long time for anyone to notice the numbers were changed because"—he gives his gargantuan backpack a shrug and gestures at the long row of lockless lockers—"nobody uses them."

"*What?*" Dani says, continuing to scan the locker numbers.

"That's just a recipe for future back problems. My dad's an orthopedic surgeon. He'd have an aneurysm if he saw what was going on here." Her eyes suddenly go wide. "Aha! Here we go."

Dani knocks on a locker with the number 234 at the top. Right where it should be, between 312 and 472. She whips out a combination lock, opens the door to the locker, slides the lock into the handle, and starts shoving all her stuff inside—books, jacket, backpack— leaving her pretty much unencumbered. Which, I have to say, with my shoulders in constant cramp mode, looks like the smart choice.

"There we go," Dani says, holding out her empty arms like she might be expecting a hug. "Free and easy." She shakes her head. "Oh. I almost forgot." She quickly smacks her locker door once, opens it, and reveals a steaming cup of Starbucks coffee on the top shelf. A coffee that was definitely not there before. "Now we're talking." She takes the cup and raises it in cheers.

"Nice one," I say, laughing. She must have had the cup hidden somewhere in all her stuff, although that would have been a difficult balancing act.

"Oh, sorry," Dani says, mocking dismay. "How rude of me. Did you guys want coffee, too?" She *double* smacks the door to her locker this time, opens it again, and there, on the top shelf, are two more steaming Starbucks cups.

"Aren't we full of surprises?" I say.

Dani raises her eyebrows as she hands us the coffees. "I like to keep things interesting."

Perry takes a sip of his drink and laughs. "Holy moly. Almond Honey Flat White. How'd you know?"

Dani smirks and shrugs. "Lucky guess?"

I take a taste of mine, already knowing it'll be my regular Starbucks order, a Caramel Macchiato. "Wow, OK." I nod. "Very impressive. And a little terrifying, if I'm being honest."

This pleases her, apparently, because she beams and her cheeks go rosy.

I suddenly realize that Dani's been playing us this whole time, because not only did she have to social media stalk us to find out our favorite coffees, but she also had to have planted the drinks earlier, which means she must have discovered our homeroom was on this floor, chosen a random locker nearby (I never did see any locker number on her phone screen), and planned on running into us.

Or at least, that's how I work it out in my head. She also could be an actual wizard, but the chances of that seem pretty slim.

"To a formidable opponent," Perry offers, raising his cup.

"Hear, hear!" I say, taking another sip of my coffee.

First bell rings and the Fernwood Marching Band's version of "Girl from Ipanema" starts to squall over the PA system.

Perry gives my ankle a little kick, his eyes darting in Dani's direction.

It doesn't take a mind reader to figure out what he wants me to do.

"Oh, so, hey," I say, mustering up as many crumbs of courage as I can. "I was wondering if you might want to, I don't know, maybe, sometime, you and me—"

"Listen," Dani says, her raspy voice dipping low. My heart plummets accordingly. "I think you guys are great and all. Really sweet, actually. And if things were different, if we weren't each other's main competition, who knows? Maybe we could all be pals or . . . whatever." Her eyes flick to me. "But I have to stay focused on the only thing that matters right now. The audition. That's how I get things done. Got to put the blinders on if I'm going to win this thing." Her expression hardens. "And I *am* going to win." The smile is back, and her voice is chipper when she says, "No hard feelings?"

"Oh," I say, feeling like December's jack-o'-lantern. "That's . . . yeah. Sure. Of course." I gesture at Perry and myself. "Us, too. We have to stay focused, too. Absolutely." The embarrassment is like a physical force, causing me to back away . . . and bow for some reason, like I'm Japanese or something. "Only a couple of weeks till the audition, right?"

"That's right," Dani says. "And after that, who knows what'll happen? The world is a mystery." She turns to go and . . . did she just wink at me? Or does she have a nervous twitch? "Gotta run." Dani waves over her shoulder. "I'm sure we'll see each other around."

Perry and I watch her walk away until she disappears down the stairs. And even then we continue to stare in silence, sipping our coffees.

Until Perry finally says, "You are in a world of trouble, my friend."

"What are you talking about?"

He turns to me, gives me a you're-kidding smirk. "Admit it. You had no idea she was *that* good a magician."

"So?" I say, still watching the stairwell where Dani ducked down.

"*Soooo*," Perry says, "you're head over heels for the girl who is *clearly* our main competition. That never ends well."

"Yeah, well, it doesn't matter, does it?" I shrug. "You heard what she said. It's all audition, all the time. No distractions. Which means nothing can end badly, because nothing can *end* if nothing is ever started."

"I see." Perry nods mockingly. "And that little flirty wink she gave you before she took her leave? That isn't going to get inside your head? And haunt you for the rest of your days?"

"No," I say. "At least not for the next two weeks while we crush this audition." I shoot Perry a smile and a wink. "After that, who knows what'll happen?"

9

I TURN MY BIKE INTO THE PARKING LOT OF THE HERITAGE
Acres Assisted Living Facility. It's an old converted Holiday Inn
Express and it looks the part, all brick and beige. The gardener here
must love honeysuckle because the place is scrambling with the stuff.
When the little white flowers are blooming, like they are now, the
whole front yard smells like cotton candy.

There are no bike racks at Heritage Acres, so I have to chain my
Schwinn to one of the faux-Victorian lampposts. I'm running a little
late—it's already 4:05 and my pre-dinner performance is at 4:15—
which means I'm not going to have much time to set up.

I shouldn't have tried to find Dani after school. I was hoping she
might show up in one of my classes, but no such luck. I kept an eye
out in the halls but never spotted her. I made one last-ditch effort
to see if I might catch her boarding one of the school buses, but it's
like she just vanished into thin air. Which, considering her talents,
would not be out of the realm of possibility.

I'm not even sure what I would have said if I'd run into her. Ask
her what she meant by her departing wink? If she was hinting that

we could possibly be friends *after* the audition? Or, maybe, *more* than friends?

Yeah, in hindsight, it was probably better I didn't find her. I would have just made an ass of myself. She made it perfectly clear she didn't want any distractions. And to be honest, I'm glad she did. Because I don't need any distractions right now, either. I've put everything I have into getting this audition. And that's where my focus needs to be.

Particularly now, knowing just what a formidable opponent Dani is actually going to be. Which is why it's a good thing I'm here this afternoon. I need as much real-world practice as I can get.

I click the lock on my bike chain, hoist my backpack onto my shoulders, and do a hunched-over hustle toward the front door.

Every Monday for the past year I've been coming to Heritage Acres to do an afternoon performance for the residents. It was never supposed to become a regular volunteer gig when Perry and I did the initial show. It was just a onetime thing as part of our school's forty-hour community service requirement. But Margie Atkins, the director of extracurricular activities, kept emailing me, telling me how much everyone loved the show, how it was the highlight of their week, asking us, again and again, to please come back. I dodged her for a while, but then one day—when Perry had football practice and I was really bored—I just sort of went and did a show by myself.

I wasn't sure what was going to happen that first solo performance, but I found that I really liked it. The atmosphere is so loose and easy here, so it's hard to get self-conscious. Plus, the residents are very appreciative. At least the ones that stay awake. It's the perfect testing ground for new material. I can mess up, stumble and bumble around, drop billiard balls from the sleeves of my jacket, and no one seems to care or even notice. It's just smiles, snores, and shaky applause all around.

"Here's your water," Margie says, trailing me into the Bistro. She sets three mini bottles of Poland Spring on the table in front of the giant bingo board.

Margie is the tiniest woman I've ever met. Barely five feet tall and maybe eighty pounds draped in wet seaweed. She has a perfectly round, topiary-like mass of curly red hair perched on her head, making her look like she's trying out for *Annie: The Middle-Aged Years!* For some inexplicable reason—a charming saleswoman with an evil sense of humor?—Margie's gone with a pair of windshield-wide, attention-grabbing, red-white-and-blue glasses that cover a third of her face. It's not the look I would rock, but she's so sweet and full of energy you almost forget that you're speaking with a cartoon character.

"Thanks," I say, cracking a bottle of Poland Spring and taking a sip. "Packed house today, huh?" I raise the bottle toward the traffic jam of wheelchairs and walkers gridlocking the entryway.

"Ukulele Larry had a testicle explode," Margie says.

"Explode?" I shiver and wince in sympathy pain. "Yikes. How?"

Margie wrinkles her nose. "Something about a grumpy donkey. I didn't ask for details. His wife was pretty hysterical. I don't know if he was riding it, got kicked by it, or . . . whatever. But it sounded just awful."

"Wow," I say, blinking away the images zipping through my mind. "So many ways I'd rather not picture Ukulele Larry."

"Tell me about it," Margie says, sighing. "Anyway, you're the only game in town today, so enjoy your newfound popularity."

"All right, cool. Some fresh faces. This should be fun."

Margie's cheeks suddenly drain of color. "Oh my. What is Mrs. Swinick doing here?"

I turn to see who Margie is looking at. I'm guessing Mrs. Swinick is the overtanned, sinewy woman flipping a twiggy bird at one of the health-care aides.

"Don't think I've ever seen her at one of my shows," I say.

"She only comes out of her room to see Ukulele Larry," Margie says, then gives me a knowing look. "He flirts with her. It's cute. When she hasn't been drinking. I think it brings back memories. She tells me she was a pretty wild groupie back in the day. The band names change—Mott the Hoople, Grand Funk Railroad, Hoodoo Rhythm Devils—but the racy stories always end the same way." She shrugs. "Who knows? Anyway, I expected her to head right back to her room when she got the news about Larry's . . . misfortune."

"Well, maybe I'll win her over with some magic," I say.

"Mmmm." Margie pulls her lips to the side, then quickly clears her throat into her fist. "*Maybe*, yeah. You never know. Though her 'ex-has-been' is also a magician, so . . ." Margie makes a *yikes* face. "I heard an affair on the road and a secret second family. Which would color anyone's opinion of an occupation, I think . . . But, hey, maybe she doesn't hate *all* magicians. *Anymore*. You could be the very thing that turns her around." Margie looks over at Mrs. Swinick, who grabs her pendulous breasts and bobbles them at a man shaped like a sun-warmed candle. "Oh Lord, it looks like she's exceeded the two-cocktail limit again."

"Booooo-hisssss," Mrs. Swinick slurs through cupped hands. "I've seen better tricks in a Tijuana whorehouse."

Despite her obvious state of inebriation, Mrs. Swinick has been allowed to stay in the Bistro and ruin my performance because— according to Margie—she's a Royal Premier Super Donor.

She's a royal *something*, all right.

"You *are* a magician!" Mrs. Swinick hollers. "*Poof*"—she waggles her skeletal fingers in the air—"you've made my desire to live disappear."

This gets a raspy, hiccupped hoot from some guy with tubes up his nose.

I've never had to deal with a heckler before at Heritage Acres. I'm not exactly sure how to handle this. I'm hoping maybe Margie or one of the other staff will step in eventually.

"For my next illusion," I say, continuing to pretend I'm not being owned by a rich, boozy eighty-year-old, "I would like to ask for some help from the audience—"

"Robert Oppenheimer called!" Mrs. Swinick shouts at me. "He wants his bomb back."

This actually makes me laugh. But it's getting out of hand now. I turn toward her. If no one else is going to address this, then I guess I have to.

"Mrs. Swinick." I nod politely. "May I call you Mrs. Swinick?"

"Depends," she says. "Are you selling me shoes or are we two bottles of champagne into our wedding night?"

I smile. "Neither. We're doing a magic show."

She smirks. "Well, *that's* debatable. We're not *paying* you much for this ridiculous drivel, I hope. I donate a butt-load of cash to this shithole and I sure as hell hope we're not wasting it on you."

"You'll be happy to know I'm performing on a volunteer basis, completely free of charge."

Mrs. Swinick lip-farts. "It's still a rip job. At this point in life, time is much more valuable than money. And I'd like a refund on the last fifteen minutes. Can you make *that* happen . . . *magician*?" She says this last word like it's something foul and hot on her tongue.

I glance over at Margie, who is pinching the bridge of her nose so hard I'm worried she might snap the dam separating her eyes.

"Do you like to drink, Mrs. Swinick?" I ask her, like this isn't as obvious as Margie's mortification. "A cocktail before dinner, maybe? A glass of wine with your meal? An after-supper *digestif*?"

Mrs. Swinick beams. "Yes, yes, and who's pouring?" she says.

"Funny you should ask," I say, reaching back for the unmarked half-gallon milk carton sitting on the table. "Because *I'm* pouring. Any drink you'd like, Mrs. Swinick. Right here. From this one carton. You want milk, I've got milk." I reach into my prop box, grab one of the twenty clear plastic cups I've prepared, hold up the glass, tip the carton, and pour out some milk. No one seems surprised. It *is* a milk carton, after all. I set the milk down, grab another cup. "You want orange juice, I've got that, too." I tip the carton again and pour out some orange juice. This time the residents gasp. "Or red wine?" Another glass, another pour, another gasp.

Everyone who can applaud does. I set the red wine on the table and step up to Mrs. Swinick, brandishing the milk carton. "So, what's it going to be, Mrs. Swinick? Give me your best shot. What would you like to order?"

"Bahama Mama," Mrs. Swinick says with evil glee. "My stick-up-the-ass ex-has-been hated when I'd order that drink. 'So *sweet*! So *pink*! So *déclassé*.' As if he ever had any *classé* to begin with. No way you're pouring *that*"—she jabs a finger toward the container—"out of your magic juice box there."

"Bahama Mama, huh?" I say, glancing skeptically at my carton.

Mrs. Swinick makes a face and crosses her bony arms. "Didn't think so."

"OK, OK, just wait, now." I hold up a hand. "Give me a chance." I walk over to my prop box, my mind spinning. I have no idea what a Bahama Mama is, but I'm guessing it's something tropical. It's sweet and pink, so that helps. With rum, maybe? "You're sure you don't want to change your order? A Bloody Mary, perhaps? Gin and tonic?" I reach into the box, grab a couple of cups, and do a little surreptitious mixology.

"You'd like that, wouldn't you?" Mrs. Swinick says. "A little presto-change-o misdirection. Well, guess what? I know your game, mister. You say order anything, but you don't really *mean* anything. My ex was a shitty magician, too. You're all just a bunch of lying fraudsters."

"Not all of us, Mrs. Swinick." I remove a clear cup from the box, raise it in the air, and half fill it with a punch-pink liquid.

"Holy crap," someone coughs from the back of the room.

"One Bahama Mama," I announce, bowing and presenting the cup to Mrs. Swinick. "I don't mean to step out of line or anything, but your ex-husband was a fool." I hand her the drink. "There's nothing *déclassé* about a strong woman who knows what she wants and sticks with it."

Mrs. Swinick marvels at the drink, holding it up to the light in her birdlike hand as though it were a holy chalice. "That's . . ." She lifts the cup to her nose, takes a sip. "Delicious." Her tongue darts out and smooths her painted lips. "I haven't had one of these in years. How did you . . . ?" Her brow furrows. "How many compartments do you have in that thing?"

"Compartments?" I tilt my head and hold up the milk carton. Then I tear the cardboard apart, revealing absolutely nothing inside. "There are no compartments in here."

I smile at Mrs. Swinick as her rheumy, bloodshot eyes start to well up. She nods at me, raises her glass in approval, and takes another sip of her Bahama Mama.

10

"YOU GONNA EAT THAT?" THE WAITRESS SAYS, POINTING AT the swirl of raspberry sauce and pancake mush on my plate. "Or paint with it?"

I'm at some skeevy diner a block away from Heritage Acres. Despite the thrill of heroically salvaging my performance, my thoughts are in chaos and I figured I'd grab a quick snack before heading home for dinner, clear my head a bit, maybe tap out the email to the Magic Society on my phone.

I freeze my fork midstir and look up at the woman with the makeup mask, the smiling eyes, and the JANICE name tag. "Oh. I'm . . ." I glance down at the neon-red swamp shimmering in front of me. "Sorry. I was just . . . thinking."

Janice laughs. "Hey, you're paying for it. No law says you actually have to eat it." She narrows her gaze. "You *are* paying for it, right? I had a group of girls skip out on their ticket last week. Comes out of my paycheck, you know."

"No. Of course not. I'd never . . . I have money. Forty dollars." My cheeks burn as I wrestle my wallet from my pants pocket and show her my last two weeks' allowance. "See? Plus, my parents gave me a credit card for emergencies, so . . ." I close my wallet, aware that I'm nervously oversharing here.

"Well, that's just good parenting," Janice says. "I'll leave you to it, then. I will tell you, though"—she leans in conspiratorially and whispers—"I *have* heard that working the jaw helps work the old noggin. Plus, there's the blood-sugar thing. Maybe take a few bites and see how it goes."

"Oh. Right. Sure." I scoop up some sludge and slide it into my mouth. The sickly sweet raspberry puree glides unimpeded across my tongue and down my throat. I smile and raise my fork in appreciation, even as my stomach flinches from the syrupy onslaught.

"There you go." Janice stands up tall like she's done her civic duty for the day. "Now, I bet a solution to your problem reveals itself in no time."

"I hope you're right," I say, suppressing a retch.

"I usually am." Janice winks and starts to walk off. "You give a holler if you need anything else, 'kay?"

What is it with all the winking today? Am I someone who looks like he enjoys being winked at? I mean, sure, I might, if the wink actually *meant* something. But how do you even know? You *don't* because winks don't come with subtitles. They just hang in the air, open for interpretation.

And just like that, I've got Dani on the brain again. What if there really was some kind of after-the-audition promise in her wink? It's not so ridiculous an idea. Is two weeks really that long to wait for such an amazing girl?

Of course, the audition muddies everything, now that I think about it. Not just the wait time. The results could also affect how things play out between us. Each outcome poses its own set of challenges. Because, if *Dani* wins, she might be happy but think less of me as a magician. And if *Perry and I* win, she might be impressed but also pissed off and want nothing to do with me. Although, if *she* wins, maybe *I* would be impressed but pissed off. And then there's always the possibility that if Perry and I win, *Perry* gets all the credit and Dani just looks at me like a hanger-on. Which might be the worst outcome of all.

I rub at my face. Oh God. Why does my life have to be so complicated? Perry's life isn't this complicated. How could it be? He's always right. About everything.

He was even right about this: Dani's wink is haunting me. Even though I told him I wouldn't let it.

All right. *Enough is enough.* I need to shut her out. Dani's focusing on the only thing that matters. *I'm* focusing on the only thing that matters.

I grab my phone and open my email. I find the message from the Magic Society and hit reply. Let's get some clarification on those rules.

My thumbs hover over the keyboard. I write and rewrite the email in my head a dozen different ways, but I can't seem to commit any of the actual words to the screen.

After a few minutes I place my phone back on the table. I hate to admit it, but now that the initial dread of thinking we couldn't perform as a team has passed, I'm starting to wonder if the prospect of performing solo could possibly be a good thing. I mean, what if I actually won by myself? *Without* Perry? How would *that* look? Pretty impressive. Especially to Dani.

Still, how would it *feel*?

Empty, of course. Not having my best friend by my side.

I mean, sure, I doubt Perry ever feels empty winning things without me, but . . . this is different. This is something we do together.

Mostly.

Except when I'm researching the effects. And designing the tricks. And rehearsing it all at Heritage Acres.

But other than that . . .

I grab my phone. Better to just write the email and be done with it. Then it's not even up to me. They will respond either yes or no to our team audition and we can go from there. Whatever's meant to be, if you believe in that sort of thing.

My eyes waltz around the diner, as though I need to be sure I have total privacy before drafting my message. There's only one other customer here, sitting in the back booth, and I'm about to return to my phone when something about this guy captures my attention. He's a grizzled, droopy-eyed, buzzed-bald white dude with a dirty, overstuffed backpack propped up on the seat next to him.

But that's not what's interesting about him. What's interesting is what he's doing. And what he's doing is sitting there, sipping his coffee, mindlessly dropping a single six-sided die into a glass of water. Over and over and over again.

It's funny, once you're locked in to the guy's rhythm it's hard to take your eyes off him. The smooth tilt of his hand as he lets the die roll from his palm and *bloop* into the water. The concentrated stare as he examines the leisurely tumble of the plastic cube, rotating its way to the bottom of the glass. The careful, cautious way he lowers his spoon into the water to retrieve his test subject for the next round.

It's hypnotizing.

And also, really fucking weird.

I slide myself from the booth and make my way toward the back of the diner. Call it what you will, procrastination or following my natural curiosity, but I have to know what the hell this guy is doing.

"Hey," I say when I approach his table, hands tucked in pockets, gaze averted, trying to act all casual but failing miserably. "I was just wondering . . ." I lift my chin toward his glass. "What are you doing with that? The water and the die?"

He's either hard of hearing or too focused to notice my presence, because he says nothing.

I clear my throat into my fist. "Excuse me," I say a little louder. "I don't mean to bother you, but—"

"Then why are you still here?" The guy drops the die into the cup of water again and watches it float down.

"Oh." I laugh, because that's what I do when I'm nervous. "I didn't . . . know if you could hear me or not."

"Oh, I can hear you." His voice is nasal, gravelly. Like a snow shovel on asphalt. "I only *wish* I couldn't." He fishes the die out with his spoon, not even glancing my way.

"Right." I start to back away. "Got it. Sorry. Wasn't trying to disturb you. Just interested in your experiment." I turn on my heel.

"Trying to see if it's hinky," he mutters.

I turn back toward his booth. "Hinky?"

"Yeah. Weighted. Loaded. Crooked." The guy holds the wet die between his thumb and forefinger and peers at it.

"Well?" I say, feeling myself leaning forward. "Is it?"

He narrows his eyes like he's trying to see through the plastic. "Almost imperceptibly. Three to four percent, maybe. Enough to tilt the game in his favor." He tosses the die at me and I catch it. "Don't be using that to cheat your friends, now. However, if you find yourself in a game with your *enemies*, put your money on three."

I hold up the little white cube. "You don't want this?"

The guy glares at me. "I'm a lot of things, kid. But a cheat is not one of them."

I roll the die on his table and it lands on three.

The guy raises a bushy eyebrow and smiles. "On second thought." He grabs the die and drops it into the pocket of his blue denim shirt. "You're too young to have that kind of power."

I study the guy's ruddy, sagging face. His watery, pool-blue eyes. His liver-spotted nose. The four days of patchy white stubble surrounding his mouth, threatening to become a goatee. He's got a bulldog quality about him. But not a purebred. There's some Labrador in there as well. Maybe even a little dachshund.

"What the fuck are you staring at, kid?" the guy says.

"You remind me of someone," I say, because it's true. It just hit me. I've seen him before. On TV, I think. A commercial, maybe. Selling electronics. Someone who has the deal of all deals for you. Maybe an actor from one of the old shows Mom and Dad like to watch. *Or*, seeing how Heritage Acres is right around the corner, he could just be a resident that I recognize. But I don't think so. "I don't mean to be rude or anything, but . . . are you . . . *someone*?"

"Am I *someone*?" the guys says, rumpling his brow. "I'd hate to hear what you'd ask if you *were* being rude."

"No, like someone famous . . . *ish*," I say. "You look familiar. Were you ever on TV?"

"God, I hope not." He glances around like there might be cameras nearby. "I try to keep a low profile."

I squint at him. "Are you sure? You didn't do infomercials or something?"

"I get it all the time," the guy says. "Just got one of those faces, I guess." He reaches into his swollen backpack and plucks out a deck of cards. "Hey, you like games, kid?"

"Sure," I say.

"Wanna play?" he asks.

"What are we playing?" I probably shouldn't get involved with some stranger I just met. But I size him up, and even though I definitely couldn't take him in a fight, I could probably outrun him if I had to.

The guy sticks out a well-callused hand. "Bob."

"Quinn," I say, reaching out and giving him a firm handshake because it shows strength and confidence. Or so I'm told.

Bob cranes his neck and looks past me to my booth. "Why don't you go grab your grub and bring it over here?" He starts to shuffle the cards. "I'll show you a little distraction I picked up in Quebec. Who knows, maybe you'll even get a free meal out of it. Game called Bonneteau."

11

"BONNETEAU." BOB MAKES A SWEEPING GESTURE ACROSS the three facedown cards in front of him on the table. "Find the lady."

I study the three-card spread, tapping my lip, pretending to give this some real thought. Turns out Bonneteau is just three-card monte. Also turns out, this grumpy old man is just a scam artist who unknowingly picked a magician for a mark.

"That one right there," I say, pointing to the middle card.

Bob flips the center card over, revealing the queen. "You got her again. That's three in a row. You're good at this."

"I imagine it gets a little harder if you mix it up more," I say. *And I bet it becomes almost impossible for most people when there's cash on the line and you finally do the false throw.*

"A little bit more challenging, yeah." He nods reflectively. "But if you pay attention, you can get it most of the time." Bob turns the queen back over and snaps up the three cards. "Want to go again?"

"Sure, why not?" I eat another spoonful of my pancake paste. I've suddenly regained my appetite. It's kind of fun watching someone go through their underhanded motions when you know exactly what's coming next.

"I'm going to really make it tough this go-round," Bob says.

He might go through this routine a half dozen more times— letting me win five out of six just to show how fair and fun it is— before he ups the stakes. Everyone's method is slightly different, but the idea is always the same. Give the mark a false sense of confidence so when the wager is at last presented, he's all in for some not-so-easy money.

But I don't have time to wait for Bob's whole drawn-out play. I need to get home for dinner or I won't hear the end of it. So I figure I'll just fast-forward this a bit.

"I think I've really got the hang of this now," I say. "What do you say we make it a little more interesting?"

Bob's eyes narrow. "More interesting? How do you suggest we do that?"

"Oh. I don't know. A small wager?"

"Hey, I don't gamble with kids, kid," Bob says, throwing up his hands. "I have grandchildren. I'm a lot of things, but someone who takes candy, *or cash*, from babies is not one of them."

"Not money," I say, feigning innocence. "What about a meal? Like you suggested earlier." That's right, *Bob*. I spotted that little mind worm you planted before. "Then it's just a new friend buying another new friend a snack." I gesture at our respective food items. "Loser picks up the tab."

Bob strokes his bristly chin. "When you put it like that . . ." He lifts his mug to his lips. "Even my grandkids make me coffee."

"There you go," I say, watching his shaky moral foundation crumble before my eyes. "We'll just have Janice combine the bills. What do you say?"

Bob sniffs loudly, working his tongue around his mouth like he's trying to get something out of his teeth. "All right. You convinced me. But just this once." He starts to shuffle the three cards. "You get one shot, so stay focused." The right side of his mouth curls up in a little smirk, which makes my chest tighten. "Ready for this?"

I nod. "Go for it." My heart starts to thrum, my mouth going dry. Maybe this is a bad idea, messing around with a con artist. What if he has more than just cards and dirty clothes in that backpack?

Bob holds the two of clubs and the three of spades in his right hand, and the queen of hearts in his left. "Same rules apply. I move the lady, you have to find her. *Bonneteau.* Here we go."

He throws the cards, one at a time, facedown onto the table. I know exactly which one the queen is because Bob hasn't done any trickery. *Yet.* It's a little odd because generally the money card— queen, ace, king, or jack—is almost always held in the hand with a second card so you can simulate the throw. Meaning, the observer *thinks* you've thrown down the queen when really you've thrown down the other card. It's a classic play on expectations. But he didn't do it here. Which immediately raises my antennae.

"Now, before I start to shuffle," Bob says. "You got your eye on your card?"

"Yup."

"All right, kid. Pay close attention. Royalty can be elusive." Bob starts mixing up the cards very quickly. To the point where they're almost a blur. For an old man with such quivering, arthritic hands, he sure is dexterous. I can still follow the queen, but it's harder than before, no doubt.

"Wow," I say, my eyes starting to cross as I study the smear of cards and hands flying across the table. "That's pretty impressive."

After about a dozen seconds Bob abruptly stops and wafts his hands over the three facedown cards. "The choice is yours. Find the lady. *Bonneteau.*"

I know which one it is. Although now I'm starting to second-guess myself. Did he do a swap in the blur of the shuffle that I missed? He *must* have.

Unless . . . maybe this guy doesn't actually know *how* to play this game. Maybe he thinks the idea is just to shuffle really, really fast in hopes of confusing the observer.

Oh well. It's just the price of a coffee. "This one," I say, as confidently as I can, mashing my finger on the rightmost card. "That's my choice."

"Are you sure?" Bob asks. "I went pretty fast there. I'll give you one chance to change your mind."

I shake my head. "I'm sure."

Bob reaches forward, grabs the edge of the card, and slowly turns it over to reveal . . . the queen of hearts.

"Huh." He knits his brow, staring at the queen, looking truly baffled. "That's . . . wow. OK. Nice work. You've got some eagle eyes there, kid." He flings the queen facedown onto the table, then lifts his chin toward my soupy plate. "I'll get Janice to pack that up for you if you want."

"That's OK," I say. "It's just raspberry sauce now."

All right, I'm confused. I thought for sure he was trying to play me. But he didn't even try. He just . . . mixed up the cards.

No sleight of hand.

No misdirection.

Just . . . fast shuffling.

"Look," I say, glancing over at his soiled and torn backpack sitting on the booth bench beside him. "I changed my mind. I'd like to pay for my own meal."

"*You will not.* We had an agreement. I'm a man of my word. It's one of the last things I've got left, my word. Don't take that from me, too." He exhales and glances over his shoulder. "I'm gonna go take a piss. If you would be so kind as to watch my stuff"—Bob tilts his head toward his belongings—"we can get the bill when I return."

"Sure," I say. "OK."

"Much obliged." Bob presses his fists into the vinyl seat, slides from the booth, and hobbles off toward the back of the diner.

As I watch him go, I think about just paying for my food and his coffee and getting out of here. A random act of kindness. But then, I worry that he might be insulted. Might feel like I don't think he can afford it. Which he can't. Obviously. But still, I don't want to hurt his feelings.

As he makes his way to the bathroom, he leans over to Janice and says something to her. I watch his mouth move. *We'll be settling up soon,* I think he says, though I can't actually hear him from this distance.

Bob moves along and Janice heads over to our table with a full pot of coffee.

"How you doing, sweetie?" she says.

"I'm good."

"Bobby's not bothering you too much, is he?" she asks.

"No," I say. "He's fine. What's his story, anyway?"

Janice shrugs. "Heck if I know. I don't ask too many questions. You get a feel for the fellas who want to talk and those that don't. Bobby, he doesn't like you to pry." She bends forward with her pot and refills Bob's cup. Some coffee dribbles on the table and all over the facedown queen of hearts. "Jeez-o-Pete, Janice, now look what you've done. What a little danga-langa ding-dong you are." She puts down her coffeepot, tugs a bar rag from her apron, and wipes up the spill. In the process of drying the queen, she accidentally folds back one of the corners. "Oopsie." She grimaces and tries to fix the bent corner by flattening it on the table. Then she pulls her hands away like it never happened and nods. "There. Like new." She smiles at me. "Please don't tell. Bobby's very particular about his things. Once, he left his reading glasses on the table and I thought I'd do him a favor and clean them for him. They were filthy. Speckled with food and who knows what else. Well, let me tell you. I did *not* get the attitude of gratitude one might expect."

"Your secret's safe with me," I say, studying the bent corner on the queen. A surge of adrenaline spikes my blood. Synapses in my brain fire like crazy. Something's off. Warning bells clang every-where as I try to work out what's going on here. "I won't tell a soul."

"Thanks." Janice picks up her pot of coffee and scuttles away.

I stare at the damaged card on the table, my stomach clenching. Of course! Janice is obviously a shill for this guy. I glance over at her, laughing with one of the customers at the counter. She looks so innocent. Like someone's mom. But there's no other explanation as to why she would perform the classic shill move, marking a card so I'll think I have an upper hand on the next game.

Now I just have to wait here for Bob to return so he can offer me another, *larger* bet. A chance for him to get even. But really, an opportunity to fleece me completely.

Well, at least I don't have to feel so bad about winning anymore.

"All right, I've gotta skedaddle," Bob says as he approaches the booth. "Got a podiatrist appointment to get to. Gout's been grousing again."

Huh. OK. Maybe I'm wrong. Maybe my fevered brain is just jumping to conclusions. "Should we ask Janice for the bill?"

"We could and we should." Bob checks his watch. "*However.*" He slides back into the booth and slaps the table with his hand. "As I have just a few minutes to spare, would you be averse to giving a poor old man one last chance to save his dignity?"

Ha! Right. Here we go.

I smile. I don't know whether to call this guy out, right here and now, or just give him enough rope so that he hangs himself.

"What do you have in mind?" I ask.

"A one-sided wager in your favor," he begins. "If you win, I will still cover our bills as per our last game. However, I will *add* to that a hundred-dollar credit that you can use here anytime. Conversely, if *I* win"—he places his hand on his chest—"and you *don't* find the lady, you'll only have to cover our bills. Sound fair? Still, no money is exchanged."

"Sure," I say, biting my tongue. "Sounds good." But what's in it for Janice? I wonder.

"Plus tip," Bob says, holding up a finger.

Ah, there we go. "Of course," I say.

"We don't want to forget about that," Bob says. "I come here all the time. Janice is one of the good ones. Doesn't get paid half of what she deserves. Tip has to be included. Twenty-five percent."

"Twenty-*five*?"

"I'm not cheap," Bob says. "Are you?"

"No," I say. "It's just, I thought fifteen to twenty percent was standard."

"Janice works her tail off," Bob says. "She has a family to feed. It'll mean the world to her. Besides, what's an extra five percent to you?" He gestures at me like I'm made of money or something.

"Fine," I say, because really, it's not going to matter one way or another, since I won't be paying. "Why not say thirty percent? Since we're being generous."

"I like how you think, kid," Bob says, snatching up the three cards once again. "Shall we review? We have the two of clubs, the three of spades, and the queen of hearts." He shows me all three cards once more. The two and three in his left hand, the bent-cornered queen in his right. Once again, I'm not sure how he plans on doing his sleight of hand, but I'm going to be extra focused this time because it's sure to happen; at some point he is going to have to swap out the bent queen for a bent two or three. "Your mission, if you choose to accept it, is to find the lady. *Bonneteau*."

Bob throws the cards down and immediately begins mixing them up, not asking me if I know where the queen is this time. But he knows I won't protest. The queen is easy to follow. It's the one with the bent corner.

Except that it isn't.

Because he swapped it out.

And I know exactly when he did it.

Bob releases the cards and pulls his hands back. "Now it's your turn." He motions toward the spread. "*Bonneteau*. Find the lady."

12

I SMILE AT BOB AND SHAKE MY HEAD. "ARE YOU SURE YOU don't want to call off the bet?" I don't know why I feel like I need to give him an out. He's the one trying to scam me. But still, if he's hustling kids, he has to be pretty desperate.

"Why would I want to do that?" Bob says.

I shift my gaze from the cards to Bob's watery eyes. I can't do it. I can't take this guy's money. "Because I know the trick, OK? You switched out the queen."

"I don't know what the hell you're talking about, kid."

"This card here." I press my finger into the leftmost card. "*Should* be the queen. It has a little bend in it so it's easily located."

"Wait." Bob narrows his eyes at me. "Are you saying you marked my cards?"

"No." I shake my head but keep the card pinned to the table with my finger so he can't switch it out again. "I'm saying you had *Janice* mark the card. But you switched it out so I would only *think* the queen was marked and therefore choose the wrong card."

"So, wait." He laughs, smiles, waggles a finger at me. "Let me get this straight. You're saying that you think this *isn't* the queen?" Bob nods toward the card I'm touching.

"I don't think it. I *know* it. Listen, call it what you want—Find the Lady. Three-card monte. Chase the Ace. Running the Red. Bonneteau. They're all the same. I'm familiar with the scam. I happen to be a magician."

"Oh, OK, this is going to be fun." Bob scoots forward and taps the marked card I've got pinned to the table. "How certain are you that this *isn't* the queen?"

I press my finger so hard into the card that the tip under the nail goes white. "As certain as I am that you're trying to figure out how to switch it out again before offering me another bet."

"I'd be happy to up our bet if you want. But only if you are absolutely, one hundred percent sure that you *do not* have a queen of hearts pinned to the table there."

"Look," I say, shaking my head, "I don't want to take your money."

"Ooooh." Bob leans back, nodding. "I see. So you're a coward."

"I'm not a coward."

He shrugs. "Circumstances would dictate otherwise."

I clench my jaw. Screw it. I gave him a chance. "I get to flip it over."

Bob smiles and leans forward. "I wouldn't have it any other way. But we *definitely* have to raise the stakes a bit. Like you said." He grins. "How about this? I will *double* my credit for you to two hundred dollars. All you have to do is pay our bill, give Janice that nice thirty percent tip we discussed, and hand over those two sweet, crisp twenty-dollar bills in your wallet."

Wait, *what*? How did he know—?

Janice, of course.

Bob stares at me. "Do you want to take the bet or not, Mr. I-Happen-to-Be-a-Magician? Or are you now questioning your superior expertise?"

I scrunch up my eyes, trying to work this whole thing through again. Could I be wrong? I was sure I saw the swap. He's got to be bluffing. He wants me to back down. That's the only answer.

"I don't have all day," Bob says. "Come on. You think you're so smart, that you have me, and Janice, and this whole game figured out. Maybe so. *Orrrrr* maybe I was right all along, and you just don't have the balls to turn that card over."

"Fine," I say, tugging my wallet out with my free hand and slapping it on the table. "Deal. There's no way this is the queen of hearts."

I pull my finger away and flip over the bent-cornered card.

My stomach drops the instant I see the scarlet Q.

I look up from the table and stare at Bob, who's got a mobster's half grin on his face. "I don't understand," I say.

"*That*," Bob says, pointing at me, "is the first intelligent thing you've said all afternoon." He sweeps up the cards and lifts his chin toward the cash register. "Now go settle up with Janice. She's all ready for you."

I leap the curb, cut past the stop sign, and rip onto our street. Sweat courses down my back, and my thighs burn like crazy as I try to outbike the late-for-dinner lecture that's nipping at my heels. I got a text from Mom while I was at the diner saying to be on time tonight because we were having guests. They'll be either new home buyers or people from their theater group, the Lilting Librettos. Either way dinner will be interminable. Normally I'm able to feign interest and pretend to be engaged in adult conversation, but tonight my brain is on fire.

The whole ride home I've been trying to figure out how Bob did it. I know I saw him swap out the bent queen for a different marked card while he was shuffling—at least I *think* I know—but for the life of me I can't figure out how he switched it *back* to the queen while I had the swapped card pinned to the table.

He didn't even go near it.

Or did he? I can't remember now. I *feel* like he didn't come near the card, but that doesn't mean anything. The only thing reliable about memory is its unreliability. Magicians prey on this all the time. It's very possible that Bob misdirected me at some point and I didn't even notice him making the swap. Could have been while we were negotiating the bet.

It's kind of shaken my confidence, if I'm being honest. I felt all puffed-up after astonishing Mrs. Swinick with her Bahama Mama. But if I can't even beat a basic three-card monte game . . . I thought I was better than that. Thought I could spot the trick in a trick almost every time.

I missed his little sleight of hand with the diner bill, too. According to Janice, "Monday's settle-up-for-the-week day, dontcha know?"

Luckily I had my credit card on me. I'm not exactly sure how I'm going to explain what a $63.27 food emergency was to Mom and Dad, though. Maybe I'll just tell them I bought a homeless man a meal. A *big* meal. They'll like that. And who knows, it *could* be true. He certainly looked the part. Although you'd think someone with such mad magic skills would be able to parlay it into some kind of job or—

Bam! The realization hits me like a bazooka-rifled dodge ball. My bike wobbles and I wrestle control of my handlebars, course-correcting before I steer myself into a parked car.

Holy crap.

That's why he seemed so familiar to me!

I stop pedaling and glide, my heart galloping like a spooked horse. I can't believe it took me this long to figure it out.

Bob is *Robert*.

As in Robert *Lazlo*.

As in the Dazzling *Fucking* Lazlo!

Of course he was able to fool me! It totally makes sense now. He's one of the best magicians I've ever seen!

I run my hand through my wind-tangled hair. This is so wild. Robert Lazlo, the creator of the Monkey's Paw, the single greatest illusion I have ever witnessed, just scammed me for his restaurant tab and two weeks' allowance. I don't know why I'm smiling at the idea, but it feels like a sign. A magician's hazing or something.

I coast up my driveway, past a gold Mercedes I don't recognize, dismount my bike, tap the code into the glowing garage keypad, and watch as the door rises with a rattling groan.

I'm literally shaking, every nerve in my body firing at once. This kind of thing *never* happens to me. We're talking Perry-grade luck here. If he came up to me one day and said *he* ran into Robert Lazlo at some random diner, I'd just shrug and say, "Of course you did." But *me*? Something going *my* way for once? It's unprecedented.

And just as this thought washes over me, another idea crests right behind it: the Monkey's Paw. The idea of it literally makes me gasp. Because if we actually *do* have to perform as solo magicians—I mean, sure, sure, I'm still going to write the email, see if they'll let us audition as a team—*however*, if the MSA still insists we go on as solo magicians . . . well, then, the Monkey's Paw is the absolute pinnacle of solo magic acts.

If I could get Robert Lazlo to show me the secret to his trick . . . well, then, forget about it. With a mind-melting effect like that?

I'd be unbeatable.

I chuck my bike in the garage, shut the door, and bolt into the house. I have some googling to do. As certain as I am that Bonneteau Bob is the Dazzling Lazlo, a little confirmation would not be unwelcome. Plus, I still have to write that email to the Magic Society of America before I get too ahead of myself.

"I'm home!" I bellow as I kick off my shoes, then duck my head into the kitchen, the rich, savory smell of Mom's beef stew completely enveloping me. "I just need to run upstairs for a sec," I say breathlessly. "I'll be down for dinner in half a min—"

"Meet the Darlings," Dad cuts in, gesturing at a midforties, gray-flanneled couple who look like they're here at gunpoint. "We just sold them the Goldsteins' house, right around the corner on Alpine."

83

"Nice to meet you," I say, offering my hand. "Mr. and Mrs. Darling."

"*Doctor and Doctor* Darling," Mom says with an impressed laugh. "He's an orthopedic surgeon and she's a dermatologist."

"Wow," I say. They sound rich. Wonder why they bought in our crappy neighborhood and not over in the Uplands. "Cool."

"And this is their daughter," Dad says, motioning toward the kitchen table to a girl who I hadn't noticed until now. "Dani."

Wait—what? Dani Dani? No way. How's that even—?

But there she is, sitting in my kitchen, silently cutting a deck of cards with one hand. I open my mouth to say hello, but the sight of her has choked off my oxygen supply, making it impossible to speak.

Mom must notice my deer-in-the-headlights look because she offers up some helpful prompting. "Dani says you two already met at school?"

I work some air through my lungs to try to acknowledge this as a fact, but all that comes out is a little balloon squeak.

"The magic shop, too," Dani says, showing me the ace of spades on the bottom of her deck of cards, giving it a little shake, and turning it into the jack of diamonds.

"Yeah," I choke out. "We've . . . met."

"Well, then," Mom says, touching my shoulder and corralling me over toward Dani. "Magic *and* high school. You two seem to have a lot in common. Why don't you go into the family room and chat about it all? Dinner will be ready in a few minutes."

13

CODE RED. NEED HELP. DANI'S HERE. MY HOUSE! LONG STORY. FREAKING OUT. HIDING IN BATHROOM. WHAT DO I SAY TO HER?

I sit on the closed toilet lid, the calming scent of lavender air freshener having no effect on me. I stare down at my phone screen, willing Perry to answer me.

"Quinn, honey," I hear Mom call from downstairs. "Don't get lost on your phone in there. You have a guest."

"I'm not on my phone," I mutter-shout.

Goddamn it. *Come on, Perry. Write back.* I shake my phone like Perry's response is sand stuck in an hourglass.

I can't believe Mom and Dad did this to me. I mean, I know their intentions are good and all, but seriously, inviting a girl from school over? With no warning? They know I hate being ambushed. Have they already forgotten the Great Surprise Party Puking of Seventh Grade? I know I never will.

If I'd had a little prep time, if Mom had just warned me while I was at the diner, I could have googled some interesting topics of conversation. As it is, I'm working without a net.

Unless Perry can supply that net.

"Quinn!" Dad hollers up the stairs. "Let's go. Don't be rude. Pinch it off."

Jesus Christ, Dad. Thanks for that!

I haul myself off the toilet, then flush and wash my hands for effect.

As the water runs, I stare at my reflection in the mirror. The best you can say about my face is that it's inconspicuous. Like clip art. The kind of mug you might use in an advertisement for nine-dollar haircuts. "You've got the best face of all," Mom said to me once when I was feeling particularly loathsome. "It's a blank slate. The kind of face every performer wants because you can make it your own."

Mom and Dad try. They do. But this parenting thing does not come naturally to them.

I puff out my thin lips. Press my weak cheeks up with my fingertips. Furrow my brow seductively. Trying to make my face my own. Handsome. Sexy. Confident.

Instead, I look like I have a secret . . . and that secret is that I just shit my pants.

I release my face and sigh. Perry used to be a blank slate, too. Until he woke up breathtaking.

I step from the bathroom and make my way to my room. I should really head straight downstairs to join everyone, but I have to change out of this sweaty T-shirt and put on some more deodorant.

I don't need Mom and Dad pointing out my pungency at the dinner table with an oh-so-clever rendition of "Smell-o Dolly" or "There's No Business Like BO Business."

Besides, it'll give me a little more time to maybe get some help from Perry.

"Howdy," Dani says the second I step into my bedroom.

"Holy shit!" I shout, my heart seizing up. I look around like we've entered an alternate reality where girls actually visit my bedroom. "What are you doing up here?"

"Apparently there's been a biscuit tragedy," she says. "Dinner's postponed another fifteen. Your parents said you'd entertain me." She regards my messy, cluttered room and grins. "So far, I'm pretty entertained."

"Sorry," I say, quickly plucking clothes off the floor and furtively flinging them into my equally messy closet. "I wasn't expecting guests."

"It's fine," Dani says, laughing. "I've seen worse. Trust me." She does a slow pirouette, studying the place. "I could help you organize." She shrugs. "If you want."

"You want to help me clean my room?" I say, equal parts horrified—because even *I* don't know what we might find under some of these piles—and tempted—because at least it'll fill the time.

"It's something I'm good at." Dani forces a smile. "I'm a big fan of orderliness. Lists, schedules, calendars. Bins, baskets, boxes. You know what they say. A cluttered room is a cluttered mind."

"Yeah, no, that's true," I say, suddenly remembering some of the more personal things I've got squirreled away. "And as much as

I'd appreciate it, my parents would be absolutely appalled . . . right before they incorporated it into their musical. How about we do some tricks instead? See if we can fool each other?"

Yes, good idea, Quinn! Magic will keep me distracted. Stop me from wondering what to say to her, and what *not* to say to her. And what her soft, wet, perfectly formed lips must taste like.

"Oh. OK. Sure." Dani shrugs. "You first, though. Show me something you're working on."

I grab a deck of cards from my desk—one of several I've prepped for "impromptu" performances such as this—and start to shuffle them.

"So, uh, I was . . . wondering," I say, stalling for time as I furtively search for the nine of spades. "I'm a little confused. Because . . . I thought you said you needed to focus on the audition. Blinders and everything. That you didn't have time to hang out with people. And yet here you are."

"Maybe this is me focusing," Dani says, waggling her eyebrows. "You know. Friends close, enemies closer. Studying the competition. Learning all your habits and insecurities. That sort of thing."

I study her, trying to figure out if she's kidding or not. But her expression is masterfully unreadable.

"Seriously?" I say.

Dani shrugs. "I won't lie, it did cross my mind." She furrows her brow. "Like, why didn't I put up a fight when my parents told me we were coming over here? Normally I would have at least made an attempt to get out of it. That alone makes me suspicious of my intentions."

"Wait." I stop shuffling the cards. "So . . . you're *not* joking? You came here to spy on me?"

"I don't really know. I don't *think* so." Dani winces adorably. "Probably not? Could be I was just grateful for the interruption. Sometimes when I get on a roll I don't know when to stop myself. Like, when I first started learning how to play the mandolin, I would practice until my fingers bled. But then I'd just superglue the wounds shut so I could practice more." She laughs. "Still, the fact that I wasn't more adamant about not coming tonight, I can't rule out the possibility of duplicity on my part."

"Wow. OK." I blink at this odd girl. Is she messing with me? Or is she being, like, *super* honest? "*Thanks*, I guess? For being . . . up front about it. I'll be sure to be on my guard. Just in case."

I start shuffling the cards again, wondering why I'm not more upset about the idea that Dani might be spying on me. Instead, her bald-faced honesty just makes me like her even more.

Which immediately makes me wary. What if that's her play here? Make light of the fact that she's trying to get close to me so that I won't think she's actually trying to get close to me. It would be a brilliant bit of mind-fuckery.

Just the fact that she's already scrambling my thoughts to an unsettling degree should make me really dislike this girl.

And yet I don't.

Quite the opposite, actually. The more she confuses me, the more I want to be close to her.

14

"PICK A CARD," I SAY, FANNING THE DECK OUT ON MY DESK. My mouth is a bit pasty and my hands are a little slick, but considering my near meltdown in the bathroom earlier, I'm much calmer than I should be. It doesn't make a lot of sense. I've never performed magic one-on-one for a female who wasn't my mother. Why am I able to speak in full sentences? Why am I not shaking like a spooked whippet? What kind of real-life wizard is this girl?

"Mine's a card trick also," Dani says, studying the spread. "Just so you're aware. So you don't think I'm copying you."

"That's fine," I say, wondering why she's telling me this. Is she trying to throw off my rhythm? Or is this more of her radical honesty? "Let's get through mine first." I nod at the desk. "Any card."

Dani's eyes flit up from the desk to meet mine. "I'm not going to make this easy on you. I'm going to study every move you make. That's the only way to get better at anything. To pull it apart. Dissect it. Examine the minutiae."

"Right," I say, trying to work up a little saliva in my mouth. "Except there's no minutiae to examine yet. I just asked you to pick a card."

"Not true," Dani contradicts. "Consider the setup: You spread the cards out on the desk. You're not holding them in your hand. You didn't flip through the deck and ask me to say stop at any point. The setup is always important, as you well know."

I shake my head. "Not in this case. I could have held the cards in my hand. Or flipped through them. Wouldn't make a difference. I just thought this way you wouldn't think I was forcing a card on you."

Dani smirks at me like I'm full of it. "Is that so?" She slowly, cautiously begins to reach for the bottom card. "So you wouldn't be averse to me taking"—she snatches the last card in the spread and holds it up triumphantly—"this one?"

"Absolutely not," I say, scooping up the rest of the deck and handing Dani a Sharpie. "Please, sign the card for me."

Dani takes the marker, uncaps it, and turns away. "Don't peek." She signs the card, recaps the marker, and spins back. "Here," she says, holding out the card and pen. "Go on. Set up your double lift, or whatever."

"No, no." I shake my head, take only the Sharpie, and point at her signed card. "You hold on to that. Keep it facedown on the desk. I'm not going to touch it."

I shuffle the deck of cards, do a few fancy flourishes for effect, then stop suddenly, like something just came to me. "You know what? Now that I think about it, after what you told me earlier, I'm not sure I trust you with your card exposed like that." I reach out and snatch it up from the desk, just like I said I wouldn't do. "You might try to switch this out on me to throw me off my game." I fold the card over twice into a little square. "Bite down on this with your teeth." I mime placing the card in my mouth. "That way, we both know it can't be tampered with."

Dani smiles as she takes the square. "The old kissing trick, then, huh? That's pretty forward of you."

"Uh, no, not the kissing trick," I say, though, I won't lie, the thought did occur. "It's a variation. Without the . . . you know . . . physical contact."

"Oh," she says, and I could swear she sounds ever so slightly disappointed. She slips the folded card between her teeth. "OK, let's see where this goes."

"Now I'll pick one." I flip over the top card on the deck and show Dani the nine of diamonds.

"All right," she says through clenched teeth.

"I'll sign mine just like you signed yours." I uncap the marker, sign my name to the nine, recap the pen, fold up my card, and place it in between my teeth so that Dani and I are mirror images.

She giggles. "I'm so curious," she says, her words slightly garbled by the card. "*Clearly*. Since I've stopped nitpicking everything."

"All right, now," I say as seriously as I can while holding a folded-up playing card between my teeth. I look straight into Dani's radiant green eyes. "Slip the card all the way inside your mouth." I flick out my tongue and pull the folded card into my mouth by way of example.

"It sure as hell *seems* like the kissing trick," Dani says, laughing as she pushes the card into her mouth with her finger.

"More like a pelican trick." I quickly tilt my head back and make a big show of swallowing the card, like a giant seabird gulleting a fish. I drop my chin and open my mouth to show her it's empty. I dart my tongue this way and that to prove there's nothing hiding anywhere. "Go on. Check yours."

Dani pulls the moist card from her mouth, already grinning excitedly, knowing what she's going to find. She unfolds the card and sees the nine of diamonds that I signed. She shows it to me. "That's impressive," she says. "Where's mine?"

I smile because I was just waiting for her to ask. "Why, it never left the deck." I fan the cards out facedown on my desk, the queen of hearts with Dani's signature on it, the only faceup card in the row.

Except—

—she didn't sign her name on the card. I pluck out the card and read the note Dani wrote: QUINN PURCELL WILL CHOOSE AND SIGN THE NINE OF DIAMONDS.

"Ta-da!" she says, holding out her hands like a game show hostess. "And there's *my* card trick. Are you astonished and amazed?"

"Uh, yeah," I say, examining her swoopy, sexy handwriting, feeling a little woozy, confused, but excited, too, my heart racing, like I just stepped off a Tilt-A-Whirl. "I am. Very much so."

Dani grins impishly. "I told you I was watching your every move. Some pretty nice misdirection with all that spying-on-you talk, huh?" She winks at me. *Again.*

And with that, I fall helplessly, hopelessly in love.

15

THE DINING ROOM IS FILLED WITH THE WARM, COZY smells of Mom's beef stew and Dad's buttermilk biscuits and mashed potatoes. It's their signature meal—and something that impresses everyone who eats it. Which is good, because the more time I spend with Dani, the more I want to impress her.

The entire time at dinner Dani and I have been ignoring the adult conversation. (It's their own fault for seating us side by side.) Instead, we try to make each other giggle by performing clandestine magic tricks: vanishing the saltshaker, using our minds to bend the cutlery, levitating napkins, and serving spoons, and water glasses.

It feels an awful lot like . . . flirting.

Something I've never been able to do successfully before. Which is why it makes me suspicious. This isn't me. This is Perry's domain. Cute girls volleying cute things at him. Perry casually lobbing something adorable back.

Dani's done something to me here. Made it too easy to talk to her. Made me too comfortable. Why would she do that if she's already said she doesn't want to be friends? Is it the spying thing after all? I know she said it was just misdirection, but what if it wasn't? What if her saying it was misdirection *was actually the misdirection*?

I could drive myself in circles like this. And yet all I know is, right here, right now, at the dining room table, as Dani and I are showing off for each other . . .

I'm having more fun than I've had in a very long time.

"For my taste," Dani's father says in response to Mom asking if the Doctors Darling have seen any good musicals lately, "I find that musicals simply ask too much of the imagination."

"How so?" Mom asks, genuine curiosity in her voice.

"*Honey,*" Dani's mother warns, patting her husband's hand. "The Purcells *perform* in musicals. They invited us to one next week, remember?" She forces a smile. "The lovely, colorful, caveman brochure they gave us? The Stage Hollow Dinner Theater?"

"*Sage* Hollow," Mom corrects, as if they'll somehow end up at the wrong theater, watching the wrong musical, and eating the wrong plate of Filet Misérables. Or Fried Okrahoma! Or the always popular Linguinally Blonde.

"It's fine," Dad says, waving this off. "It's good for us to hear criticisms from the outside. We're always trying to convert the uninitiated. I'd like to hear why you don't enjoy musicals, the most joyous form of entertainment ever created by humankind."

"It's only my opinion," Dani's father says, chewing his food and swallowing. "But I find it hard enough to suspend disbelief when regular people are up onstage acting ridiculous. Make them break out into a song-and-dance number about the glorious bran muffin they're eating"—he shrugs and starts cutting his meat—"it's all a bit much. *For me.* That's all I'm saying. It's probably just my own lack of vision."

Dani nudges me with her elbow. Shows me a knife with three dots of butter on the blade. She spins it over to show me there are three dots of butter on the other side, too. This is a classic. Jumping Spots on a Paddle.

She licks a finger and wipes away one of the dots on the top. When she flips the knife over, the same spot on the back has disappeared as well. She does this two more times, until both sides of the knife are blank. Then, with a little flick of the knife, the three butter dots reappear. On both sides!

It's so silly and simple that it makes me laugh, this basic of basic tricks.

But Dani's not finished. She holds up a finger, gestures at the knife with the three butter dots on it, gives it another shake—

And turns it into a spoon with three butter dots down the center of the scoop.

I nod, giving her a silent round of applause under the table, impressed by her original spin on the effect.

"OK, well, I don't want to sound too full of ourselves," Mom says, glancing over at Dad. "But when you come see *The Hominid's Lament*, I bet you come out the other end a musical convert." She throws up her hands. "That's all I'm going to say about it. You can form your own opinion. Tickets are available at the Sage Hollow box office."

"Well," Dani's mother says, "we are very much looking forward to the performance." She shoots Dani's father a look that could choke off his airway, but then quickly twists her face into a smile. "Isn't that right, honey?"

"Yes," Dani's father drones. "We are very excited about it."

"Speaking of exciting performances," Dad says, seeming very happy that he's been handed an exit strategy, "I guess we're going to have a little friendly competition between our two families."

"Mmmm, yes," Mrs. Darling says, taking a sardonic sip of her Chardonnay. "The magic camp auditions. That's a bit of a sore subject in our house."

"Oh?" Mom says, her spoon clinking the side of her bowl. "How so?"

"They don't want me to audition," Dani says, popping a piece of biscuit into her mouth. "Even though they know it's the most important thing in the world to me."

"That's not true and you know it," Mr. Darling says. "But then, you hear what you want to hear."

"*Gary,*" Mrs. Darling snaps through clenched teeth, giving her head a quick shake.

Mom's head swivels between Dani and her parents. "I don't understand."

"They think I'm spreading myself too thin," Dani says, starting to pick at the ragged cuticle on her thumb. "But I'm still getting straight As—like I promised—so I don't see what the problem is."

"The *problem*"—Mrs. Darling returns her daughter's glare—"is not something I want to discuss in front of people we just met."

"You brought it up," Dani says, still digging at her finger. "I just don't think it's fair, you making me feel guilty about it, that's all. But whatever."

Everyone at the table suddenly finds the minutiae of their beef stew incredibly interesting. The uncomfortable utensil-clinking and awkward silence that pollutes the air is suffocating.

Until, finally, Mr. Darling sighs. "Dani is an overachiever." He glances sympathetically at his wife. "And we're worried she'll burn herself out. That's all. It isn't some big, dark secret."

"She gets it from us, unfortunately," Mrs. Darling says. "I'm afraid we aren't the best models of balance."

My eyes dart between Dani and her parents. Would they really stop her from auditioning? I'm gonna be honest, the prospect of that is not unappealing. She's going to be tough competition, and it would solve a lot of complications in my life. Also, if she dropped out, I'd know pretty quickly whether or not she's been messing with my emotions.

I wonder if Dani's parents know the *extent* of her obsession with the auditions. Do they know about her working for free at the smoke-filled magic shop all weekend, for example? About her refusal to make any friends till the auditions are over? They must be aware of her unhealthy mandolin-practicing habits, at least. Unless . . . they aren't.

These are the kinds of things that could push parents over the edge. Could make them put their feet down in order to do what they feel is best for their kid.

The more appealing the thought becomes, the more disgusted with myself I get. I am a lot of things, but a devious, underhanded snitch is not one of them.

Right?

16

As much as I enjoyed dinner, I have important work to get to. It's a testament to the effect Dani has on me that she almost made me forget about what happened at the diner today.

Almost.

I tap the keyboard on my computer to wake the screen, open the browser, and type ROBERT LAZLO, MAGICIAN into the search bar. My results come back immediately. The first thing Google wants to know is if I meant LASLO DJERE, SERBIAN TENNIS PLAYER.

I did not.

I scan the first page of hits. There isn't much here. I've searched for Robert Lazlo before. Particularly his Monkey's Paw effect, even asked about it on magic forums. Everyone agreed it sounded like an amazing illusion, but no one offered a satisfactory explanation for how he could have pulled it off.

The first titles that have anything at all to do with the Dazzling Lazlo are a string of social media accounts—Twitter, Facebook, Instagram—that have no photos, have never been filled out with any details, and have only ever been updated with a few test posts. His grandchild's one attempt to nudge the struggling magician into the current century, possibly? "Here, Grandpa, I set it all up for you. Just take a picture or video with your phone and post it. Easy sneezy."

There are a few reviews of the ten-cities-in-ten-nights Three Magi show. The one on the *Fernwood Community Caller* website called it "bland and mostly forgettable, save for a pretty neat trick at the end where Robert 'the Dazzling' Lazlo used vapor blown from his mouth to accurately predict a word sealed in an envelope by a randomly chosen audience member."

First of all, the illusion was *way* more than just "pretty neat." *Second of all*, words cannot accurately describe how impossible this effect is to pull off without an accomplice. And the Dazzling Lazlo made sure we knew he wasn't resorting to that by having a tossed beach ball choose the volunteer. *And finally*, the reviewer mentions nothing about the entire reason it's called the Monkey's Paw to begin with.

It pisses me off every time I read it. And I must have read it over a hundred times. Which makes me either a masochist or a fool. Probably both.

I drag my cursor over to the search bar and click on IMAGES.

The only thing Robert Lazlo–related that comes up is a fuzzy picture of the playbill from a show he did at the Mahaiwe Performing Arts Center in Great Barrington. Someone sold it on eBay three weeks ago for the initial $.75 opening bid. This particular copy was "grease-stained with missing center staple, loose pages, heavy crimping, and an unidentified odor (mouse?)."

I scroll down the page of images on the screen. There's a Roberta

Lasso, a redheaded woman who looks like a prop comic, a Robert Leslie if you want Mr. Potato Head's uglier brother to do your taxes, and a Phillip De Lazlo, a Hungarian painter played by Johnny Depp.

But no pictures of Robert Lazlo. No publicity stills, no show posters, not even a single fan photo. Which is weird. Even my parents have head shots and production stills online. It sure was fun when someone at school found *that* out and printed hundreds of their "mime" shots to wallpaper the lunchroom with. It's been two years and I still get people doing jazz hands when they pass me in the hall.

Perry eventually ferreted out the culprit and "took care of the situation." I never found out who it was or what happened to that person—Perry assured me it was nonviolent, and also better if I didn't know—but I've had a pretty smooth ride ever since. Sometimes it really is nice being best friends with the benevolent Godfather of Fernwood High.

And then, just as if Perry can hear me thinking about him, a message pops up on my phone: SORRY, MAN. JUST GOT YOUR MSG. WAS OUT TO DINNER WITH PARENTALS. LEFT PHONE AT HOME. HOW'D IT GO? YOU GUYS BOND OVER BIDDLE GRIPS AND FALSE CUTS? THAT WOULD HAVE BEEN MY ADVICE.

I grab my phone and text him back: WENT WELL. BETTER THAN EXPECTED. I THINK. I DON'T KNOW. TELL YOU EVERYTHING TOMORROW.

COOL. CAN'T WAIT. HEAR BACK FROM MSA YET?

Shit. Hanging out with Dani may not have made me forget about meeting Robert Lazlo, but it did elbow that little piece of business from my mind.

NOT YET, I message back, which is not a lie. CLOSED NOW. MAYBE TOMORROW?

I've already opened the mail app on my computer and am typing a note to the Magic Society of America before Perry can ask me what I said to them.

Instead, Perry shoots me a thumbs-up emoji. Then: ENGLISH ESSAY DUE TOMORROW. GOTTA HIT IT. LATER.

Phew. I exhale and continue to write.

To Whom It May Concern:

I am writing about your rules and guidelines for the upcoming MSA Fantasy Camp auditions. My partner, Perry Larsson, and I entered the competition as a team and have received separate invitations to audition. However, it appears the rules require that every magician perform on their own. Are we reading this correctly? If so, is it possible that we may still audition as a team, since that is how we registered? Any clarification you can provide on the matter would be greatly appreciated.

Sincerely,
Quinn Purcell

I read over the email and nod approvingly. I'm not sure what response I'm hoping for. Of course it would be great to audition with Perry. But if this guy I met is indeed Robert Lazlo, and he's willing to show me how he performed the Monkey's Paw . . . well, that makes things a little more complicated.

But I'm getting ahead of myself.

I need to make 100 percent sure that my memory isn't playing tricks with me and that Diner Bob really is the Dazzling Lazlo. Sure, there's his magic skill and the Bob/Robert connection, but that's circumstantial at best. I want to see hard evidence.

I click on the next page of images. Then the next. Then the next.

I realize that the Beltway Theater isn't the Bellagio and that I may have overinflated the Dazzling Lazlo's reputation a bit over the years—I *was* just eight when I saw him—but I wasn't aware I'd given him an entire career he never had. Did I do the same thing with the Monkey's Paw? Did I make the illusion more impressive than it was? Could it really just have been a "pretty neat trick" after all?

I shake my head. *No way.* I remember what I saw. Even the less-than-astute Maureen F. Starkwell at the *Fernwood Community Caller* thought it was the standout effect of the night.

I grab the back of my neck. Crap. Maybe I should forget about the whole thing and just audition with my best friend, no matter what the MSA says. We entered as a team and so we should be able to audition as a team. Perry's right. He usually is. It's hard not to be when everything just falls in your lap.

Sometimes literally.

I once saw him catch a toddler who had fallen from the upper level of the Fernwood Mall. There we were, strolling past Wetzel's Pretzels, a lady screams, Perry looks up, and the next thing you know he's cradling this two-year-old girl in his arms, the kid completely unharmed. Like he was some sort of guardian angel. And the most amazing thing about it? It wasn't all that surprising. My best friend walks around the world performing heroic deeds on a regular basis. Which is why, if *he's* not worried about the vaguely worded rules and regulations, I shouldn't be, either.

I've nearly convinced myself to give up on the idea of auditioning solo when I click to the next page of pictures.

And there it is. A thumbnail image. Slightly out of focus.

A tiny black-and-white shot of the Three Magi cast on the Magnificent Marissa's webpage. I certainly wouldn't call it ironclad. Sure, the guy in the grainy photo on my computer screen *could* be the Bob I met yesterday, but you'd never get a conviction based on it.

Still.

I tilt my head this way, then that, trying to mentally overlay Diner Bob's gray stubble and disappointed scowl onto the Dazzling Lazlo's dyed goatee and intense glare.

I'm nodding before I even realize I'm nodding. It's in the scowl. The three little crow's toes at the corners of his crinkled eyes. And the same mole—is that a mole, or lens dust?—just below his left ear. I squint hard at the screen.

Yeah, it's him.

Definitely.

I think.

17

"And this is?" Bob says, staring down at the grainy photo of the Three Magi that I printed out and placed in front of him.

"You don't recognize anyone in that picture?" I ask.

Bob regards me, his eyes tiny slits. "What's your play here? Are you one of those baby-faced undercover kid cops you see on TV but don't believe exist in real life?"

"*What?* No." I shake my head. "I was at this show." I poke my finger into the paper. "The Three Magi. That's you with the goatee, isn't it? Robert Lazlo. The Dazzling Lazlo. You performed the Monkey's Paw illusion, the best trick I've ever seen."

Bob screws up his face. "I don't know what they're putting in the pot these days, kid, but I think I preferred it when it was less legal." He shoves the picture across the diner table.

I leave it sitting there between us. "What's your last name, then? If it isn't Lazlo."

Bob leans back in the booth and crosses his arms. "Smith."

"Bob *Smith*?" I say. "Seriously? *That's* your name?"

He shrugs. "Sorry to disappoint you, kid. Law of averages says everyone'll run into a Bob Smith at some point in their life. Now's your time."

I blink at him. I'm not sure what to do here. I figured he'd either shyly admit it or plausibly deny it. I didn't expect such a blatant, straight-up lie.

It's almost like a dare.

"So you're *not* a professional magician?" I say. The gamey smell of frying bacon that wafts from the kitchen is starting to make me feel nauseous. "And you didn't perform at the Beltway Theater eight years ago with the Wonderful Wonder Phil and the Magnificent Marissa?"

Bob laughs. "Listen, I've burned a lot of brain cells in my day, but I think I'd remember something like that."

I sigh. "Oh, come on. This is ridiculous. You're obviously Robert Lazlo. Just admit it."

Bob leans forward, interlacing his fingers on the table. "I'm sorry, do I *owe* you something?" He glares at me. "Am I *indebted* to you in some way, form, or fashion?"

My insides shrivel. "No."

"Then fuck off, because I'm not going to 'admit' anything." Bob cocks his head and plants his tongue inside his cheek. "Least not for free. Now, if you want to talk *bartering*, then OK, I'm open for business. But information has a price tag." He rubs his thumb and first two fingers together. "Know what I'm saying?"

"You want me to *pay* you to admit that you're the person I already know you are?"

"That's not what I said," Bob insists. "I *said* information comes at a cost. For a nominal fee, let's say five bucks, just for shits and giggles, I will tell you whether I am, *or am not*, the person in that photograph." He points his hairy finger at the printout.

"Fine. OK." I remove my wallet, produce a five-dollar bill, and hold it out to him. "You feel good about this, do you?"

He plucks the money from my fingers and folds it up into a square. "I would have felt a hell of a lot better if it was a twenty, but I'm a fair businessman." He slips the money into the breast pocket of his blue denim shirt, then flashes a closemouthed smile.

I wait for him to talk, to confirm my suspicions. But he just keeps smiling at me.

After an incredibly long and uncomfortable amount of time has passed, I shoot him an expectant look. *"Well?"*

"Well what?" he says, licking his teeth.

"You said if I gave you five dollars you would tell me if that was you in this picture." I poke at the paper on the table.

"I've already told you, kid," Bob says. "Again. And again. And again."

"Yes, but that was before I paid you."

"Oh." Bob squints at me. "Sorry. Did I not make that clear? The information is the same. It's just the price tag that went up. Next time, same answer is ten bucks."

"So you're saying, right here, right now, for one hundred percent, after you've accepted money for your truthful answer, that you are *not* Robert Lazlo, the magician? You just happen to look exactly like him—right down to the mole under your left ear—are able to do magic, and have the same first name?"

Bob shrugs and takes a sip of his coffee. "The universe is a mysterious fucking place. What can I tell you?"

There's something about the twinkle in his eyes. Like he's really having fun messing with my head. I mean, it's *definitely* him. He knows it. I know it. And he knows I know it.

I have to give it one last shot. It's nearly the end of the business day and I have yet to hear back from the Magic Society. Which doesn't bode well. Perry says he's still not worried, but the more I read over the rules, the more it seems clear they don't want Perry and me onstage at the same time. And if that's the case, I'm definitely going to need the Monkey's Paw trick if I want to even have a chance of competing—with him *or* with Dani.

I pull out my wallet again, yank out my last bill—a twenty—and slap it on the table. "Look. I get twenty bucks' allowance every Saturday if I complete all my chores and submit to watching my parents' weekly musical rehearsals. I can offer you that *and*, I don't know, any help you need around your house—if you have a house—or your car, or running errands or whatever, for the next two weeks, if you will *just* admit that you're Robert Lazlo and agree to teach me how to perform your Monkey's Paw illusion." I watch Bob's eyes dart down to the money and back up again. "This is very important to me. Seriously. I'll do anything. What do you say? Do we have a deal?"

"Let me get this straight," Bob says, pinching his brow. "For significantly *less* than minimum wage and a couple of weeks of your slave labor, you would like me to pretend to be this Robert Lazlo clown and teach you some magic trick based on a short story that I didn't bother to read in high school? Do I understand the terms of the negotiations here?"

Suddenly I'm not feeling so confident about this anymore. I peel my tongue from the roof of my bone-dry mouth.

"If you *are* Robert Lazlo," I say. "If you're really him . . . then yes."

"Uh-uh-uh." Bob shakes his head. "We've already established I am not your guy, remember?" He pats his breast pocket. "However, if all you want me to do is *say* I'm your guy, make up some simian-themed effect to show you, maybe throw in a few hard life lessons along the way . . . for your money and your muscle, *plus expenses* . . ." He nods. "I suppose we can give that arrangement a trial run."

Oh, crap. I don't know what I'm agreeing to here. Maybe I got it wrong. Maybe he really *isn't* Robert Lazlo.

Or maybe, *just maybe*, he doesn't want people to know who he really is. The scraps of information I could find on him mentioned rumors of bankruptcy. And *someone* bought that greasy, mouse-scented playbill, which now seems less like the act of a devoted fan—even *I* wouldn't have bid on it—and more like the act of a desperate has-been trying to scrub the internet of all traces of his existence. So he might be in some kind of trouble with the law.

"You do know magic, though?" I say, trying to get at least this out of him. "I mean, you fooled me pretty good the other day."

"You kind of fooled yourself on that one," Bob says, grinning at me. "But then again"—he strokes his bristly chin—"isn't that what all magic relies on? The observer's self-deception."

"So you *do* know magic," I say, practically pleading. "Right?"

Bob sits back in the booth and crosses his arms again. "All these questions and I haven't even been officially hired yet."

I don't know what kind of game this guy is playing—trying to screw with my head, I guess—but I trust my eyes and my deductive reasoning. He's definitely Robert Lazlo. I know it in my gut.

I slide the twenty-dollar bill across the table and leave it in front of him. "Consider yourself officially contracted."

Bob casually rocks forward, picks up the twenty, folds it, and slips it into his breast pocket to keep my five company. "Nice. It's been some time since I've been gainfully employed." He gives me a closemouthed smile. "I have to say. It feels good. Does the job come with dental benefits?"

"Excuse me?"

Bob laughs. "Relax, kid. I'm just yanking your chain. I never go to the dentist." He smiles big, showing me his mahogany-stained teeth.

"So, when can we start?"

"*You* can start tonight." He sniffs loudly and takes another slug of his coffee. "With a little homework. Write up a description of this Monkey's Foot trick."

"Paw," I correct.

Bob stares at me coldly. "I don't carry my *Merriam-Webster's* around with me, kid, but last I checked a paw *is* a fucking foot. But whatever. Just write it down. The whole thing. From start to finish. Don't leave out any details."

"Wait," I say, blinking like he just flicked lemon juice in my eyes. "You don't remember the trick?"

"Of course I remember it." Bob smirks. "I'm the Amazing Robert Lassington, right? The point is not whether *I* remember it. I want to see how well *you* remember it. Be specific. Patter, props, gestures, volunteers. Anything and everything that happened on that stage. I want to see how closely you pay attention." He points a gnarly finger at me. "If you leave anything out, I'll know." He cocks his head and smiles. "Or at least, I'll pretend to know."

"OK, just a second," I say, opening my clenched fists. "First of all, the show was eight years ago, so I don't know if I can remember absolutely *everything* about the act. Second of all"—I hold up a finger—"I would *really* like to clarify something. I know that you know that I know who you really are, and that we're sort of acting as if you're *not* really this person. However, it's kind of *vitally* important to me that you actually *are* indeed this person . . . this person that we're pretending you're not. Do you understand what I'm saying?"

Bob sighs, rolls his eyes. "So much pissing and moaning. I'm getting bored of you already. Maybe we should reconsider this arrangement. I don't want to waste my time with whiners."

"Sorry, sorry, sorry," I stammer, my heart thundering in my chest. I'm going to lose my prize fish before I've had a chance to reel him in. "Forget what I said. I'll do it. I will. I'll write out the trick. No problem."

Bob nods. "Good. I'd prefer it to be typed, double-spaced,

Helvetica font, fourteen point, please, because it's easier on my old, rheumy eyes. Also, my mother was an English teacher, so I'm a stickler for grammar and spelling. Might I suggest you give it a good going-over before you hit print?"

"OK, sure, yes, fine," I say, ignoring the nagging warning bells going off in my head. "When do you want it by?"

He stares at me blankly. "When do you *think* I want it by?"

"Tomorrow?" I say, squinting up an eye.

"Sure, OK, I'm free tomorrow," Bob says. "Meet me here, same time. Be prepared to perform a few tricks so I can evaluate your abilities." He sniffs again. "Also, lose the attitude."

"What attitude?" I say.

"*That.*" He points at me. "Right there. The defensiveness. The questioning. Correcting me when you know damn well a paw is a foot. If you're going to challenge everything I say, this is not going to work out well for you, I promise."

"OK," I say. "Sorry. I just . . ."

"You just *what*?"

I just hope I'm right about all this. I shake my head. "Nothing." Time to get out of here before I completely screw this up. I grab my backpack and slide out of the booth. "I'll see you tomorrow, then. With my homework." I start to leave, then turn back and flash him a smile. "Thank you," I say, choking back the emotion that's rising inside me. "You have no idea how much this means to me. I've never met someone like you before. In real life."

Bob pulls a toothpick from his shirt pocket and starts working on his back teeth. "I'm beginning to understand that."

"I mean it," I say, feeling a hitch in my chest, my throat starting to close. "Nothing like this ever happens to me."

"Oh, good Christ," Bob says, looking heavenward. "I hope you're not one of those weepy, whiny, huggy kids, because this"—he pivots his index finger back and forth between us—"does not end in an avuncular embrace. *Ever*. That I can assure you."

18

I TRUDGE THROUGH THE EMPTY SCHOOL PARKING LOT, hunched over, the morning chill penetrating my bones. I slog past the overstuffed, overripe dumpsters, pinching the shards of sleep crust from my eyes as I make my way toward the rear doors.

I am not feeling my best this a.m. My legs seem heavier than they did last night, and the stale 7-Eleven coffee I gulped down on the ride over is burning a hole in my stomach.

I hate getting up early. I really do. I usually have to peel myself out of bed when my alarm goes off at a *normal* wake-up time, but getting up *an hour earlier*? That's a real commitment for me. Something I would do for magic and magic alone.

I reach out for the door handle and miss it by several inches, which makes me stumble backward and groan like Frankenstein's monster. I wish we could practice our audition later in the day, but before school is the only time Perry doesn't have some other obligation: sports, sports, sports, band, chorus, the *Fernwood Herald*, Italian Club, Future Business Leaders of the World, and, oh, also sports. Fortunately Mr. Carlyle lets us use the theater rehearsal room whenever we want, as long as he's not prepping a production.

The hallways are dead empty; my squeaky sneakers are the only sound reverberating off the locker doors. There's a peacefulness to being here now, without all the bustling bodies and voices. But it's slightly unsettling as well. Like the world has died and you could run into a brain-eating zombie at any—

Oh Jesus!

I jerk to a stop, nearly emptying my coffee-bloated bladder, before I clock that it's only Mr. Zuzzolo, our forever-weary, saggy-eyed custodian, turning the corner, slowly pushing his giant hall mop like it weighs more than he does. Which it just might.

"Morning," I croak out, trying not to sound like I nearly soiled myself.

"'Morning without you is a dwindled dawn,'" Mr. Zuzzolo rasps, marching forward, not even glancing my way.

Aw, that's sweet. (Of course, the screw-off attitude does take something away from it.) You can say anything to Mr. Zuzzolo and he'll toss you a line of poetry that somehow relates. I once told him about a urinal in the boys' restroom that wouldn't stop flushing and he just stared at me and said, "'He took my father grossly, full of bread; With all his crimes broad blown, as flush as May.'"

The rehearsal room is just behind the theater, up a small flight of five steps. Normally I can take the stairs in two strides, but today, so early in the morning, my backpack weighed down with props, it feels like ascending Mount Everest. Not that I'll ever know what that actually feels like.

Not like Perry. Who for real put it on his bucket list. The bucket list he continually has to update because he keeps achieving all of his . . . buckets.

I grab the doorknob and pull. It opens way easier than I anticipated and I have to catch my balance so I don't go down hard.

"Oh, hey!" It's Dani, standing on the other side of the door, towing a huge, back-saving rolling suitcase behind her. "It's all yours. I cleaned up after myself. Left it just like I found it."

I blink at her, unable to reconcile her presence in front of me. "What are you . . . ?" My brain sputters. "When did you . . . ?" I point at the room. "You were . . . using the rehearsal space?"

"Yeah," Dani says, grinning like it isn't *way* too early to be this peppy. "Mr. Carlyle said you and Perry were using it at seven, so I asked if I could use it at five."

"In the morning!" My eyeballs nearly pop out of their sockets.

Dani shrugs. "Needs must. Can't get anything done when you're sleeping. Lucky for me Mr. Zuzzolo starts work early."

Standing this close to Dani, I can smell the minty-rosemary of her shampoo.

"That's . . . wow. And I thought I was being dedicated." I quickly comb my fingers through my bed head and run my tongue across my coffee-lacquered teeth.

"Hey, do you have a sec?" Dani says, her expression growing serious. "There's something I wanted to ask you."

"Oh," I say, an excited charge coursing through my body. "Sure. What is it?"

"OK, so"—Dani winces—"this really isn't even any of my

117

business. But I was reading over the audition rules again last night, just to make sure I was following the guidelines to the letter, and I found something that . . ." Dani bites her lower lip. "Never mind. I should stay out of it. I'm sorry." She nods like she's made a firm decision. "You need to get to work, so I'll go ahead and let you do that."

She starts to move past me, but I step in her way.

"Wait," I say, way too curious to let this go now. "What did you find in the rules?"

Dani looks at me, scrunching up her face. "OK, but you have to promise me that you'll take what I say with a grain of salt, because there's a strong possibility that my telling you might be completely self-serving. I don't *think* that it is. And I don't *want* it to be. But I don't really trust myself with stuff like this. I can be pretty ruthless when important things are on the line."

This makes me laugh. "Like how you might have agreed to come to my house so you could spy on me?"

"Yes, *exactly*. Just like that." She sounds serious. Looks *really* serious.

"Wait. I thought you said you were joking about that. That it was misdirection for your card trick."

She smiles tightly. "Yes, but was that just another misdirection?" She shrugs. "We can't be sure. My subconscious might have another agenda."

I study her through narrowed, baffled eyes. "Are you telling me that you sometimes do stuff . . . and you don't know why you're doing it?"

Dani looks deep into my eyes. "Do *you* always know why you do everything you do? *Really?* The true, underlying reasons why you say all the things you say to people? All the time?"

"I think so, yeah." I shake my head, my brain feeling like scrambled eggs. "I mean . . . I guess I hadn't really thought about it. But I'm *me*, so . . . why *wouldn't* I know why I'm doing something? How would that even work? Doing something without knowing why you're doing it?"

"I'll tell you exactly how it works," Dani says, exhaling like she was hoping it wouldn't come to this. "Third-grade science. Mrs. Killington had just taught us that the sinuses and esophagus were connected. I didn't believe her, so I talked Austin Gerber into putting a popcorn kernel up his nose just so I could see if it would really come out of his mouth. The kernel got jammed up there, became seriously infected because he was too embarrassed to tell anyone, and—two weeks later—Austin had to go to the hospital to have it extracted."

"Wait." I shake my head. "You told a kid to put a piece of corn up his nose and he did it and that proves, *what?* That the kid's a jackass for listening to you?"

"That's the thing, though," Dani says, looking at me dubiously. "I *didn't* tell him to do it. I only sort of . . . *suggested* it." She wrinkles up her nose adorably. "Which is even worse, right? Because if someone *tells* you to do something, you know what they're trying to do and you can just say no. But if someone makes you think it was your idea in the first place . . . isn't that even more devious?"

I crack up. "How do you *suggest* someone put a popcorn kernel up their nose?"

Dani shrugs. "I may have been playing with a popcorn kernel at snack time, wondering out loud what might happen if someone— *not necessarily Austin specifically*, though I must have known deep down he'd be the one to do it—put the kernel up their nose. If it might come out in their mouth." She grimaces. "Then I *maaaaay* have pretended to put the corn up my nose and done a little sleight of hand to have it appear on my tongue."

"Oh." I nod, finally getting it. "And then Austin—who, I'm guessing, had a crush on you?—did it for real. Because he wanted to impress you."

She nods somberly. "It was only after that, looking back on it, that I really understood what I was doing." She grimaces again. "So now you can see why I'm worried about my motives here. It's no secret that I want to win the auditions, and that you and Perry are my stiffest competition. So even though I *think* I'm telling you this to help you, we can't rule out the possibility that I'm *actually*—subconsciously—doing it to help *me*."

I study her, trying to connect words to my thoughts, my feelings, but it's like putting together a puzzle in a windstorm. Dani is the strangest person I've ever met in my life. I still can't tell if this is an elaborate play—it feels like it must be—or if this girl is just the most blatantly honest, self-reflective human being on the planet.

Either way, I'm way too curious not to see where this leads. As long as I keep my guard up, what's the harm in playing along?

"Consider me properly warned," I say, holding my hand up in a three-finger Boy Scout salute. "I take full responsibility for any kernels of corn that I shove up my nose—literally or metaphorically." I raise my eyebrows. "Now, what is it about the audition guidelines that has you so worried?"

19

"ALL RIGHT, SO," PERRY SAYS, OPENING HIS LEATHER-BOUND notebook, "I've jotted down all the illusions and effects we've ever done and I've highlighted the ones we've gotten the best responses from. We'll only have five minutes, so we need to decide if we do one big effect—like Drill of Death—or several smaller ones linked together, to showcase different techniques."

I look at his notebook page. The list is written in the most beautifully perfect cursive anyone has ever laid eyes on. If you didn't know Perry's skill with a fountain pen, you'd think it was computer-generated.

"That's great," I say, feeling all skittery, like a spooked housefly.

I need to talk to Perry about our audition. As it turns out, the thing that Dani's concerned about is the same thing we're all concerned about—namely, that we'll be disqualified if Perry and I perform as a team. I haven't heard back from the Magic Society yet, but it seems fairly obvious what they're going to say. What I'm most worried about now is that if we wait too long to decide one way or the other, we won't have enough time to rehearse before the audition.

I'm just wondering if it would be easier and cleaner to tell Perry that the MSA said it was a no-go. That we have to do solo acts. It wouldn't be a *real* lie. That *is* what they're going to say. Even Dani reached the same conclusion. And if I'm wrong, if they respond that it's fine for us to audition as a team, well, then, I can just tell Perry that they changed their minds.

"Of course, there is another option," Perry says, tapping his pen on his notebook. "This was Gwen's idea, actually, when I asked her which of our shows she liked the best. She said she couldn't choose just one. *Soooo*"—he twists his face into an embarrassed smile— "if we—i.e., *you*—could design a brand-new centerpiece effect but incorporating a lot of our older effects, we could give the audience an exciting 'wow' ending but also show the judges a lot of skills along the way."

"Sure," I say, my eyes dancing around the cavernous rehearsal room: the flickering fluorescents, the worn-out hardwood floors, the tattered prop furniture pushed into the corners. "It's just, there's something . . . I think we need to talk about? Something to . . . decide on first?"

A flash of doubt shoots through me. *Dani warned you not to do anything rash based on what she told you.*

But this isn't based on what she told me. It's based on my own interpretation of the rules.

I think . . .

My mind flips back to double-check:

"I've already written to the MSA," I said to Dani when she *finally,* reluctantly, *told me she was worried I might be throwing*

away the biggest opportunity of my life. "But, considering it would have benefited you enormously if we were disqualified . . . it was very unselfish of you to mention it."

"Mmm," Dani said skeptically. "Was it unselfish? Or am I just trying to break you two up because I know, together, you're twice as formidable?" She wagged a cautioning finger at me. "That's where things get sticky with my conscience."

"Yeah, well, I'm not Austin Gerber," I assured her. "And I've already been thinking about shoving the popcorn kernel up my nose. So your conscience is clear."

"OK, good," she said, exhaling. "That makes me feel much better. But I would definitely wait to get confirmation from the Magic Society before you do anything rash." Dani nodded firmly, like this was the only decision to be made. "It might seem like lost rehearsal time if you end up having to go solo, but you'll be really grateful if they say you can perform as a duo, right?" She laughed self-consciously. "Of course, that's just the sort of advice I would give if I was try-ing to undermine you! Ugh! Sorry, Quinn. I'm being super unhelpful, aren't I? Talk it over with Perry. He definitely has your best interests at heart!"

I shake Dani out of my head. She's in there a lot lately. I'm won-dering if simply "having my guard up" is enough to keep things clear in my mind. Although, in this particular situation, it seems pretty straightforward: I had the thought before Dani told me her thoughts. So it can't be manipulation if I had the idea first.

"I'm really starting to get anxious about our act," I say, swallow-ing the guilt that's rising like bile in my throat. "The Magic Society says no partners. So . . . we have to decide . . . if we're going to risk being disqualified by auditioning as a team."

"Wait." Perry furrows his brow. "You heard from the MSA?"

"Yes," I say, tiptoeing around the truth. Because, yes, I *did* hear from the MSA—when they sent my invitation. "They made it pretty clear that partner acts are not allowed." Again, this is not technically a lie. Both Dani and I believe that this is what the rules already state.

"Jeez," Perry says, his shoulders slumping. "That's too bad. I thought for sure they'd let us. No wonder you're in such a strange mood this morning. I thought it was just because you were tired."

"Yeah, no, it sucks," I say. I didn't know I was in a strange mood, but I'll take that baton and run with it. "It doesn't seem fair. At all. Even Dani thinks so."

"*Dani?*" Perry's expression shifts, slowly clouding over. "You talked to her about this? Before talking to me? When?"

My cheeks go hot. "This morning. Out in the hall? I ran into her as she was leaving. It just . . . sort of came up."

"You do realize she's our competition, right?" Perry says. "Possibly our *main* competition. I told you this might be a problem for you. You really shouldn't be talking to her about our act—or *acts*."

"Yeah. No. I know." I drag a sweaty palm down my pant leg. "I didn't tell her . . . that I'd heard back from the MSA." *Because I haven't.* "She was just worried about us, that's all. She doesn't want us to blow our shot."

"That's all?" Perry says, heavy doubt lacing his tone. "No other agenda on her part? Nothing in it for Dani if we don't audition as a team?"

"*As a matter of fact,*" I say, feeling myself starting to bristle, "there's more in it for her if we *do* audition as a team. Because if we get disqualified, two of her biggest threats . . . *gone.*" I try to snap my fingers, but it just comes off as a flaccid puff of air. "Anyway, it's a moot point. The rules say we can't audition together."

Perry's stance softens. "Yeah, I guess. You're right. I'm sorry." He runs a hand through his hair. "It's just . . . it's a colossal letdown, that's all. I was really looking forward to going to the fantasy camp *together.* I don't even know if I want to go if you're not going, too."

He pierces me with his baby blues and I nod along, trying to compose my features into an expression that says I'm *also* deeply conflicted about attending the camp without my best friend. Which I *am* . . . though maybe not quite as much as Perry clearly is.

He swats a hand at the air and forces a smile. "Forget it. If those are the rules, those are the rules. There's no decision to be made really. We'll audition solo." Perry grimaces. "As long as you agree to let me use some of our old effects?"

"I'll do better than that," I say, waves of relief and shame washing over me all at once, catching me up in an emotional riptide. "I'll do just like you said. I'll design something new and incredible for you using tricks and techniques you're already familiar with. And for my act . . ." My mind flashes to me performing Robert Lazlo's Monkey's Paw effect to a standing ovation. "I'll come up with something else for me."

I wrench a smile onto my face, trying to ignore the ballooning guilt in my gut.

20

"YOU WANT TO GIVE ME A HINT AS TO WHERE WE'RE GOING?"
I ask Bob, who's driving us somewhere in his pre-internet, powder-blue Mercury Grand Marquis.

"You'll know it when we get there," Bob grunts.

The car bobs along like an enormous boat riding the high seas. Every once in a while, a loud explosion blasts from the tailpipe, causing us to lurch forward. Bob affectionately calls this his stealth mode.

The seats and the dash are all cracked and split, the ceiling fabric torn and dangling. The cabin smells like stale coffee and dirty clothes, which makes sense considering the vast amount of empty Dunkin' Donuts cups, moist napkins, and old socks coagulating on the floor.

I met Bob at the diner after school and immediately handed him my full description of the Monkey's Paw illusion. It took a lot longer than I thought it would to write out: trying to remember all the details, agonizing over every word, checking over my spelling and grammar. But Bob didn't even look to see if I properly formatted it (which I did). He just folded up the paper and tucked it into his shirt pocket.

Instead of discussing my homework, Bob said we had an errand to run. *"Stat."*

We've been driving now for around twenty minutes, most of it in silence. Which is getting a little tedious, if I'm being honest.

I check my phone for the umpteenth time, scanning Perry's social media feeds like I'm his stalker instead of his best friend. I feel a little bad that I misled him this morning. Even if all I really did was speed up the inevitable. Still, I don't like that I wasn't completely honest with him.

And so, to ease my guilt, I flip through Perry's Instagram posts. Just to remind myself how much better his life is than mine.

Most people's feeds are not accurate depictions of their real experiences. They're curated, polished, Facetuned versions of reality. Not so with Perry. His life really *is* as incredible as it looks. Better, actually, because he can't capture every wonderful thing that happens to him. Though he does seem to get a lot of them. Shot after video after shot after video: being hoisted on the shoulders of his adoring teammates; posing with every hot, eyelash-batting girl in Fernwood; doing a series of shirtless back handsprings down the football field.

There's a reason more than a hundred thousand people—*including my own parents*—follow him.

Sometimes—and I would never admit this to anyone—but sometimes . . . I secretly wish Perry is a serial killer and that one day it comes out that he has dozens of bodies buried under his award-winning blueberry bushes. Then I would be the blindsided best friend who goes on talk shows and is showered with sympathy, compassion, and movie deals.

And Mom and Dad would see they loved the wrong person all along.

And I would win.

For once.

I put my phone away, still feeling guilty but now, also, feeling like a dick for being so petty and jealous of someone I love so dearly.

I sigh and stare out the passenger-side window. The rhythmic smears of color are hypnotizing, distracting me momentarily from my nearly all-consuming envy.

"You can talk, you know," Bob grumbles.

"Hmm, what?" I say, my focus dragged back to the car.

"Just because I need to concentrate on my driving," Bob says, gesturing at the road ahead, "doesn't mean you have to sit there like a boil on a butt cheek. You've been staring at your phone the whole time, hardly said five words to me the entire ride."

"Oh," I say, having completely misread the situation. "Sorry. So, OK, well, do you want to talk about my homework, then? The Monkey's Paw illusion?"

"No," Bob says, jerking the car into the parking lot of a strip mall. "Anyway, we're here."

He pulls the Mercury into a space between a brand-new red Porsche and a sparkling silver Audi, jams the car into park, and grins at me.

"I always like to find a spot between the fanciest cars in the lot," Bob says.

"So they won't ding your car?" I ask, wondering how he could even tell.

"Uh, *no*." He laughs. "I just like to put the fear of Jesus into these snobby, rich bastards. Who the fuck pays two hundred grand for a depreciating asset? The Bible got one thing right. A fool and his money are soon parted. If you want, we can wait. They all make the same exact puckered anus mouth. It's pretty hilarious. But the best part, the sweetest nectar of all, is when they *say* something to me. 'Careful getting out of your car.' Like I'm a five-year-old. That's when the fun really starts."

"Yeah, that's OK," I say, reaching for the door handle. "I don't do well with confrontation. Let's just run your errand and go."

Very cautiously, I open the massive, hundred-pound door. I don't know how much a little ding in the side of a Porsche 911 Targa costs, but paying it off would probably involve me having to do things I wouldn't be proud of.

I have started to hoist myself from the seat when Bob grabs my arm and pulls me back.

"Where are you going?" he asks.

"Out," I say. "I assume whatever we're doing doesn't take place in your car." I swallow hard, then blink. "I hope."

"I haven't told you the plan yet," he says. "We have details to go over."

"Details?" I say, narrowing my eyes. "What kind of errand is this?"

Well, at least it involves magic. I figured we were just going to Walgreens to pick up some Anusol and nose hair clippers, but the idea of being Robert Lazlo's confederate is *way* more exciting.

Still, I'm not exactly clear why he wants to perform illusions for a bunch of happy-hour drunks. But I'm not supposed to ask questions. So I don't.

"Split off," Bob grumbles as we step into the dark entryway of Father Flannigan's Tavern. All the heavy wood and stained glass give the restaurant an air of gravitas despite the cloying steak-house smell, a thick stew of onion rings, charred meat, and beer.

The lounge is peppered with a mix of suits and jeans. Several of the tables are occupied and nearly every seat at the bar is taken. Celtic music jingles over the speakers, just loud enough to be heard over the hum of conversation.

"Where should I wait?" I say.

"The john. Stay there for fifteen. Put a timer on your phone. Then come out and dissolve into the crowd. Don't be early. But don't be late, either."

I open my mouth to ask if he wants me to signal when I exit the bathroom, but Bob shuts me down with a murderous stare before making his way over to the bar.

The bathrooms are just off the entry, down a short hall. I push through the door to the men's room and am immediately bathed in a warm, uriney breeze. Lovely. I yank out my phone and start the countdown.

Fifteen minutes feels like fifty. In that stretch I watch a Penn and Teller video, take a pee, wash my hands, jot down a few audition ideas for Perry (just because I plan to smoke my competition with the Monkey's Paw trick doesn't mean I'm not going to try to come up with something impressive for him), and listen to a man giving birth to his intestines.

The second my timer rings I bolt from the bathroom.

As I step into the tavern, I can feel a difference in the air. An electricity. An excitement. People are laughing and oohing and aahing.

I approach the dozen or so spectators crowded around Bob just as he pulls a three of diamonds from the pocket of his blue flannel shirt.

"Holy cripes!" I hear a lady squeal as everyone breaks out in applause. "That's the exact card I was thinking of. Whaddya know?"

"Thank you, thank you," Bob says, holding court at the center of the group. "Much appreciated."

"Do another one," a middle-aged woman in a red leather skirt calls out. "You're amazing."

"All right," Bob says. "Last one, though. I don't want to wear out my welcome." He taps his stubbly chin. "Now, let me think here. We need something spectacular for the closer."

I start to work my way into the small crowd, slowly and casually wending toward the center.

Bob gestures at the barrel-chested bartender looking on. "Hey, Charlie. It's Charlie, right? You got a fifty in that register of yours?"

"Sure," Charlie says. "But I've got to account for all the money in there at the end of the night."

"I'm not going to *steal* your money," Bob says, looking genuinely insulted. "I'm a lot of things, Charlie, but a crook is not one of them. Go on, get the fifty. It'll be worth it, I promise."

I watch Charlie's expression shift from wary, to curious, and back to wary again. "I . . . I don't know," he stammers.

"OK, I see you're nervous," Bob says. "How about this? I won't even touch the money. You'll be the one handling it the entire time. What do you think about that?"

Charlie knits his brow, mulling over this new bit of information.

The impatient crowd breaks into a cheer. "Char-*lee*! Char-*lee*! Char-*lee*!"

Finally the bartender nods. "OK. I can do that." Charlie trots to the far end of the bar, rings open the register, and pulls out a fifty. He jogs back down to where Bob is standing.

Bob regards the money. "So. Here's how this is going to work. Since I'm not touching the bill, *you're* going to be the one who does this trick."

"Me?" Charlie says, grimacing.

"Yes, you, Charlie," Bob says. He leans in a little closer to the bartender. "I don't say this to everyone, but I see something special in you. A gift. Tell me something. Do you ever have flashes of insights that later turn out to be true? Or a dream that seems *so real* you can't believe it was just a dream?"

Charlie nods. "Yeah. Sometimes. Also déjà vu, too. I get that one a lot."

"Well, there you go," Bob says, like the matter is settled. "That's what I mean." He turns to the crowd. "Would everyone like to see Charlie learn how to use his special gift?"

Roars from the patrons. *"Yes!" "Yeah!" "Unleash your gift, Charlie!"*

I use the distraction of everyone's excitement to angle my way right to the front of the crowd. Exactly where Bob wants me.

Bob looks at the bartender with deep intent. "Are you ready for this, Charlie? It could be a life changer for you."

Charlie shrugs. "Yeah, sure, I guess."

"OK, good, because we need a positive attitude if this is going to work." Bob pulls a Sharpie from his pants pocket and uncaps it. "I want you to take this pen and I would like you to sign the back of that fifty-dollar bill. Can you do that for me?"

"Sure." Charlie grabs the marker and scribbles his name on the bill, then hands the pen back to Bob.

"Excellent. You're doing great, Charlie." Bob recaps the Sharpie and slips it back into his pants pocket. "Now, I need you to look deep inside yourself, searching your innermost beliefs about reality, and answer this one question. *Do you*, or do you *not*, think that I can help you dematerialize that fifty-dollar bill—with *your* signature on it—and have it rematerialize back inside the register?"

Charlie laughs and shakes his head. "No. I don't think anyone could do that."

"OK. OK." Bob nods. "But if I could *help* you do that. Lead you to an awakening of the powers within yourself . . . would you be so amazed that . . . oh, I don't know . . . you would agree to cover the round of drinks I've offered to buy this lovely group of people?"

Charlie smiles incredulously. "Before I agree to anything, let me make sure I've got this straight," he states. "You're telling me that the bill will disappear from here"—he gestures at the money on the bar—"and reappear inside the register? I don't move. You don't move. Only the bill moves?"

"Yes," Bob says, nodding. "You have the power inside yourself to do that."

Charlie laughs. "All right, fine. Hell, if it happens the way you described, it'd be worth *two* rounds of drinks."

Bob perks up. "You hear that, everyone? The man says he'll buy us *two* rounds! Hooray, Charlie! What a sport!"

Everyone cheers, raising their glasses high, the thick arms of the two brawny guys I'm standing between sandwiching my shoulders. Charlie's eyes dart around at the crowd, his face a little pale now.

Before the bartender can protest, Bob grabs a red cocktail napkin from the bar and hands it to him. "What do you want me to do with this?" Charlie asks, holding the napkin like it's a dirty diaper.

"I want you to unfold it and cover the bill," Bob says. "You can't look directly at the bill or it will seem *too* real to you. *Too* solid. Part of this is battling with our belief system. We have to *break* your belief in what you think is possible. If not, you won't be able to work with the bill on a molecular level."

"Molecular level?" Charlie scrunches up his face like Bob has asked him to puzzle out a calculus problem.

"I'll lead you through it," Bob assures him. "Don't worry."

"If you say so." Charlie gently unfolds the napkin and lays it down on the bar, covering the signed fifty-dollar bill. He looks at Bob. "Now what?"

"Now"—Bob grins and waggles his bushy eyebrows—"the real magic begins."

21

"OK," Bob announces after two people have felt under the napkin, verifying the presence of the money. "Let's have one last volunteer. That'll make three *independent* verifications. No one can argue with that."

That's my cue. I take a breath and try to clear my mind. Wipe my moist hands on my pants and part my dry lips with my drier tongue.

Bob searches the crowd, then chin-gestures to me. "You. Kid. Go ahead. Reach under the napkin and tell me if you can feel the fifty-dollar bill."

I nod and step forward, keeping my head down, like I'm shy instead of completely terrified. I'm supposed to be as forgettable as possible and not draw any attention to myself. Hopefully I don't pass out. That would probably draw some attention.

I step up to the bar and smile at Charlie. Then I grab a corner of the napkin with my left hand and carefully slide my right hand underneath.

"You feel it?" Bob asks.

"I do," I say as I quickly palm the bill and swap it out with a piece of sweat-soaked flash paper. I sure hope the moistness doesn't stop it from burning. That would *not* put me in Bob's good graces.

"Excellent, thank you very much," Bob says, stepping forward. "And thank you again to our first two volunteers." He gestures at the bearded Jamaican guy and the potbellied white dude who checked under the napkin before me. And while everyone's looking at *them*, I slide my hands into my pants pockets and disappear back into the crowd.

"Now, Charlie," Bob says, "what I'm about to ask you to do *may* sound unwise . . . but I assure you, it is vital that you follow my instructions precisely if you want to complete this amazing feat. Are you prepared to do this?"

"Uh . . ." Charlie's gaze darts around the room. "I guess?"

"All right," Bob says. "Listen up. Keeping your mind perfectly clear, quickly grab that napkin, along with the bill underneath, and fold the entire thing into a small square. Can you do that for me, Charlie?"

Charlie looks unsure, but he nods. He snatches up the napkin and starts folding like crazy, until he has a sloppy square about the size of a matchbook.

"And now," Bob says, holding a lighter out to Charlie, "you have to do the bravest thing of all."

This is my chance. While everyone is focused on Charlie and Bob, I slip away unnoticed and head down to the register at the other end of the bar.

The idea is simple. While everyone watches Charlie light the napkin—and, supposedly, the money—on fire, I will get an unsuspecting server to make change for the real, signed fifty-dollar bill, safely returning it to the register.

Unfortunately I don't see any waitstaff milling about at the moment.

I check down at the other end of the bar, where Charlie is shaking his head and leaning away from Bob.

There's a blur of motion in my peripheral vision. I turn to see the back of a tiny, frizzy-haired waitress scurrying by me.

"Excuse me," I say, but get nothing. Not even a peek over the shoulder.

I twist around, looking for anyone—another bartender, a manager, a hostess—who might be able to help me. But this is not a well-staffed establishment. And I'm running out of time. Once Bob convinces Charlie to burn that napkin, I will only have a few seconds to get this bill planted.

I stare at the register. I could just leave the cash on top. But that's not what Bob told Charlie would happen, and what if Charlie refuses to buy those two rounds for everyone? Something tells me Bob wouldn't be happy to be stuck footing the bill.

I crane my neck over the bar. There's a tiny slot at the top where the drawer fits into the register. I might be able to carefully slip the bill inside. The problem is getting around to the other side of the bar without being noticed.

As I dither, Charlie slowly raises the lighter up to the napkin, his shaky hands making the tiny flame dance.

With the flash paper inside—even sweat-moistened flash paper—that thing will burn in seconds.

It's now or never.

"Can I help you?" the curly-haired waitress asks just as I start to duck under the bar counter.

"Oh," I say, midcrouch. "I just . . . dropped my money." I hold up the fifty-dollar bill as proof.

"Huh, interesting," the woman rasps. "Because it sorta looked like you were trying to sneak behind the bar."

"No, no," I say, straightening up, my neck starting to feel a little bit rashy. "I was definitely just . . . picking up my money." I show her the fifty again.

"That's a lot of scratch," the waitress says. "You steal it outta Mama's pocketbook?"

"No," I say, so unconvincingly that I almost start to think I did actually steal it. "My uncle gave it to me. For my birthday. Last week. He's a pilot. In San Diego. He doesn't have kids of his own."

"Oh, really?" the waitress asks. "Is he a boxers or a briefs guy?"

"Uhhh . . . I have no idea," I say, confused. "Why?"

"I don't know," she says. "You seemed in the mood to share a bunch of useless information about someone I could give two craps about."

I stare at her, momentarily stunned. Like she just reached out and slapped me with a rubber chicken.

She sighs wearily and gestures at my hand. "You're holding that cash like you're ready to do something with it. You want a Coke? A Shirley Temple? What?"

I shake my head. "Uh . . . no. I just need . . . some change. For a tip."

"That I can do." The waitress presses a button and the register rings loudly, the cash drawer flying open with a substantial *clunk*.

I whip my head to the left to see if the noise caught anyone's attention, but all eyes are focused on Charlie as he drops the flaming napkin into a glass of water.

Shit, shit, shit. This needs to be done *now*.

I thrust the bill at the waitress. "Just some change. Yes. Please."

The woman takes the fifty-dollar bill and examines it, flipping it over, holding it up to the light.

"This funny money?" she asks, squinting at it.

Oh boy. I don't have time for this.

"*Funny?*" I say. "As in fake? No. Definitely not."

She points at the signature. "You always write on your bills?"

"That's not mine." I clench my fists, pressing half-moons into my palms. "I didn't do that."

"Well, whose name is it, then?" The waitress brings the bill closer to her face.

Oh, crap. How well does she know Charlie the bartender? Has she ever seen him sign his name? Maybe I should just confess. Tell her about the trick. Bring her into the fold. Give her a tip for helping out.

But what if she calls bullshit?

Either way, Bob would never forgive me. And I can't have that. Not on my first tour as his confederate.

I check the crowd once more and catch Bob's eye for a split second. He furrows his brow and I give him a little head shake, hoping he realizes I need him to stall a bit longer.

"It's a *C* and an *H* for sure," the waitress says, her face contorting as she tries to sound out the name on the bill. "Ch . . . Ch . . . Chuckles?" She looks at me. "Who's Chuckles?"

"My uncle," I blurt, because I have to heave this thing forward. "The one who sent me the card—for my birthday."

"The briefs-wearing, childless pilot from San Diego?" The waitress peers at me. "Your uncle's name is Chuckles?"

"Yeah, good old Uncle Chuckles," I say, wondering if my fingernails are actually drawing blood or if my palms are just slick with sweat. I look over at Bob again. He's holding the murky glass of water and ashes up in the air for everyone to gaze at, swirling it around so it catches the light. I can't hear exactly what he's saying, but I *can* see that his forehead is getting sweaty.

"His real name is Chuck. But we call him Chuckles. 'Cause he laughs a lot. He's super cool. Hundred percent."

I don't know why I feel the need to defend my fictional uncle to a woman I will never see again, but it seems important.

"Well, tell your 'super cool' Uncle Chuckles it isn't super cool to defame United States currency." The woman waves the bill in the air for all the world to see. "I do believe it is illegal *and* punishable by up to six months in prison. Although I might have that confused with bear wrestling." She looks down into the register and exhales heavily, like this is going to take some real effort. "What denominations would you like?"

"Anything is fine," I croak, struggling against the thick mass that's swelling in my throat. "Whatever you've got."

She looks down at the cash drawer again. "All right, then. One of everything it is."

22

"IF I PUKE UP ALL THAT ASH, YOU'RE MOPPING UP THE MESS," Bob says as we thump out of the strip-mall parking lot.

"I didn't tell you to drink it," I say, wincing at the thought of him swallowing the gray, cindery water.

"No," Bob says. "You just left me swinging in the wind, so I had no other option."

I shake my head. "The waitress was chatty. You should have factored in more time for that."

Bob turns his head, his dark eyes like hard, threatening bullets. "Beg pardon?"

I avert my gaze, feel my soul shrinking inside. "Nothing."

"You have to learn to think quicker on your feet," Bob mutters. "Otherwise this isn't going to work out."

We sit in silence for a while until I notice Bob coasting over the center yellow line.

I point at the road. "You're straddling."

"Oh, now you're going to tell me how to drive, too? Do you even have a license?"

A loud, blaring horn howls from behind us. Bob wrenches the steering wheel to the right just as a black truck zooms by us. The young female passenger shoots her arm out the window and gives us an overly aggressive middle finger.

Bob shakes his head, muttering, "The whole world is going to shit in a shoe."

I clench my jaw, resisting the urge to point out that you don't need a license to see who was driving unsafely.

"The cash," Bob says, thrusting his callused palm out toward me. "You did get the change, yes?"

"Yeah." I lean back and burrow my fingers into the front pocket of my jeans, pulling out a mass of bills and coins. "Here you go." I carefully place the crumpled wad of money in Bob's hand, unable to stop some of the change from spilling off and falling into the cracks between the seats.

Bob clutches his fist around the cash and glares down at it. "What is this, Monopoly? I've got every fucking denomination known to God or man here."

I wince. "There was no time to argue."

Bob rolls his eyes, grumbles, and jams the money into the breast pocket of his denim shirt.

"Sorry," I say. I stare out at the passing neighborhood, berating myself for not being quicker, for not doing a better job. If I were Perry, I'd have charmed the pants off that waitress and had two twenties and a ten in my hands lickety-spli—

Wait a second.

I whip my head back toward Bob. "That was *their* fifty. The restaurant's. The one I got change for."

"It was," Bob confirms.

"So, I didn't actually get *change* for a fifty. I *stole* fifty dollars from them!"

He rolls his eyes. "I wouldn't exactly call it *stealing*. We did provide a certain amount of entertainment. Generally you expect to get paid when you offer a service."

I hunch down in my seat like the cops are already after us. "I can't believe we scammed them. I can't believe I didn't even realize that we were scamming them." I turn and look at Bob. "When did you stop doing magic and become a thief?"

"Hey!" Bob glares at me. "I worked damn hard for that money. I didn't walk in with a gun and take it. If people are too oblivious to hold on to their cash, far be it from me to stop them from giving it to me."

"Yeah, but you're tricking them into giving it to you," I say. "They don't have all the information. It's not fair."

Bob laughs. "*Fair?* Life isn't fair, kid. I hate to break this to you, but you and me"—he wags his finger back and forth between us— "we weren't born rich, athletic, *or* handsome. So we leverage what we *were* given. Our talents. I don't see what's so wrong with trying to even the playing field a little."

"Yeah, well"—I clutch my arms around my chest, my stomach twisting around itself—"I wish you would have said something. I feel very uncomfortable with this." My breath is shallow and shaky.

"The only thing I ever stole was a Spider-Man comic from a drug-store when I was nine. I still have nightmares about the Slender Man pharmacist chasing me down and grabbing my arm with his spindly fingers."

"Would you like me to turn the car around so you can return the money?" Bob asks. "Tell everyone in that bar that you played them for fools? Beg their forgiveness while someone takes a steak knife to your gut?"

I shake my head. Just the thought of going back there makes me want to dive under a blanket.

"Good, because there's no fucking way I'm doing that."

"Maybe we can mail the money back to them," I say, sitting up hopefully. "Anonymously. Call it a donation or something."

Bob looks at me like I've just asked him for a kidney. "Listen, kid. I get it. You have a conscience. It's cute. But the simple fact of the matter is that the twenty dollars a week you're paying me—while an *enormous* sum—does not pay the bills. That is why you agreed to run these errands with me for the next two weeks."

"Wait," I say. "You want us to do this again?"

"And again. And again," Bob says, nodding. "Not the same story line, of course. That gets boring. However, the results should all be consistent." He pats his money-stuffed shirt pocket.

"I'm not OK with this," I say.

Bob laughs. "You will be, kid. Don't worry. The guilt abates pretty quickly. Really what you need to do is reframe things. We're putting on a show. They're paying us for that show. End of story."

I bite my lower lip. "I'd really rather not."

Bob shrugs. "Suit yourself. But I can't help you if you don't help me." He fumbles around in his shirt pocket, then flashes the folded-up Monkey's Paw description I gave him earlier.

Panic grips my chest. "Can't we do other errands? Grocery shopping? A trip to the pharmacy?"

"Sorry, kid," he says, turning his attention back to the road. "Thing is, my regular partner's been . . . sidelined since January. Been rough sledding since then. So I'm afraid you're going to have to check your pair of Goody Two-shoes at the door. Price of doing business."

23

I STAND IN THE HALLWAY, LOOKING THROUGH THE TINY window in the rehearsal room door, watching Dani practice her audition routine. She has a string of Christmas lights in her hand and has been doing the same sleight—changing a small red bulb for a large red bulb—over and over and over again. It was near perfect the first time I watched her do it, but there's clearly something she isn't happy with because fifteen minutes later she's still doing the same move.

It's hypnotic. The repetitiveness of it. The swoop of her hand. The focus on her face. The intensity in her eyes. I've tried to break the spell, look away for a second, but there's a physical pull I can't seem to resist. The fact that I could happily stand here for the rest of my life, my legs going numb, my eyes raisining, scares me a little.

I had no intention of getting here this early, but I had a terrible night's sleep, filled with dreams of SWAT teams swarming my house, submachine guns drawn, coming to take me in, dead or alive. I'd wake every time with a start, breathing heavily, immensely relieved that I was only dreaming, until I'd hear the pounding on the front door again, the sound of squealing tires, the flutter of heli-copter blades.

And the nightmare would begin all over again.

Finally, at around five thirty, I crawled out of my sweaty, tangled sheets, took a scalding-hot shower, got dressed, and rode my bike to school so I could . . . *what?*

Maybe talk to Dani before Perry shows up? Dani, our chief competition? Dani, who has told me—repeatedly—that she can't be trusted?

Yeah, that sounds like something a sleep-deprived me might do.

Dani does one last bulb swap, blinks at her work a few times, then puts the string of lights down. She grabs her phone and starts tapping away, which seems to break the tractor-beam-like hold she had on me.

I spin from the window and have just checked the time on my own cell—6:52 a.m.—when a green message balloon appears on my screen: YOU SPYING ON ME?

Shit! I squat down, fumbling my phone, barely catching it before it smacks the floor. How'd she get my number? I don't remember giving it to her. I press my back into the wall, slowly, slowly, slowly raising myself up, cautiously twisting my head to peek in the small window—

"*Boo!*" Dani shouts.

"Oh *Jesuscrapfuck!*" I scream, reeling back from Dani's grinning face on the other side of the glass.

She shoves the door open, cracking up. "Sorry. When I saw you duck down like a cartoon character, I couldn't resist."

"I wasn't . . . spying," I stammer, holding my hands up in surrender. "I swear. Not on purpose, anyway. I just . . . got here early, is all. I didn't really see anything . . . much."

"Relax," Dani says, laughing. "I don't care if you see my act. I've been practicing it for six months. If you can steal it and perform it in two weeks, more power to you." She cranes her neck, looking past me. "Perry's not with you?"

"He's coming," I say. "We're still rehearsing together. But we've decided to audition separately."

"Oh, so you heard back from the MSA?" she says.

I could lie to her—I probably *should* lie to her—just to be sure word doesn't get back to Perry. But instead I find myself confessing the truth. "No. Not yet. We just thought . . . we didn't want to risk it. Better to play it safe, you know. With the time crunch and all."

Dani winces. "Please don't tell me I had anything to do with that."

I laugh. "Perry and I talked it over. It'll be good. For both of us. Seriously. We can practice on our own schedules. It'll free up some time, actually."

"Phew." Dani pretends to wipe sweat from her brow. "Well, I know *one* girl who's going to be happy to get her hands on some of that free time."

My immediate thought is *Dani*. Dani wants to get her hands on my free time. But then a second thought arrives on the heels of the first: *Tread carefully here, Quinn. This girl still baffles you.* Of course, isn't that also part of the attraction here?

"Oh yeah?" I say, an electricity dancing across my skin. I avert my gaze, trying to think of something witty to say. Something funny and flirty. But my bovine brain gives me nothing, as usual, and so I have to freeform. "What . . . girl?"

"Perry's girlfriend," Dani says, giving me whiplash.

I blink at her. "I'm sorry . . . *who?*"

"Gwen," Dani says. "Perry's girlfriend? We're in chem together. It's like a nonstop monologue with her. Perry this and Perry that. How he's always so busy. How they hardly ever see each other anymore."

"Oh, yeah, no." I shake my head. "They broke up, like, three months ago. *That's* why they don't really hang out all that much anymore."

"*Really?*" Dani says, her eyes wide. "That's . . . wow. OK. Well, you wouldn't know it, the way she talks about him."

"Tell me about it," I say. "Perry's the same about Gwen. They were totally into each other. Perfect match, actually. Which is why they broke up, I guess? Too much, too young. I don't know. It still confuses me."

Dani laughs. "Yeah, well, that's not going to last. It's like trying to keep two industrial-strength magnets apart. They'll be back together again eventually."

"You're probably right," I say, feeling a pang that's part envy and part jealousy, remembering how Perry would go AWOL for days at a time, responding to most of my texts with a lazy thumbs-up emoji.

"Anyway, since you're here so early . . ." She tilts her head toward the room. "I'm doing this holiday mash-up thing that I wouldn't mind getting your opinion on."

"Oh," I say, my head suddenly filled with helium. "I'm . . ." I stare at Dani, whose bright, wide emerald eyes whisper the only possible answer to her question. "Sure. I'd love to."

"It's . . . outstanding," I say, shaking my head, gesturing at the long string of illuminated Christmas lights that Dani's holding. My jaw nearly fell from my face when she dragged her hand down the string, instantly changing every bulb from small to large with an effortless sweep of her hand. Absolutely nothing like what she was practicing. "I don't even know what to say. You clearly don't need *my* help."

Dani looks at me sideways. "Seriously? Come on. The move is so simple. It's right there for anyone to see."

"Yeah, well, *I* barely saw it," I say, not completely confident I *did* see it. I'm fairly sure the lights must be gimmicked, maybe they flip over from small to large when you activate a switch, but I wouldn't put money on it. "And I was looking. Carefully. Maybe that's why it works so well. You know, a hidden-in-plain-sight sort of thing."

"You think?" she asks. She tips her head to one side, then nods, apparently satisfied. "Yeah, maybe you're right. I mean, if you barely caught it when you were looking so closely, then maybe it'll slip past the judges." She reaches out and squeezes my arm. "Thank you."

It's amazing how a few words and an arm squeeze from a beautiful girl can change the entire tenor of your mood.

"Do you think it's weird, though?" Dani asks, screwing up her face. "A holiday act in June? Do you think the irony will be lost on the judges?"

It's lost on me, but then I'm not even sure what irony is. "The effect is so good, I wasn't even thinking about the fact that they were holiday lights."

"Really?" Dani says, sounding a little disappointed. "That's a problem. I want the audience to be puzzled. I want them to wonder about it. Otherwise why call it *A Very Hannu-Kwanzaa-Christmas*?"

"I don't think you have anything to worry about," I say, suddenly realizing that it's *me* who should be worried. It's quite possible that Dani is a better magician than me. And I already thought she was amazing.

Between her mad skills and Perry's otherworldly charm, I'm not even sure something as off-the-charts as the Monkey's Paw can compete. But it's the best (and only) shot I've got.

24

Dear Charlie,

My wife and I accidentally left your restaurant on Tuesday without paying our bill. Please accept our apologies. I believe fifty dollars will cover it. Thank you.

Best wishes,
Douglas Henning

I tuck two twenties and a ten into the folded letter, seal the letter inside the envelope addressed to Father Flannigan's Tavern, and drop it into the mailbox.

The relief is almost instantaneous. I wish I could have done this three days ago when the idea first struck me, but I had to wait until I could sell a few things on eBay. Finally I can breathe all the way to the bottom of my Goody Two-shoes again.

Granted, if I really were a Goody Two-shoes, I wouldn't be assuaging my guilt so that I can justify teaming up with Robert

Lazlo again. But Perry's the perfect one, not me. If I'm going to have a shot at winning the auditions, I need the Monkey's Paw—and the only way to get the trick is to be Bob's confederate. I'll just have to find a way to repay anyone else he scams along the way.

I check the time on my phone. I've got to hustle if I'm going to make the Fernwood Festival in time. I've been so preoccupied lately—between figuring out what I was going to sell on eBay so I could repay Charlie, working on Perry's and my acts for the auditions, and daydreaming about a future in which Dani and I tour the world as a magic duo—that I totally forgot I volunteered to man a booth at tonight's charity fund-raiser until Perry peeled off to lacrosse practice with a "See you at the Fest!" His Charity Club puts on one of these wonderful (but, if I'm being honest, horribly dull) events every year, and every year I have to pretend to care about the disappearing red-lipped shit beetle or the unethical treatment of bushes and trees.

"Wouldn't miss it!" I'd called back.

Though I would give anything not to have to be there. Spending an entire night manning an empty psychic booth while watching an endless gaggle of giggling girls line up for Perry's Dunk-A-Hunk stall is not exactly my idea of fun.

Still, a promise is a promise. And those shit beetles aren't going to save themselves.

By the time I burst into the county-fair-festooned gymnasium, the place is swarming with churro-eating carnival-goers, stilt-walking clowns, and raffle-ticket-selling volunteers.

I jog around the ticket booth and dash past the line of food stalls, breathing in a rainbow of scents as I go: burnt sugar, charred meat, fried dough, spicy mustard, pepperoni pizza. My hungry stomach stirs for a second, then just hides its head in confusion.

The fun-and-games stalls are all lined up by the windows. The balloon dart throw and ring toss seem to be the popular choices. Not so much ping-pong fish cup or the very appropriately titled Sand Art with Mrs. Borring.

The main draw here is clearly Perry's wet white long johns at the Dunk-A-Hunk (and-See-His-Junk) booth. He has a line of groupies that snakes right out the gym door, down the main hall, and past the library. With the money they pull in from Perry's heroics, they'll not only be able to cure rectal cancer—this year's very poster-friendly charity cause—but every other kind of cancer, too.

I catch Perry's eye on his soggy perch and give him a wave. He immediately leaps up and steps down from the dunk tank. A loud, disappointed moan erupts from the Dunk-A-Hunk line as Perry pulls on a robe and slips on some flip-flops and makes his way over to me. I didn't mean to interrupt the proceedings. I only wanted Perry to see that I was here. That I'm a good friend. That I keep my promises.

"Hey, man," Perry says, lifting his dripping chin as he approaches. His hair is plastered across his face in a long straggly swoosh that would make anyone else look ridiculous but makes Perry look like the handsomest lifeguard in a beach movie. "You shut off your phone?"

"Uhhh, no. Maybe. I don't think so. Why?" I reach into my pocket and pull out my phone to check.

"You didn't respond to my texts," Perry says. "You didn't get them?"

"Yeah, no, I did." I gesture at my phone screen, just remembering now that I meant to remind myself to write back. "I was frenzied today and I figured we were seeing each other tonight, so . . ." I point at the phone again. "You said you wanted to talk about the audition?"

Perry looks at me. "Are you OK, Quinn?"

"Yeah. Of course. I'm great. Why?"

"I don't know. You just seem a little . . . off lately."

"*Off?*" I say more defensively than I'd intended.

"Yeah. You know. Distant. Distracted. Not your usual jaunty self."

"Really?" I say, trying my best not to seem distant. Or distracted. "It's probably just"—I motion at Perry's text messages on my phone screen, sneak-reading their actual content for the first time—"the audition. Same as you. I'm getting anxious about it." I clear my throat. "Anyway, you said you had some new ideas?"

"Can't now." His teeth chatter as he peeks over his shoulder at the ever-growing line of girls at the dunk tank. "Charity Club wants to raise over two thousand dollars this year and I need to do my part if we're really going to 'stick it to rectal cancer.'"

"Yeah, you've got to change that slogan," I say, glancing up at the banner over the gymnasium stage. "So, afterward, then. We'll go over your whole act."

"I think I'm just getting nervous, is all." Perry rubs his hands together and blows into his cupped palms. "It's hard for me to imagine performing magic without you. I realized the other day that I've never actually done it before. Not in public. Which is why . . . I don't know . . . I'm second-guessing everything now. Maybe instead of doing the tricks I've already performed with you, we could come up with something completely fresh. So I won't keep comparing my performance to the ones we did together."

"Oh. OK. Sure." I nod, not exactly certain what "fresh" trick he has in mind and who (me, of course) is supposed to design it. But we can probably work something out. "If you think you have enough time to perfect something new." Who am I kidding? This is the kid who learned how to play a Bach concerto in a single afternoon just diddling on his Casio keyboard.

"Perry! Perry! Perry!" the crowd of dunk tank patrons chant.

"The donors are getting restless," Perry says.

"We don't want a riot on our hands," I say. "We'll catch up later." I clap him on his well-muscled shoulder. "You go stick it to rectal cancer, my friend."

It takes me a few minutes, but I finally find the psychic readings booth the Charity Club has set up for me, tucked away next to a stack of hay bales, just beside the door to the boys' locker room. Not exactly the prime location I was promised, but that's OK. I'd rather not be in the midst of Perry's libidinal, softball-hurling madness. I can see the debauchery just fine from where I'm situated.

My whole stall is tilting slightly and has been sloppily decorated with purple tissue paper and two sagging, half-deflated gold balloons. Someone has printed out a generic eye-in-hand

FORTUNE-TELLER sign—on what looks like a dot-matrix printer—and taped it crookedly to one of the plywood posts.

Not exactly the kind of storefront that sucks in the customers. Which is why I'm shocked to see that I already have one waiting when I arrive. Even more surprised to see who it is.

"*Gwen,*" I say as I shrug off my backpack and move to the stool inside my booth. "Nice to see you. Have a seat." I gesture at the folding chair on the other side of the table.

"Thank you," Gwen says. But she doesn't sit. Instead, she scans the area like she's being followed, clutching her string of pink carnival tickets like they're a rosary. "I've been waiting for you."

"Oh," I hear myself croak. My heart beats triple time. All the dials on my senses spin to ten. I swallow back the I'm-talking-to-a-hot-girl nausea that threatens to derail my good fortune. This is far too important to vomit away. *I've been waiting for you.* How many times have I fantasized about hearing Gwen Wilson—or any girl, really, but especially Gwen Wilson—say those very words? Her voice is slightly hoarse, which makes her British accent even sexier.

"I wanted to be first in line."

I force a laugh, glancing past her. "Guess you overestimated the demand for my services."

Gwen doesn't even crack a smile, just pulls the chair out, looks around again, then sits and stares at me. "How much?"

"Sorry?" I say, my pulse pounding in my ears. My tongue feels like a dehydrating slug in my mouth. *Get a grip, Quinn. So the most beautiful girl in school has been waiting for you? Big deal. You can talk to her without dissolving into a puddle of goo.*

"How many vouchers?" She holds up her crumpled coupons. "For the reading?"

I could listen to her say "how many vouchers?" all night long. Actually I could listen to her say *anything* all night long. The way she pronounces things, it always sounds just a little bit dirty. I wonder if Carter ever asks her to read random things to him for fun. Cereal boxes. Kitchen appliance manuals. Medication warnings. I can just hear her now, sounding like a naughty Mary Poppins: "A spoonful of sugar helps the medicine go down. However, side effects may include headaches, skin rash, hair loss, bloody stool, and, in rare instances, explosive gas with oily spotting."

All of a sudden I feel guilty and my gaze darts around the gymnasium, looking for Dani, wondering how this will look to her. Me sitting and chatting with a British supermodel. I *am* working my psychic booth, but still . . . *Although* why do I even care? I don't. I shouldn't. There's nothing to feel guilty about. And yet—

Gwen's other hand, the one not strangling the tickets, is crossed over her chest, fiercely clutching her opposite shoulder, like if she let her arm go it might drop off. You don't have to be a detective—or a psychic—to know something's bothering her.

"Five tickets for five minutes," I croak, making up a number because no one told me what I'm supposed to charge.

"OK, here," Gwen says, handing me her wad of coupons, fifty or sixty at least. "Take them all. I don't want to be interrupted."

"Oh." I stare at the stack of slightly warm, moist ticket strips in my hand, knocked dizzy-headed by how intimate this feels. "I don't think we're in any danger of that, but OK." I fold up the coupons and drop them into my empty glass jar. I can't believe this is real life. This can't be happening to me. I scan my surroundings to see if anyone's filming this with their phones, but nobody is.

Come on, now. Act professional. You can do this. I interlace my fingers and smile at Gwen. "So, what aspects of your life would you like to explore? Would you like me to read your palm? Or just your mind?"

That's right. There you go. You're an actor pretending to be a psychic. Simple.

"I don't want a psychic reading."

"Oh . . . all right." My eyes slide over to the sign taped to the wooden post. "You are aware you're sitting at a psychic booth?"

"I don't really believe in all that grot. I mean, a little, I suppose. Superstitions. Broken mirrors and spilt salt and all that. But just, you know, I imagine it's all a bit rubbish."

"OK," I squeak. Suddenly my mind is a cascade of fireworks, all the beautiful possibilities of what she *does* want exploding in my thoughts. "If you don't want a reading"—I push the words past my lips before I faint—"what . . . do you want?" *She wants me. She wants me. She wants—*

"Your advice," Gwen says, checking over her shoulder again. "About Perry."

"Perry?" I slump in my chair. It's my life in a nutshell: I get to sit across the table from a smart, gorgeous, amazing girl, staring into her forever-blue eyes—while we discuss the flawlessness of my best friend. "What about him?"

"It's just . . ." She scrunches up her face like the words are

162

physically painful to get out. "Why did Perry call me up onstage? At the talent show last week? Out of everyone in the audience?"

I've opened my mouth to reply when something—some*one*—catches the corner of my eye.

It's Dani, dressed like an adorable scarecrow clown, wearing patched overalls and a straw hat. She wanders around the fair, entertaining random children by making game tickets magically appear out of their ears, noses, and pockets.

I track her as she stops in front of a little girl, crouches down, and pulls an endless string of coupons from the belly button of the delighted, giggling toddler. She hands the tickets to the beaming child, then heads over to the ticket booth, where she proceeds to buy another huge roll of charity vouchers.

I could watch her all night. Smiling at the cashier. Laughing. Counting out her change. Adjusting her scarecrow hat and—

Change? Oh no. No, no, no. Wait a second. Could she be . . . ? No. She wouldn't scam a charity just to get some giggles from kids. Would she? I study her hands closely and watch as the ticket booth guy hands her some bills . . . which she immediately drops in the donation jar.

Aaaaand . . . I instantly feel like a complete tool. Of course she's not stealing from rectal cancer patients. Her parents are loaded. They probably give more to charity than my parents make. It's just my own guilty conscience, projecting my misdeeds onto her.

"Earth to Quinn," Gwen says, waving a hand in front of my slack-jawed face.

I shake my head. "Sorry," I say, forcing my eyes to stay on

Gwen—which was never something I had to work at before. "I really don't know why Perry called on you, Gwen." Which is the truth. Perry and I never discussed who he should choose. It just needed to be someone the audience wouldn't be suspicious of. "He trusts you, I guess. You're honest. Also, people like you. And . . . he probably thought it would be good theater."

Gwen nods, like she's warming to that idea. "Yeah, perhaps that's it. Perhaps it was simply good theater. It's only that . . ." She stalls again at the same spot. "I was wondering . . . does he talk about me? Ever?"

"Of course he talks about you," I say, stating the obvious. "You keep inviting him to things and then he says to me, 'Hey, Quinn, wanna come with me? Gwen just invited me to a barbecue, a cookie-making party, her cousin's bris.'"

"Not like that," Gwen says. "Not casually. I'm just . . . He's not dating anyone. We said we were both going to snog a few frogs to make sure we weren't missing out. He's not doing any snogging."

My eyes slide to regard Perry's endless line of groupies. "Maybe nobody wants to date him."

Gwen just shoots me a don't-be-daft look. "I'm serious. Look, Carter's a sweetheart, truly, it's just . . . he's not Perry. He can't help that. It's a puzzle-piece thing. We don't fit as well as Perry and I did. So I need to know"—she bores her stare into me—"if he's choosing not to date anyone because he's not ready yet or . . . if it's because he still fancies me as much as I do him."

What I wouldn't do to have someone this hypnotizingly gorgeous say something like this about me.

"Maybe you should ask him." I lift my chin toward the dunk tank. "He's gonna have to take a bathroom break soon. Just . . . tell him how you feel."

Gwen shakes her head. "I can't. We promised we'd be strong for each other. *However*"—she leans toward me, her gaze intense—"if I knew for sure that Perry was having second thoughts . . ."

Oh man. I do *not* want to be in the middle of this. Plus, Perry has specifically told me not to get involved.

I'm about to tell her that I don't feel comfortable betraying my best friend's confidence when I'm once again captured by the sight of Dani. She's holding a bouquet of drooping flowers in front of a little girl. A quick swoop of a scarf and the flowers are now a giant cloud of pink cotton candy. The little girl's eyes saucer, her entire body shaking with excitement as Dani hands her the paper cone.

"All right, then, fine. I get it. You're a loyal friend." Gwen thrusts a palm at me. "Why don't you predict my future, then? That's what I paid for, and no one can blame you for doing your job, right?" She gives me a conspiratorial wink. "So, tell me. What does my love line say?"

Jesus, why is everyone winking at me all of a sudden? And as soon as the thought occurs, my mind is conjuring up images of Dani. The wink in the hallway. The wink at my house. How each wink seemed to crack my heart open a little.

"Well?" Gwen says, wiggling her fingers at me, snapping me back to the gymnasium. "Have I met my soul mate yet? Or is he somewhere far off in the future?"

I take Gwen's hand and am about to feed her some ambiguous

Barnum statement—*You think that you're struggling with your love life. However, deep down in your gut, you know what you have to do*—when a thought occurs: if Perry and Gwen are going to end up together again anyway—and it seems obvious to everyone that they are—why put it off? They are clearly perfect for each other. What does it matter if they're sixteen or sixty? Perfect is perfect. They're like magnets, right? Whatever I say isn't going to change the inevitability of them getting back together.

And so I look into Gwen's eyes . . . and "predict" her future.

25

"SORRY, MAN," PERRY SAYS, SITTING ON THE BACK OF Gwen's Harley (I didn't even know Gwen rode a motorcycle) and holding on to her waist as she revs the engine. "Gonna have to bail on the audition. No time to pretend magic, not when I've got real magic in my life."

And with that, Gwen guns it and the two of them ride off into the sunset.

I awake with a jolt, then fling back the comforter and waft the blankets around to try to dry the sweat that's soaking through my T-shirt and boxers.

Jesus, I stink like a game farm goat.

I roll over and grab my phone off the nightstand. It's 3:33 a.m. Half of 666. That feels like a bad omen. I stare at the screen until it changes to 3:34. I'm becoming superstitious. A sure sign I'm starting to lose my grip.

I swing my legs around and sit on the edge of the bed, feeling like I might yurk up the three churros and the pile of soggy nachos I ate for dinner.

I press my palms into my aching eye sockets, trying to recall everything I said to Gwen. All I can remember for sure is seeing Dani walking around like Johnny Appleseed, spreading joy and carnival snacks wherever she roamed. And then, when I turned back to Gwen, I decided to . . . what?

Sell out my best friend? Sure, I can pretend I was just nudging along the inevitable, but let's be honest here. I had an agenda. I didn't know I had an agenda, but my dream sure did. I want Perry to get back together with Gwen because I know that if he does he won't have time to practice. Which means he won't be a threat.

The realization hits me like a shower of space debris. I wanted something and I made it happen, even if I didn't know I was making it happen. Just like Dani and the popcorn kernel.

My hand shoots up to my gasping mouth.

Wait a second! Wait. One. Second. Holy crap.

Dani.

Dani was the one who said that Gwen and Perry were inevitable. That they were like industrial-strength magnets. Didn't I even think exactly this as I was talking to Gwen? *Perfect is perfect. They're like magnets.* Is it possible . . . ? Did Dani plant that thought in my head? Did she hope I might say something to Perry about Gwen? Or, like I did at the fair, say something to Gwen about Perry? Because, yes, it benefits me if Perry blows his audition, *but it benefits Dani as well.* And, as she has stated loud and clear: nothing is more important to her than this audition.

I grab my forehead, massage my aching brain.

No, no, no. You're jumping at shadows now. She's messing with your mind. Or you're letting *her mess with your mind. Or you're messing with your own mind. Or whatever.* Clearly I'm a bit scrambled right now.

Let's think this through. Gwen came to me. To my psychic booth. Out of the blue. I wasn't looking for her. She asked *me* about Perry. I had nothing to do with any of that. *Dani* had nothing to do with any of that.

I scrub my face with my hands, making tortured animal noises through my fingers. I can't think straight. If I could only get a little sleep. But there's no way I'm sleeping. Not with my mind on fire like this. I hop off my bed and start to pace my room like a trapped tiger.

I need to figure this out. If Dani's manipulating me like a master mentalist, then I need to shut it down. Not see her anymore. Steer clear. However, if it's *me* that's the devious one—which, Occam's razor and all—and if it's *my* subconscious that's done this all on its own? Then I don't know what I'm going to do.

I stop pacing before I wear a deer path in my carpet. I sit at my desk, prop my elbows, and support my heavy head with my hands.

They'll be back together eventually, Dani said. Yes, she did say that. But it was me, my brain that thought about how Perry would go AWOL for days at a time because he was always with Gwen. I didn't mention that to Dani. Sure, I said they were really into each other, but Dani didn't know just *how* consumed Perry ended up getting.

I really want to blame it on Dani. But maybe I can't. *Oh God. What have I done? I'm the worst friend ever.*

I grab my stomach, the hot blade of remorse piercing my gut. I slowly spill from the chair, collapse to the floor, and curl up in the fetal position. I rock my body back and forth, letting the self-loathing wash over me.

Maybe this all works out fine.

Maybe nothing comes of it.

Maybe Gwen doesn't even mention anything to Perry at all.

26

"DO WE HAVE TO DO THIS TODAY?" I GROAN, RUNNING MY hand through my bed-tangled hair. "I didn't get a lot of sleep."

"Do you want your allowance?" Mom asks, knowing there is only one answer to this question. "Then you'll be our audience." She motions to the armchair in the corner of the living room.

Mom and Dad have moved the coffee table aside and pushed most of the furniture toward the walls to make room for their performance. I don't know how I forgot it was Saturday morning. If I'd remembered I would have hidden in my room for a few more hours, foraging for dusty sunflower seeds and M&M's in the bottom of my backpack, until this afternoon when I have to go meet up with Bob.

"We had to switch up the ending of the third act last minute," Dad says, carrying a potted plant into the living room and placing it stage left. "Our test audience *hated* the saber-toothed tiger mauling."

"I didn't hate it," I say. "I just thought it was . . . abrupt." They continue to move furniture, clearly not listening to me. I head toward the kitchen. "I'm going to get a Pop-Tart."

"Be quick about it," Mom says. "We're almost set up here. We've only got three days to get this ironed out. Opening night's Tuesday. Don't forget."

"I won't," I say as I trudge past the fridge. How could I? There are programs all over the house, posters on every lamppost in town, flyers on every store countertop.

I yank open the cereal cupboard, grab a package of raspberry Pop-Tarts, pour myself a glass of milk, and drag my grouchy, tired butt back into the living room.

"Do I need to know anything here?" I say, taking a bite of sweet, lab-created berries. "Story's still basically the same?"

Their "story," from what's managed to seep past my apathy, is a star-crossed lovers' tale set during the Paleolithic age. Never mind that Early Man could barely speak, let alone sing. Mom and Dad never let reality or logic get in the way of their art. Apparently one of them got the "great idea" when they read about Europeans having Neanderthal DNA.

You might be surprised to learn that there have already been several attempts at staging a caveman musical. I know I was. But none, according to Mom and Dad, with the depth and scope of theirs.

"It's a completely new finale," Dad says, microadjusting the placement of the houseplant. "Finn has just learned he will never get to be with his one true love because they're different species. He, a *Homo neanderthalensis*. She a *Homo sapiens*. Finn is distraught and—instead of luring a man-eater into the Sapiens' settlement as previously planned—he decides—having recently discovered fire— to burn down the Sapiens' forest in protest."

I take a sip of milk. "That doesn't seem any better than the wild animal. He could still end up killing the girl of his dreams."

"Yes," Mom says, pointing at me like I hit the nail on the head. "It's bad judgment. To set tigers free *or* to burn things down, without thinking of the consequences. Something *Finn* will have to learn the hard way."

Ah yes, I see. So I make a small negative comment about their musical and they decide to write a song based on the time I accidentally burned down our hundred-year-old laurel hedge. Except that *I* didn't burn it down for love. Just, you know, because I was six and thought it'd be a good idea to cook my Ball Park frank over a campfire.

"All right," I say, exhaling audibly, not even trying to hide my irritation. "Let's get this over with."

Dad connects his phone to the Bose speaker on a side table. "We want honest feedback," he says. "Like always."

This is a lie. They don't want honest feedback. *Clearly.* They simply want a warm body sitting in front of them. Anytime I offer even the tiniest critique, I get two days of them explaining to me why my opinion is wrong and/or another one of my life's humiliations used as "inspiration" for the rewrite.

"Quiet on the set!" Dad calls out like he's Martin Scorsese.

Mom gets in position, lying on the floor beside the potted plant. Dad moves to the fireplace and grabs two sticks from the kindling rack. They both do a series of phlegmy, voice-clearing exercises that go on interminably, like they have TB or something.

Finally, when I've nearly finished my first Pop-Tart, Dad taps his phone and the music for their brand-new musical number begins.

He starts to circle the room, waving his sticks in the air, grunting like an ape. I have to stifle a laugh because it seriously sounds like he's trying to work out a nugget.

Just as Dad hunkers down next to the plant, furiously rubbing his sticks together, my phone buzzes. I slide it from my pocket and see a text from Perry.

STRANGE CALL WITH GWEN. CAN YOU CHAT?

Oh, crap, that was fast. I thought maybe she'd ease into it over a few weeks, not dive right into the deep end. My palms go insta-slick, my stomach flopping over. Did she tell him what I said? Is he pissed? Happy? Hard to read the tone in his text.

EARNING MY ALLOWANCE, I message back. EVERYTHING OK?

CALL ME WHEN U CAN TALK.

Great. As if the next sixty minutes weren't already going to be pure torture.

I'm about to open my mouth and tell my parents I'm having painful bathroom issues when Mom starts to sing a sleepy chant, low and under her breath.

"Habilis, Erectus. Sapiens, Neanderthals. Habilis, Erectus. Sapiens, Neanderthals."

Dad hoists himself to his feet and stomps around Mom and the potted plant, huffing like an angry animal as he scrubs his sticks together in time to Mom's chant.

"Habilis, Erectus. Sapiens, Neanderthals. Habilis, Erectus. Sapiens, Neanderthals."

I furtively text: MIGHT BE A WHILE. BIG NEWS?

The second I hit send I regret it. Big news? Why would I ask him that? Unless I expected big news. Unless I was the *cause* of big news. Crap. I can just hear the questions now. "Why did you ask me if I had big news?" "What would make you think that?" "Did you tell Gwen about our private conversation? When I explicitly asked you not to?"

Dad starts in with his own singsong mantra. *"Foragers and hunters. Gatherers and herders. Foragers and hunters. Gatherers and herders."*

The music on the speaker swells with synthesized strings.

"When you play with fire, you're gonna get smoke," Mom sings from the floor with all the passion and angst of the undiscovered.

"When your act's all high-wire, you reap what you stoke," Dad responds in his best caveman crooner.

Mom clambers to her feet, squinting around like it's the middle of night. *"If love is destruction, then mine is ablaze."*

Dad crouches beside the potted plant, scraping his sticks together with an impassioned fury. *"Internal combustion, a smoldering haze."*

Then, the two of them in harmony. *"Habilis, Erectus. Sapiens, Neanderthals. Foragers and hunters. Gatherers and herders."*

I check my phone screen again. No answer from Perry. What does that mean? That he's suspicious? He is, isn't he? I can tell. I can feel his suspicion seeping over the airwaves—

This is so painful. I need to know if he's mad. But if I bolt right now, I don't get my twenty bucks. And I need that twenty bucks. I can't imagine Bob will accept an IOU for his pay this week.

I force myself to focus on Mom and Dad's performance. I need to at least sound like I was paying attention when they ask me what I think. If Perry's upset, there's nothing I can do about it. Even if I wanted to, I can't *un*-betray him. I did what I did and I'll have to deal with the consequences.

When the last notes of "Friendly Fire" have sounded, the potted plant lies on its side, Mom is dead, having been burned to a crisp, and Dad—playing the fictional, prehistoric me—squats beside her charred form, weeping in despair. There's probably a deeper lesson to be garnered from their song—other than fire is a blunt instrument—but I was too distracted to get the nuances.

"It's perfect," I say as Dad helps Mom from the floor. "I wouldn't change a thing."

"Are you just saying that so you can leave?" Mom asks, her eyes narrowed at me.

"No," I lie. "It was really good. Very dramatic. The fire. The . . . total devastation. And the song was super catchy." I point to my temple. "I'm humming it in my head right now. Hmm, hmmm, hmmm." I drone something randomly close to their melody.

"Qu*iiiinn*?" Dad stretches out the *i* in my name like it's Silly Putty. "Be honest. You didn't like it, did you? Is it because it's based on the time you burned down our laurel hedge? Is that why you're having a hard time being impartial?"

"*Ohhhh*," I say, like this never occurred. "Was it really?"

When they first started writing their musical, Mom and Dad tried to pretend they weren't stealing straight from my life, but now they just cop to it and try to flatter me by saying that it's my own fault for being so darn interesting.

"Was it the chanting?" Mom asks. "Because the chanting is important. It sets the tone for the whole piece. It's the heartbeat. This quiet thrumming of interspecies love. Different but the same. If you didn't like the chanting you just didn't understand it."

"I liked the chanting," I say, licking the sticky Pop-Tart filling from my fingers. "It really pulls you in."

"Does it feel a little slow?" Dad asks, looking at me, looking at Mom. "It feels slow, doesn't it? But it needs to build. From the soft rumble of the chant to the raging beat of the inferno at the end. If you start off faster, it detracts from the swell and ache of the anticipation. But maybe we should bump up the BPM a titch."

They'll go on like this for a while. Positing a problem and then arguing with themselves about it. It took me a while to get the drill—I honestly thought they wanted my opinion at first—but I'm finally starting to learn that I'm just the "No, it's great" guy.

"No, it's great," I say.

"Well, if it's my character's immolation at the end," Mom says, "that has to happen. They call it a tragedy for a reason, Quinn."

"Nope," I say, toasting the air with my glass of milk before sucking the rest of it down in three gulps. I swipe my sleeve across my lips. "Didn't have a problem with the death. Makes sense to me."

"Well, then, what was it, son?" Dad says, staring at me. Then, suddenly, as if lightning strikes, he gasps and whips his head in Mom's direction. "The swelling symphony. Clearly he didn't like the pomposity of it. Makes it feel cheesy. Amateurish."

"*Noooo*," Mom says, glaring at me. "The orchestra sound gives it gravitas. Importance. A real weight. I worked for hours to get the right tones on my Casio." She purses her lips, then turns to Dad. "You think it sounds pompous?"

Dad dodges his head like Mom just took a swipe at him. "*I* didn't say it was pompous." He shoots a *j'accuse* finger at me. "Your son said that."

I force a smile, knowing that anything I say can and will be used against me in a future argument. I really wish I could skip out on this part of the proceedings, but I have been reminded on more than one occasion (some of which included threats of Gilbert and Sullivan marathons) that I am being paid to be an audience. "*And sometimes that means being an audience to the creative process.*"

Mom and Dad go back and forth about the orchestra for the next forty minutes while I obsessively check my phone for messages from Perry. At last they settle on trying the song with a simple string quartet sound to see if maybe "less is more" in this case.

"All right, mister." Dad grins at me and reaches for his wallet. "That was very helpful. Your mother and I appreciate your honesty." He takes out a twenty and hands it to me. "You're free to go."

The second I step from the living room, I'm dialing Perry's number. Before it has a chance to connect, a text comes through.

GOING AFK, Perry's message says. LACROSSE PRACTICE. CALL AFTER.

No, no, no! I mash my finger into my phone screen, like somehow this physical act will make it connect before Perry shuts his phone down. But it's too late. When I finally get a ring, it picks up immediately and I'm treated to Perry's peppy greeting, inviting me to leave my name and number if I would like a return call.

27

"YEAH, YEAH, HELLO," PERRY FINALLY ANSWERS, SOUNDING like he's fumbling his phone.

"Oh-thank-God," I exhale. "I've been . . . trying you for, like . . . a few times." I shift in my chair, glancing around the food court at the Fernwood Mall, praying Perry doesn't see my fourteen missed calls as something more than the normal concern of a friend. "You sort of left me hanging on a cliff there."

"Sorry, man," he says, slightly out of breath. "Lacrosse practice. I texted you."

"Yeah, no, yeah," I say, trying to keep my voice casual. I take a deep breath, the odd mixture of international smells—chow mein, pizza, curry, refried beans—doing nothing good for the state of my anxious stomach. "I guess . . . I just wanted to make sure we had time to talk before the afternoon got too busy. Anyway. *Gwen?* What the hell's going on there, man?"

"Oh my God, it's intense," he says. "You're never going to believe it."

"Intense? In what way? Fill me in!" I look over at the hallway leading to the restrooms. Bob's gone to the men's room to "get propped-out" for our next errand. I'm not exactly sure what we're doing here at the mall—Bob's been vague with the details—but I'm certain it will involve me doing something I'm uncomfortable with. Right now I'm just trying to keep a low profile, praying I don't see anyone I know.

"OK, so, get this," Perry continues. "Gwen calls me up first thing this morning and tells me that she and Carter have split up, and that she wants us to give our relationship another shot if that's what I want, too."

"Holy . . . *wow*," I say, wincing at my bad acting, wishing I could have another take. "That's . . . such a . . . surprise."

"I know, right? She said she's been thinking about it for a while, but . . . it sure seems out of left field." Perry clears his throat and sniffs, like he's untangling a thought. "Hey, so, you didn't . . . happen to say anything to Dani, did you? About how I've been having second thoughts about the breakup?"

"*Dani?*" I'm so surprised and relieved to hear him asking about her that I nearly blurt out "No, of course not," before realizing that I *did* talk to Dani about Perry's feelings for Gwen. I think I may have even used the word *obsessed*. My stomach twists.

"Why would I . . . say anything to Dani?" This is not an answer, of course, but it's also not exactly a lie, either.

"Yeah, no, of course you wouldn't," he says. "It's just . . . I was thinking . . ." Perry takes a deep breath. "Can I ask you something? And you promise me you won't get mad at me?"

Oh, shit. My heart lodges in my chest, my head starting to swim. I have no idea what he's going to say, just that I know I'm not going to like it. "Yeah. Of course. Yeah."

"OK, so . . ." He clears his throat. "This is going to sound off-the-wall, but . . . I had this thought and I can't get it out of my head now. And I know it's ridiculous, but I have to say it so that at least I've said it."

"Okaaaaay," I say, bracing for impact.

"Do you think that maybe . . . there's any chance Dani spoke with Gwen . . . *trying* to get us back together?"

"Like, playing matchmaker?" I know exactly where he's going with this because, well, I've had the same "ridiculous" thought. About Dani. *And about myself.* "Why would she want to do that?"

"Gain an advantage?" Perry says. "Hoping I get distracted? I don't know. It doesn't make a lot of sense, but when I was talking about the auditions to Gwen, Dani's name came up. I told Gwen she was probably our biggest obstacle and that's when Gwen mentioned that Dani was in her chem class. She said she really liked her. That Dani had some real deep insights into people. It's weird. The minute Gwen said it, I got this tingling on the back of my neck. Like when you told me she talked to you about the audition rules and us not auditioning as a team. It raised the hackles, like a spider-sense or something."

"*Wait,*" I say, awash with relief that this is all about Dani and not about me stabbing him in the back. "So you think that Dani's deliberately trying to sabotage us?"

"I know, I know," Perry says, a wince in his voice. "You like her. I'm sorry. I wasn't going to say anything, but . . . I mean, come on. The thought never occurred to you? Even a little?"

"Sure, I mean, yeah," I say. "I definitely thought about it when you brought it up the first time, but I kind of dismissed it. Seems like a lot of effort to go through." *(He said about the girl who seems to go to a lot of effort about everything.)* "But you never know, right? Could be." No need to try too hard to change his mind.

"I don't know, it's a stretch, I suppose," Perry says. "But I'm glad I said it. Just so there are no secrets between us. Anyway, I gotta hit the showers. I'll let you know what happens with Gwen."

"Cool," I say, ignoring the spark of guilt stabbing my belly. "Sounds good. Later."

I've just clicked off my phone, my head still spinning from the call with Perry, when I see Bob staggering from the restroom hallway, tugging down on his dark blue dress shirt, adjusting the collar on his sports jacket, and scanning the food court.

I watch him swivel his head, furrowing his brow, searching everywhere. I do a little weave and wave to catch his attention and he heads over to my table. I set my hands in my lap and take a deep breath, trying to refocus on the task at hand.

"It's like fucking Where's Waldo in here," Bob says when he finally gets to my table. "You sure don't try to stick out in a crowd, do you, kid?"

"It's a gift, according to my mom," I say, keeping my head cast down. I tried to lobby for a different venue—this being the hangout

183

for everyone I've ever known, ever—but Bob says the food court crowd is perfect camouflage for the kinds of performances we'll be doing.

"You ready?" he asks.

"I'm still not clear on how this is supposed to work," I say, glancing over at the mall cop—a blond woman with a severe ballet bun—chatting up a pasty-faced guy working at the Cookie Nook. "You actually *want* me to call over Security?"

"Yes," Bob says, buttoning the cuffs on his sleeves.

"But why?" I ask. "What if she calls the *actual* cops?"

"You're the one who's got the guilty conscience," Bob says. "Here's your chance to turn me in."

I blink at him. "So you're not going to tell me how this is going to go down once the mall cop gets involved?"

"You want the Gorilla's Foot or not?" he says. "Do what you're told and let the rest play out as it may."

I don't even correct him anymore because I think he messes the name up on purpose just to piss me off.

At least, I hope that's what he's doing.

"Can't you even give me a hint? Am I supposed to stick around? Run? What?"

Bob waggles his eyebrows at me. "Oh, I think you'll know what to do when the time comes."

28

"HEY, HEY, WELCOME TO THE FERNWOOD MALL FOOD court," Bob says as he steps up to a group of five college kids sitting at one of the blue-and-orange tables. He looks almost managerial in his jacket and tie, which is all part of the story, I guess. "I hope everything's been to your liking so far." He points at the food on the table. "The pizza. The Hunan Surprise."

The kids all nod and mumble their satisfaction. It's a motley crew of beards, hair extensions, and Fernwood Community College sweatshirts. Two guys who look like they crawled out from under a bush in the Ozarks and three girls in various states of dishevelment. They are either all stoned or hungover or possibly both.

"Glad to hear it." Bob claps his hands together, which seems to startle the skinniest of the girls. "So, the reason I'm here: we're test-driving a new promotion. To see if people might appreciate some wandering entertainment in the food court. You know, music, clowns, magicians. If you have a moment, I'd like to give each of you fine people a chance to earn a fifty-dollar mall gift certificate." He pulls out a piece of paper—a generic gift certificate, probably purchased at the Dollar Store across the street—from his suit pocket and flashes it at the table. "Would you like that?"

The five of them look at one another with *why not?* faces and mutter, "Sure," "Yeah, OK," "I'm game, as long as it doesn't involve math."

"Excellent," Bob says, slipping the paper back into his pocket. "So, here's how this is going to work. I'm going to perform a little magic trick for you, and then I'd like each one of you to tell me if you enjoyed it or not. Straight-up simple. No hidden agenda. Be honest, though. That's important. No matter what you say, it will not offend me, nor will it affect your receiving the gift certificate in any way. Can you do that for me?"

I'm loitering in the background, staying just within earshot, waiting for my cue and trying to figure out how I'm supposed to return today's scammed money to some random mall strangers I'll never see again. If I could find out one of their names, I suppose I could mail it care of Fernwood Community College. Assuming they actually go there and aren't just wearing the sweatshirts ironically.

I jam my hands in my pockets, keeping a furtive side-eye on the proceedings. Once Bob's customers receive their "free" gift certificates, I'm supposed to call over the mall cop, loudly claiming that "the manager" is trying to pull a fast one.

I don't feel good about it. I wish we didn't have to bring the authorities into the mix. But Bob says to trust him. Which I *don't*, but what else am I supposed to do? Hopefully this is our last outing. He's promised me he'll give me the secret to the Monkey's Paw trick next time we meet, so I just have to grit my teeth until then.

As Bob does his thing, I walk by the Cookie Nook to get a better look at the mall cop I'll be dealing with shortly. She's pretty in a sort of black-widow-don't-fuck-with-me kind of way. It's the hair, I think—pulled back so tightly that it gives her a permanent look of disdain—that makes you feel like you're one wrong word from a trip to the slammer.

"Interesting factoid," the security guard says. "The first cookie was invented by a Persian in the seventh century. Lavish cakes, they were called."

"Wow," the pasty guy behind the counter says, only just barely feigning interest. "I did not know that."

"*Seriously?*" the mall cop says, her already-bugging eyes bugging even more. "How do you work at a cookie shop and not know this?" She shakes her head, as if disappointed at what's become of the world. "They really should make you take a test on your dessert knowledge before they give you the keys to the cookie cupboard."

"Yeah, it's a real crime," the guy says, rolling his eyes. "They'll give this job to anyone with a master's in engineering. You should probably write the head office and complain. Otherwise buy a cookie or get the hell out of my face."

"Whoa, hey, now." The security guard touches the billy club dangling from her belt. "Am I going to have to take you back to headquarters"—she peers at his cookie-shaped name tag—"*Sawyer*? Introduce you to Watch Commander Billingsly?"

"What the hell are you talking about?"

"I'm talking about a possible violation of Fernwood Mall Code

321.42, Sawyer." Her eyes dart to the cash register. "Employee embezzlement."

"I didn't steal anything," he says, sounding more irritated than intimidated.

The mall cop shrugs. "Maybe you did. Maybe you didn't. But a few hours stuck in an airless office with Watch Commander Billingsly and his suffocating BO and you'll confess to pretty much anything."

Great. I now know my future—and it smells like some guy named Billingsly.

I make my way back to Bob and his audience.

"Are you absolutely sure, Sanjana?" Bob asks a sleepy-eyed girl. She's holding a deck of cards in one hand, staring at a second pile of cards sitting on the table. "You can add cards. Take some away. I don't want to influence you at all."

Sanjana thinks about this, smiles, then takes two more cards from the middle of the deck and adds them to the top of her pile. "There. Now I'm done." She sets the deck aside. "No more changes."

"Perfect." Bob looks her straight in the eye. "Now, I want you to do one last thing for me, Sanjana. Just to make sure there is absolutely *no possible way* either of us could know what card you are going to pick." He gestures at the pile on the table. "Take your randomly mixed-up bunch of cards there and deal them out into two alternating stacks. One on the left, one on the right, back and forth until all the cards are dealt out."

Sanjana does as she's told, ending up with two even piles of cards on the table in front of her.

"Fantastic," Bob says. "I think we can all agree that those cards are completely random now." He nods at the stack. "Please choose one of those piles. I don't care which one. Left or right. It's all your free will."

Sanjana's eyes dart back and forth between the stacks. I can't tell which one she's going to choose, and honestly it really doesn't matter.

It only seems like it does.

Sanjana presses a finger into the stack to her right. "This one."

"Once again," Bob says, "I'll give you a chance to change your mind."

Sanjana shakes her head and grins. "No, thank you."

"All right, then. Look at the card on top of the pile." Bob pulls a pen and a scrap of paper from his pocket and hands these to Sanjana. "You can show your friends, but don't show me what you've got. Just write down the card on the piece of paper and fold it in quarters."

Sanjana does as instructed, then hands the pen back to Bob.

All of this frippery is simply a way of making the trick look more impressive than it actually is. Which is basically a pre-prep and a card force. It's all in the delivery. And Bob certainly has that down. I'm impressed with his comfort and ease. If I had a delivery as smooth and effortless as his, I might not even need the Monkey's Paw to beat Perry. Dani, on the other hand? I'm going to need the perfect trick *and* the perfect delivery if I'm even going to stand a chance.

"Now for the fun part." Bob takes a lighter from his jacket pocket and gives this to Sanjana. Any time you can add fire to a trick, it's a big win for showmanship. "Here we go. Time to tap into any psychic powers you might possess." Bob nods. "Light your paper on fire, place it on the food tray, and think of your card as you watch it burn." He points at her. "Go! Now!"

Sanjana flicks the flint wheel on the lighter, ignites the tiny square, and drops it on the tray. Everyone watches as the flames lick the paper, curling it up into a glowing ball of cinders.

"Are you picturing it?" Bob says excitedly. "The number and the suit?"

"Yes," Sanjana answers.

Bob quickly shoves the left sleeve up on his jacket—if she'd chosen the other pile he would have rolled up his right—revealing the bare skin on his inner forearm. "Now project it. Here." He pokes hard at his arm, vibrating with energy. *"Can you see it there, Sanjana? Picture your card."*

Sanjana stares at Bob's hairy arm, her eyes bulging. She nods slowly. "I do. I can see it there."

Bob shoots out his hand, grabs a bit of the ash from the food tray, and starts to rub his forearm vigorously. "I think I see it, too." As he smooths his palm over his arm, a dirty gray 8 ♣ appears on his skin.

"What the actual fuck?" Sanjana jerks her head back, blinking wildly.

A chorus of oohs and aahs sound all around as Bob shows his arm to the group. "Was that your card, Sanjana?"

"Yeah, it was," she says, looking to her left and right for confirmation.

"Thank you." Bob grins, rolls down his sleeve, and takes a humble bow as everyone applauds. "All right, well, there it is. So, did you enjoy the show?" The five of them nod enthusiastically. "Was it something you think other people would enjoy as well?"

"Some people might not want to be bothered," Sanjana says, glancing around the food court. "But I think most people would like it."

"I love the feedback," Bob says. "Now, I think I owe you each something for your participation." He slips the stack of gift certificates from his pocket, along with a pen. "Can I get your names?"

This is my signal. I'm supposed to walk straight over to the security guard, but I linger a moment, clocking Sanjana's last name—Malhotra—for future reference.

Bob will now look over his shoulder conspiratorially and ask the group if they would like him to make the certificates out for *a hundred* dollars instead of fifty. He'll need five bucks from each of them as a processing fee, so the mall isn't out of pocket on the larger amount, because they can only give a certain amount of money away each day and blahbbity-blah-blah-blah, but it's all completely legit and there's nothing to worry about. It doesn't really matter what he tells them as long as it sounds mildly plausible. Greed and impatience will be their undoing.

"Excuse me, ma'am," I croak out, reading the name on her badge: KARLEEN MARSHALL, SECURITY OFFICER.

"What is it, kid?" Karleen says, her hand pressed against the glass display counter of the Cookie Nook. "Can't you see I'm busy interrogating a perp here?"

"Sorry," I say, like she might actually be attending to a real crime. "It's just"—I clear my throat into my fist—"there's a guy over there pulling a scam on some college kids." I tilt my head in Bob's direction.

"Scam?" Karleen cranes her neck, looking past me. "Grandpa in the cheap sports coat over there?"

I look over my shoulder and see Bob collecting cash from everyone. "Yeah, that's him."

"Looks OK to me," Karleen says. "You want to know what the *real* scam is?" She points at Sawyer, standing behind the counter, angrily typing away on his phone, probably tweeting his annoyance to his eleven followers. "Wisenheimer here knows nothing about cookies. *Nothing.* Can't answer even the *simplest* question about the very product he's trafficking in. Can you believe that? They hire a cookie ignoramus to work at a shop that *only sells cookies*. It's like they want to fail as a business."

"That's, uh, yeah," I say, taking a look over at Bob again. He's going to have my head if I don't deliver this security guard soon. If I make him have to tap-dance again, I can kiss the Monkey's Paw goodbye. "I really think you should go over there. He's—"

"You look like a smart kid." Karleen cuts me off. "Let me ask *you*: What do you think is the most popular cookie in America?"

I sigh, resigning myself to failure. "Chocolate chip?"

"Exactly." Karleen slaps the display counter and smirks at the sales guy. "Chocolate *fucking* chip. It's the cookie you have the most quantity of right here."

"I don't give a shit," Sawyer says. "Go away. Clearly this person needs your help. Maybe go do your job."

"*My* job?" Karleen splutters, dragging her hand down her face. "*My* job? What about *your* job? Do you even know *why* they call them Toll House cookies? Or when National Cookie Day is?" She glares at him accusingly. "Have you ever even eaten a Little Debbie Nutty Bar?"

"Hey!" I say desperately, feeling the Monkey's Paw slipping from my fingers. "You want to know how much I know about cookies?"

"More than Gen Z here," Karleen says. "That's for sure."

I chuckle weakly. "Good one. Anyway, I bet I can guess what your favorite cookie is without you even telling me."

Karleen regards me suspiciously. "You think you can guess *my* favorite cookie? Without any clues?" She smiles. "Not a chance."

"Hundred percent," I say. "But if I do, you have to promise me you'll come over and see what's going on over there."

29

IF YOU TEAR A FOLDED PIECE OF PAPER UP IN THE RIGHT way, you can palm the center portion, chew up the remnants, and still sneak a look at what your subject has written down.

"Nilla Wafers," I say, pretending to swallow as I tuck the wet wad of paper inside my cheek. "That's your favorite cookie."

"That is incorrect," Karleen says. "Sorry. Fudgie Wudgies. *Those* are my favorite cookies. You lose. Thanks for playing." She turns back to the sales guy. "Now. Where were we? Oh yeah, that's right. Insubordination."

"You're lying," I say, having read exactly what she scribbled down. "That's not what you wrote."

"Excuse me?" She turns on me like a wolf, steps into my personal space.

I gulp. "I said that . . . your favorite cookie . . . isn't a Fudgie Wudgie. It's a Nilla Wafer."

A smile twitches at the corner of her mouth. "Prove it."

"OK, fine," I croak. "I will."

This is what Bob would call thinking on my feet. I start to retch, like I'm trying to work the paper wad up from my stomach.

Karleen takes a step back. "What the hell are you doing? You vomit on me, I'm taking you in."

"I'm proving it." I use my tongue to slide the moist mass from inside my cheek, then spit it out into the hand that's palming the piece of paper she'd written on. "Let's have a look, shall we?" I make a show of trying to pull the pieces apart and finally "find" the portion with NILLA WAFERS scrawled on it, the paper convincingly slimy from its close contact with the sodden wad. "Right there." I slap it on the counter. "Nilla. Wafers."

"Ha!" the sales guy says, pointing at Karleen. "Owned. Now buzz off, Famous Anus."

"Whatever," Karleen says. "I'm adding both your names to the Fernwood Mall no-fly list, so . . . don't bother applying for a mall credit card or . . . trying to get your picture taken with Santa."

I lead the security guard over to the table, an angry hornet's nest in my gut. I have no idea how the rest of this is supposed to play out. My only glimmer of hope is that I know Bob doesn't want to go to jail, so I imagine he has *some* sort of escape plan.

Unless . . . his plan is having *me* take the fall. My entire body flushes with heat. Could that be it? Is he pissed at me? Did he find out about me sending the money back to the bar? Does he know I'm planning to send the money back to these kids?

Am I the patsy?

"All right, what's going on here?" Karleen says as we step up to the table. "This kid tells me something janky's going down."

"Walter Becker," Bob says, thrusting his hand out for Karleen to shake. "Associate manager, Fernwood Mall. How are you doing today"—he squints at Karleen's name tag—"Karleen Marshall?"

"Let's save the pleasantries for now," Karleen says, glancing around. "You have any sort of . . . credentials I could see?"

"My word is my bond, Karleen," Bob says, nodding like this settles it. "And my job is my life. Now, if you value *your* job, you'll leave us be. I happen to be very good friends with Ivana Lakehouse at district headquarters. Head of Human Resources? Maybe you know her?"

"He's selling *actual* mall gift certificates," I say, anchoring the word *actual*, just like Bob told me to. "For five bucks they're getting a hundred. They're all basically ripping off the mall."

Karleen scans the group, looking for the weakest gazelle. She stops on Sanjana. "That true? This guy sell you gift certificates?"

Her friends all glare at her, willing Sanjana to lie.

But instead her eyes drop and she whimpers, "Yes."

"That so?" Karleen narrows her eyes at Bob. "Well, then, we seem to have a problem here, *Walter*." She grabs the walkie-talkie from her belt and clicks the call button. "Bravo One, this is Cookie Monster. We got a ten-seventy here in the food court."

"Hey, hey, lady," Bob says, holding up his hands as he slowly backs away. I look at Bob and see his eyes flick hard in the direction of the exit doors. "I don't want any trouble. I was simply"—he takes another step back, then another—"trying to help out some very kind and financially strapped students—"

Suddenly Bob turns and bolts toward the doors to the parking lot.

Karleen and I share a stunned look.

What-do-I do-what-do-I-do-what-do-I-do?

"I'll go after him," I hear myself saying before I actually know what I'm going to say. But I've already started to run, so I better think of something. "You should probably . . . interrogate the witnesses. I'll bring him back. Don't let them leave."

Karleen doesn't argue. Just shrugs and returns to the students.

I push through the exit doors, my heart beating against my tonsils. I sprint through the parking lot, past several rows of cars, wondering why the hell Bob would go to so much effort and cause so much anxiety for only twenty-five bucks.

"That was quick thinking back there, kid," Bob says as we pull out of the mall parking lot. He wags a finger at me, his face crinkling into a smile. "I knew you had it in ya. I think you might be ready to go big-game hunting."

I stare at him, feeling oddly proud but also like I've just swallowed a handful of nails. "Is that why we just did that? The whole thing? To test me?"

"Please," Bob says, rolling his eyes and turning to look back at the road. "As hard as it might be for your self-involved, teenage-addled brain to wrap itself around, I will never do anything *just* for you."

"Well, I know it wasn't for twenty-five bucks," I say.

"You're right about that." Bob springs a square of nicotine gum from a blister pack and slips it into his mouth, then clicks on his turn signal and pulls his car—

back into the Fernwood Mall parking lot!

"Wait, wait, why are we back here?" I say, scrambling in my seat, pressing my body as far back as I can. "What are you doing?"

Bob says nothing, just sweeps the steering wheel this way and that, the giant car swaying with each turn, until finally he takes us to the very back of the mall, where he cruises along a strip of loading docks and huge dumpsters.

My eyes are darting around like bingo balls, looking every which way they can for a possible clue. "I'd really feel a lot more comfortable if you told me what was going on."

"This"—Bob steers his car up beside a dumpster and shuts it off, a loud, explosive backfire erupting before the engine shuts down—"is what's going on." He looks up at the loading dock where Security Officer Karleen Marshall leans against a wall, sucking on a vape pipe.

"What the hell?" I start to hyperventilate, a pain the shape of a fist swelling below my sternum. "Are you turning me in?"

Bob laughs and grabs his door handle. "I should," he says. "Just for saying that. I'm a lot of things, kid, but a rat is not one of them. Now get your ass out of the car, clamp your muzzle, and come learn something."

I push open my door and follow Bob up the concrete steps to the loading dock.

"You ever going to get that piece of shit fixed, Bobbo?" Karleen says, glancing down at Bob's Mercury.

"Never," Bob says. "I like people to know I'm coming." He gestures at the security guard. "You've met the Cookie Monster."

"If it isn't Fudgie Wudgie," Karleen says, blowing a cloud of smoke sideways and pocketing the vape pen. "I think that should be your mobster nickname. Fudgie Wudgie." She smiles at Bob. "What do you think, Bobbo? You like Fudgie Wudgie for the kid?"

I shake my head. "I don't . . . no, thank you. Also . . . *what the hell is going on*? You two know each other?"

Karleen ignores me, stepping forward, away from the rumpled backpack that sits on the ground. "We had a near miss in there," she says. "Couple of badges waltzed in just after you left. Luckily they only wanted a couple of Sloppy Janes. Strolled right past me without even a courtesy nod. Mall cops get no respect, I swear."

"Good thing you're not a real mall cop," Bob says. "So? You make bank?"

"What do you think?" Karleen looks at Bob like he shouldn't even have to ask. "Those dupes rolled over like a pack of spanked puppies. It was hilarious. All the whimpering and sniveling." She tugs a wad of cash from her pants pocket and counts out twenty-dollar bills. *"Please. We don't want any trouble. We don't even know that guy."* Karleen laughs. "One of your best ones yet, Bobbo. It was just like you said. Plus, turns out the cops were good props. All I had to do was threaten to call them over and our little cash machines were more than happy to pay for the rest of their gift certificates. Wish I could see the looks on their faces when they try to use them."

"I prefer to picture them happily forgetting all about them," Bob says while my gaze ping-pongs between them. "Like my entitled grandkids do with the gift cards I send them."

"There's no gratitude in the world anymore," Karleen says, handing Bob a stack of cash. "There you go. Your cut. Plus"—she reaches into her backpack and removes a Cookie Nook bag—"as a congratulations on another sweet score. Get it? Sweet?" She shakes the bag at us. "I got an assortment. It used to be a dozen, but, you know, I got a little bored waiting for you."

30

"WE HAVE TO STOP MEETING LIKE THIS."

"Jesus Christ!" I whip around and there's Dani standing by the bushes beside my garage, waving at me, a Cheshire cat grin lighting up her beautiful face. Just like she looked when she showed up unexpectedly in my bedroom. My hand clutches my chest, my heart thumping against my palm. "You sure like scaring people, don't you?"

"Not in general," Dani says, brushing a curly lock from her face. "Mostly just you."

"Yeah, well," I say. "Lucky me." My pulse starts to settle as my initial terror shifts into curiosity . . . with a soft glimmer of hope underneath. "So, um, what are you doing here?"

She thrusts a small paper-bag-wrapped package at me. "I brought you a present. From the magic shop."

"Oh." I slowly reach out and take the gift from her. It's a book, I can tell by the feel. The paper bag it's wrapped in is worn and soft, like she's been holding it for a long time. "Thanks. I didn't . . . What's the occasion?"

She shakes her head. "It's nothing. Ed lets me have one thing from the shop every day that I work. As long as it's under ten bucks." She lifts her chin. "Today I grabbed that for you."

"Oh. OK, well, wow. I don't know what to say." I raise the package. "Thank you."

"I knocked, by the way," Dani says, gesturing toward my front door. "Just in case you think I'm some kind of whackadoodle who hides in the bushes. I'm not. Well, I mean, I *was* hiding in the bushes. But beyond that." Dani laughs and stares at the gift in my hands. "Are you going to open that thing or are you just going to let me babble on until I confess all my deepest, darkest sins?"

I glance at the gift, then look at Dani. "I don't know. Which is more interesting?"

This makes her smile. "Go on. Have a look."

I tear open the bag and slide out an old, barely-still-bound soft-cover edition of *Houdini on Magic*.

"You probably already have it," Dani says. "But if you don't, it's my absolute fav. Plus, Ed mentioned you were working on a version of Houdini's milk-can escape, so . . . I don't know. It's silly, right? Of course you have it. I'm such a dork. I just didn't see it on your bookcase, so . . ."

"No, actually." I clear my throat, feeling myself getting emotional for some reason. "It's not silly. It's great. I *did* have a copy. But it got stolen at school last year."

"Oh, yay." Dani smiles, then looks serious again. "Not 'yay' that yours was stolen, but I'm glad you needed it."

I start to flip through the book, the pages fragile and loose.

"Thanks," I say, smiling. "You really didn't have to get me anything."

"Yeah, but I did, though." Dani grimaces. "As an apology. I think. Maybe. For whatever part I may have played in the, um . . . Perry-and-Gwen saga."

"What?" I blink at her, my gratitude screeching to a halt, my stomach lurching from the jolt. "Your part? What are you talking about?" I know *exactly* what she's talking about! The same thing Perry was suspicious of.

Dani covers her face. "Oh God, I hate this. I feel terrible." She peeks at me through her fingers. Damn it, she's cute, even when she's acting guilty. "The thing is, I *may* have . . . said stuff. To Gwen. Not on purpose. Well, maybe on purpose. I don't know. We just started talking, and it was clear she wanted an outsider's opinion on the whole thing. To be fair. She talked to me first. I wasn't going to get involved. But after you'd told me why they broke up . . . I don't know. When she asked my opinion, I couldn't stop myself. I went in fixer mode. It's what I do. The questions just started spilling out of my mouth. Was she happier with or without him? Did she feel like she was compromising too much? Did they laugh or fight more? I was just trying to restore order to the universe. Maybe help clear the fog from her mirror." She scrunches up her face. "Unless . . . I wasn't. Oh my God. I may be awful." She grimaces, which is so adorable, but also, so confusing.

Perry was right, then. Dani *did* say something to Gwen. That's why Gwen came to my psychic booth in such a state. She was already rolling down that hill. Which means, I should be relieved, right? I'm absolved.

But I don't feel relieved because . . . who is this girl?

I stare at her. "So . . . wait. Are you saying that you think you did that . . . for what? What does it get you?"

Dani looks at me like I'm asking what color an orange is. "To gain an advantage at the audition. To get Perry out of the picture. Throw a wrench into his practice schedule. You said yourself Gwen and he were obsessed with each other."

I study her, like if I just peer hard enough I'll be able to figure her out. "And you think that you did that on purpose?"

"I don't know. Maybe. Probably." Dani looks at me and smiles sadly. "I can't sort it out in my head, Quinn. It's like . . . *this*." She gestures at the two of us. "Why am I here right now? I should be at home rehearsing, putting all my efforts into preparing for the audition. So why am I here? Is it because I genuinely felt guilty and needed to confess to you—because I actually care about what you think of me? *Or* is it because I'm trying to work an angle on you, *seeming* like I'm confessing just so you don't grow too suspicious of me?"

I stare at her. A million different questions ricocheting around my head—*Did Dani just say that she cares what I think about her? Why would she care? Is it for the same reason I care what she thinks about me?*—but only one that I need the answer to first: "So, wait . . . you *still* actually don't know," I say, really, *really* needing to get this clarified, "if you're trying to manipulate me or not?"

"I just . . ." She stares down at her hands and picks at the cuticle on her thumb. "Every way I look at this the light shines on it differently. I just wish I could trust my feelings, is all. It's like . . . sometimes I don't even know *how* I'm feeling."

She looks up and meets my eyes. Holding my gaze like a tractor beam.

Whoa. My head starts to feel floaty. There's some sort of . . . something between us. An electricity. It feels like a real thing. Unless . . . it's all in my head. And in the pink that's staining Dani's neck and cheeks.

"What about right now?" I say, the words just dropping from my lips. "Do you know how you're feeling about . . . things?"

Dani swallows. And before I know what's happening, she steps forward, grabs my face, and presses her mouth to mine. The kiss is wonderfully warm, her lips impossibly soft. A fireworks finale goes off in my head as my body is charged with electricity. I want nothing more than to stay right here for the rest of my life.

Which makes it all the more jarring and disappointing when Dani pulls away, and I come crashing back down to earth.

Her face is completely crimson now and she looks as dazed as I feel. "Omigod, I'm . . . so sorry," she stammers. "I didn't mean to . . . I should have . . . not done that." She pulls in her slightly swollen lips. "I better go."

And with that, Dani spins around and dashes off. I stare after her, light-headed with longing—and about as confused as I've ever been in my life.

31

MR. ZUZZOLO IS CROUCHED IN THE CORNER OF THE
rehearsal room, using freeze spray and a chisel to scrape a huge
wad of gum off the floor. He huffs and grumbles over his work, his
long, greasy hair dangling down, hiding his face like some kind of
demon from a horror film.

If this scene wasn't odd enough, Perry is currently tooling
around me on a unicycle—his neighbor was "just throwing one
away!" All we need now is some creepy carnival music and a severed ear and we'd be getting a call from David Lynch asking for his
subconscious back.

Adding to the dreamlike quality of the morning is Dani's kiss
from last night, lingering around me like an afterglow, the entire sen-
sory experience on a constant loop in my mind. Part of me is dying
to tell Perry what happened, but the other part of me wants to keep
it to myself. As if sharing it will diminish the excited thrum inside.

And to be honest, having already voiced his (very possibly justi-
fied) suspicions about Dani's (very possibly underhanded) motives,
I'm not sure Perry would take it in the spirit I'd want him to.

"*Wait . . .*" I say, suddenly realizing that my best friend is not only riding the unicycle but gliding around with the ease of a Cirque du Soleil performer. "Did you say you've *never* ridden before? Like, you just got on one for the first time *yesterday*?"

"Wild, huh?" Perry laughs, wobbles a bit, regains his balance, then adjusts the helmet on the top of his head.

I stare at him with equal parts amazement and envy. "How does it feel to be so good at everything you do? Without even trying?"

"What are you talking about?" Perry says, leaping off the unicycle and grabbing it by the seat post like an old pro. "I'm *trying*. It's not like I just jumped on the thing and started pedaling. Once you get your balance, though, it's really not that hard."

"Yeah, for a prodigy," I say, lifting my duffel bag of magic props up onto a table. Perry smiles and holds up the unicycle. "I can show you how to do this. You'll be proud of yourself."

I roll my eyes and laugh. "More likely I'll end up hating myself for failing. And then transferring that hate onto you. Neither of us needs that."

Perry doesn't get it. How could he? He's the only person I know who could suffer a season-ending biceps rupture and then—through a series of freak coincidences—wind up getting operated on by some super-genius, bionic-specialist surgeon and come out the other end a *better* quarterback than before.

"Suit yourself." Perry free-mounts the unicycle and starts riding backward. "But would you be averse to helping me figure out a way to incorporate this unicycle into my audition? I think it could be something that makes me stand out from the crowd."

As if he needs help with that.

"You want me to change your audition?" I say, feeling a little flare of anger as I stare at my notebook and the act he's been working on all week. "With less than a week to go? We're kind of running out of time."

Perry winces. "Oh, yeah, no, forget it. Sorry. Jeez, what am I thinking? You've already outdone yourself for me. Plus, you've got to work on your own performance. Which, by the way, I'd like to help you with, too." He starts pedaling the unicycle with one foot, jerking along unsteadily. "Why don't we go over your act today? We've been so focused on my stuff, you still haven't shown me what you're working up."

"Yeah, no, that's . . . I was . . . kinda thinking of keeping it a surprise," I say, only now coming up with this excuse. He's asked me about my act before, but I just brushed it aside, saying I was still ironing out the details. But this works better. Shuts down the conversation entirely. "It'll be fun for me. Getting your first reaction on the day. See if I can amaze and astound my partner." Although the more I blather on, the less convincing this sounds. "Besides, I'll be fine. I'm more concerned that you're all ready. And if you really want me to incorporate a unicycle into the act, I'm sure I can do that in some way."

"No, no, no, you're right, it's too much," Perry says. "I'm just flailing, I think. Looking for excuses because I'm feeling . . . I don't know . . . out of sorts. Doing this on my own. Like I said the other night. It feels so weird." He looks at me like he's trying to sort something out. "Be honest with me. Would you be totally pissed if I dropped out of this thing?"

"*What?*" I blink at him, like my blinking will somehow make my brain better able to process what he's just said. "What are you talking about?"

You know exactly what he's talking about. This is what you wanted, isn't it? When you spilled the beans to Gwen?

Well?

Isn't it?

"The thing is," Perry says, doing tight little pirouettes on the unicycle, "the more I think about it . . . I really only wanted to go to the magic camp because we were doing it together. That's what I love most about performing. You and me. So, if there's not going to be *that*"—he shrugs—"I don't know. And now this thing with Gwen. I guess I feel like I need to explore it. See where it leads. If my summer's freed up, I'll be able to do that."

Oh, crap. He's basing this all on lies. I have to tell him. That I never actually heard back from the Magic Society. And that I told Gwen that he still has feelings for her. I stare at Perry, studying his perfectly symmetrical face. He deserves to know the truth. If he still wants to quit after that, fine. But I can't have him bailing on something this big based on what I did.

I couldn't live with myself.

Plus . . . now that I think about it . . . maybe winning without Perry *wouldn't* be so great. I mean, yeah, sure, the fantasy camp might lead to a career as a successful magician, but . . . *then what?*

If we're not doing magic together anymore, would Perry and I even stay best friends? Probably not. It's the last thing we have in common. He'll just go off with Gwen and have a perfect romance followed by a perfect marriage, each helping the other achieve their perfect dreams as they effortlessly raise a gaggle of perfect children who go on to discover a cure for cancer while working on a solution to global warming.

And what would I have? A lonely, flash-in-the-pan career—and that's assuming I'm lucky enough to even make a living as a magician in the first place, which is hardly guaranteed, even *if* I attend the fantasy camp—and then . . . a life like the Dazzling Lazlo's? Running scams on the happy-hour crowd and stoned college students, spending most of my time in the back booth of some shitty diner?

"You OK?" Perry asks, canting his head to catch my downcast gaze.

"Yeah, no, I'm good." A rogue wave of emotion starts to swell inside, but I force it down. "I just . . . It'll be . . . odd. That's all. Doing this without you."

"It's not like we were auditioning together anyway," Perry says.

"I know, but . . ." I shrug. "You know what I mean. It's different, is all."

"Sometimes different is good, man." Perry claps me on the shoulder, pulls me in for a bro hug. "This is your time to shine. You go win it for both of us. Then head to that fantasy camp and show Ariann Black and David Blaine how magic is really done."

It's the perfect thing to say. Of course. I don't deserve him as a friend. And the thought of this makes me crumble. My entire body starts to tremble, Perry's firm, loving embrace completely undoing me.

"Dude, you're shivering," Perry says.

"Yeah, it's chilly in here." I step back and rub my arms like I'm warming myself instead of trying not to completely lose it. "Heat probably doesn't come on until first bell." I stare at the gym doors, willing myself to be out in the hallway already. "In fact, the cold is making me have to take a whiz. Morning coffee's run straight through me, so—" I turn and start to jog toward the exit. "I'll be right back and then we can . . . talk more . . . you know . . . about maybe changing your mind."

32

I STARE AT MY PHONE SCREEN AND THE EMAIL DRAFTS where the message to the Magic Society—asking about Perry and me auditioning as a team—sits all by itself.

Unsent.

Just as I feared.

The thought jumped me the second I burst into the bathroom. *I never did hear back from the Magic Society. Did their reply somehow end up in my spam folder, or . . . could I have actually not sent the email?*

Jesus Christ. I am the worst friend ever. How did I let myself do this? No matter what happens here, I lose. Either Perry learns what I've done—with Gwen, with this email, with everything—and never wants to speak to me again, or he never learns about it but we drift apart anyhow because . . . well . . . the one thing we shared together I just made vanish into thin air.

I blow my nose into a wad of the tracing paper they call toilet tissue in this cheap-ass school, then drag my fingers under my leaky eyes.

The bathroom smells like someone waved a lemon over a dirty diaper. I'm sitting on the toilet farthest from the sinks, leaning sideways, my head and shoulder pressed into the graffiti-enhanced stall wall. If the *Restroom Herald* is to be believed, Haisley Gergen has shigellosis, Noah eats Jacob's pube salad, and Veronica makes the best cupcakes.

Now that I'm wedged in here, I'm finding it difficult to muster the energy to unwedge myself. I wish I could just melt into the stall wall.

Be one with the poo poetry and penis pics.

And then, just as I'm circling the toilet swirl of self-loathing, thinking the world couldn't get any bleaker—

The bathroom door clunks opens and a voice calls out, "Quinn? You in here?" It's Carter. I'd recognize his Michael Bublé tenor anywhere.

What does *he* want?

"Kinda busy," I croak out, soundlessly blowing my nose into the wadded-up mass of TP.

"Sorry to bother you," Carter says. "I just . . . I saw you come in here. And I was hoping to talk to you."

"It's not a great time." I press my palms into my eye sockets, the full miserableness of what I've done to Perry stuck in my chest. I let out an involuntary groan.

What follows is a moment of excruciatingly uncomfortable silence, then—"Oh, shit. Sorry, dude. I didn't realize you were . . . I mean, it's a *public bathroom* and everything . . . But I'm not here to judge. I'll just . . . I'll let you wrap things up and catch you in the hall."

"*What?*" I blurt. "No, I'm not—"

"Seriously I didn't mean to . . . interrupt your private time—"

"*I'm not masturbating!*" I bellow, leaping to my feet, wrestling with the jammed door, and shaking it rhythmically, which makes it sound *exactly* like I'm furiously masturbating.

"I'll come back later," Carter says again, his voice retreating. "Do you want me to stand guard outside?"

"You don't have to come back!" I shout, finally getting the door open and stumbling from the stall. "I'm finished . . . *not* masturbating. Like I said. I just had"—I jerk my thumb over my shoulder—"to do normal bathroom stuff."

"OK. Good. Great." Carter nods. He's wearing his standard size-too-small-muscle-highlighting checkered dress shirt tucked into dark slacks. Like he's already settling into the role of the bank branch manager he's destined to one day be. "Because I wanted to talk to you . . . about Perry."

You and everyone else, it seems.

"What about him?" I make my way over to the sink.

"All right, so . . ." Carter clears his throat into his fist. "I know you're his best friend and everything, but . . . this thing he did with him and Gwen isn't right. We were great together. Me and her. Super smooth all the time. She's amazing. And then Perry suddenly decides . . . what? That he's bored and wants her back? And he snaps his fingers and it's done? Listen, me and him are buddies, too, but I don't even feel like I had a say in any of this."

Oh boy. This day just doesn't get any better. Is it selfish that all I

214

want to do is wallow in my own misery and have nothing to do with the misery I've caused for others?

"It sucks, man," I say, yanking a clump of paper towels from the dispenser and drying my hands. "I get it. But what are you gonna do?"

"Get her back," he says. "With your help." Carter looks at me sideways. "Maybe?"

"Look," I say, trying to save him even more heartache, "Perry didn't do anything. It was completely Gwen's choice. If it's any consolation, Perry was as surprised as you."

"Uh-uh." Carter shakes his head. "I don't buy it. Do you buy that? I mean, he kept being friends with her. And not, like, casual friends. *Good* friends. The kind of friend who is always over at her house for parties and barbecues. The kind of friend who hangs out with her parents *when Gwen's not even around*. Who does that with their ex? And then he calls her up onstage at the talent show . . ."

I sigh because it's all so exhausting. "That's how he is with everyone, Carter. My own parents want to adopt him. He's like human Ecstasy. You're near him and you love him. It doesn't mean he was trying to steal Gwen back. Some people are just all good."

"Nah," Carter says. "You're just blind to it because you're his best friend. Everyone has their motives. I mean, when you really think about it, it was underhanded of him, the way he just hung around all the time and didn't let Gwen and me have a chance."

"I can tell you for a fact that was not his inten—"

"Someone needs to teach him a lesson," Carter says, his eyes

215

glazed with a faraway look, clearly no longer in the bathroom with me. "That he can't just go around and mess with people's lives like that. And I think that someone needs to be me."

"Lesson?" I gulp. "What sort of lesson?"

He doesn't respond. Just stares off into space and cracks his knuckles.

"OK, Carter, come on, please," I say. "Violence isn't going to solve anything."

But it's too late. He's already pushing past me, headed toward the door.

33

"VEAL SCALLOPINI," MRS. SWINICK ANNOUNCES TO THE crowd gathered in the bingo room.

"*Veal?*" I say, momentarily confused because I swore I asked her to think of a fruit. "Scallopini?"

"You betcha," Mrs. Swinick says. "My ex-half-wit almost choked to death on veal scallopini. I've had a soft spot in my heart for the dish ever since."

"Right. Well. That's"—my left hand hovers above a bunched-up scarf on the table—"a fascinating story, Mrs. Swinick."

Oh boy. I should have called in sick today. I thought it would be a good idea to come to Heritage Acres, try to boost my flagging confidence, prove to myself that I can perform expertly on my own and that I still have a shot at winning this audition.

And it might have worked, except for the fact that my guilty conscience has a Vise-Grip on my attention and it's throwing off my rhythm in a big way. I've been checking my phone in between tricks, scrolling through everyone's social media feeds—Carter's. Gwen's.

Perry's—searching hashtags: #fernwoodhigh, #fernwoodhighfight, #fernwoodhighambulance.

But there's nothing. Which is good, I guess. Still, I can't shake this feeling that something horrible is going to happen to Perry. I texted him to try to give him a subtle, unincriminating heads-up. Said I ran into Carter in the bathroom and he seemed upset about the Gwen situation. That maybe he should be on the lookout for him. But Perry said it was all good, that he and Carter have worked everything out. Which didn't ease my mind at all. Because they *may* have worked everything out. Until Carter decides he is going to mete out some justice . . . with his fists.

"The man had a hair-trigger gag reflex," Mrs. Swinick says. "Made him a *very* picky eater." She gives me a knowing look. "Unfortunately. For me."

"Whoa-kaaaay," I say, trying to steer this sinking ship into port. *Any* port. "Speaking of gagging. Could you tell us, were there any *fruits* your ex-husband might have . . . had trouble swallowing?"

"His Horribleness didn't like fruits and vegetables," she says, then waggles what remains of her thinning eyebrows. "But *I* do. Very much so. They keep everything"—her eyes dart down—"lubricated." Mrs. Swinick bares her lipstick-smeared teeth at me. "If you know what I mean."

I'm not sure I *do* know what she means. Is she talking about sex? Or taking a dump? Either way, I'm not buying a ticket for that show.

"*A fruit*, Mrs. Swinick?" I press. "Any fruit at all. The first one you think of. Are you picturing something now?"

Mrs. Swinick's shoulders slump and her lips pull to the side. "I know you want me to say banana. Everyone in this room, including drooling Mr. Richards, knows you want me to say banana."

I look at her, almost pleading. "So why don't you just say banana?"

"I was trying to help you out," Mrs. Swinick says. "Pep up the act a bit. The only thing worse than a magician is a boring magician." She starts to roll her wheelchair back from the table. "Even my ex-has-been knew that you should never disrespect the audience." She stares at me, sighs, and shrugs. "Oh well. I guess I'll just await the return of Ukulele Larry. His testicle can't stay ruptured forever."

I watch as Mrs. Swinick slowly wheels herself out of the Bistro, the look of disappointment in her eyes seared into my brain. Like she was peering straight into my soul and could see how lost and hopeless I am.

34

First, there was dead silence. Now the posts and texts are coming fast and furious. On Twitter. Instagram. Facebook.

Carter has challenged Perry to a fight. Tomorrow morning. In the breezeway. He won't listen to reason. He won't listen to Perry. Or Gwen. Or any of his friends. He's gone completely rogue and is determined to see this through. Now people are going wild over it. They've even named it. The Brawl in the Hall. The breezeway isn't exactly a hall, but, you know, marketing. People have even started making bets. And T-shirts, apparently. Team Carter. Team Perry. Guess which one's already sold out?

I text Perry to see if he needs help, but he says I should stay out of this. He has a plan, but if things go south, he doesn't want me or anyone else to get hurt. I wonder if he'd still feel the same if he knew all the facts.

Did I do this? Did Dani? Did we conspire to make this happen?

Before my brain has a chance to parse this out, I am kissing Dani again. Tasting the smooth, slick saltiness of her lips. Breathing the same breath. Losing myself in the warmth of her skin—

I snap my head up. Damn it. Dani's carved a groove in my mind and I keep slipping into it without realizing it. I'm wondering now, was this part of her plan all along? The devious plot she says she's only partially conscious of because her subconscious makes her do things she isn't necessarily aware of? Or did she *actually* just kiss me because it's how she really feels?

It's enough to make you think she might be getting inside my mind.

OK, I need to prioritize my issues here. First things first. Regardless of what Dani has or hasn't done, I need to take responsibility for *my* part. Which means, I have to figure out a way to make this fight not happen.

"*Hello?* Earth to knucklehead? You still with us?" Bob reaches over from the driver's seat and snaps his fingers in my face, sending a faint scent of Everything Bagel my way.

"Hmm?" I turn and look at him.

"I asked you a question."

"You did?" I narrow my eyes, trying to decide if he's telling the truth or not. "I didn't hear you."

"Do you think you can do the trick blindfolded?" he asks.

It takes me a second to realize he's talking about the scam we're about to pull and not the Monkey's Paw. "Blindfolded? Why?"

"With the questions again. Can you do it, or not?"

"Sure. I can probably do it by feel. It's just . . . a lot more risky. Harder to control. But it can be done. Yeah."

"Good." Bob nods. "You'll do it blindfolded, then."

I open my mouth to ask why again, but Bob glares at me. "Say it and we're done. You get no trick. No advice. *Nothing*. All offers become null and void. Do you understand?"

"Yes," I say, looking down, a prickling heat dancing across my skin. I can't lose that trick now. Not after all I've been through. Not after all I've sacrificed. Even if the idea of auditioning by myself now kind of gives me a stomachache, I still need to see this through. I *have* to because . . . it can't all have been for nothing.

"I can definitely do it blindfolded," I say, turning to stare out the window. "Don't worry about me."

We drive in silence for a bit until Bob clears his throat.

"The guy who owns this restaurant bar," Bob says, like he's exhausted and can't keep up the grouchy old man routine any longer. "He's a dick, OK? The dog-kicking kind of dick. Name's P. K. Sweeney. He's even got a dick name. You get the idea. I don't know him personally, but I've heard stories. Anger issues, hitting women, running people off the road with his douche-bag-red F-150. Scumbag likes to bartend on Monday nights. Pick up young girls. Cheat on his wife. He also happens to be disgustingly rich. Doesn't need to own a bar. Just likes to dress up like a Canadian and trawl for hick chicks. Anyway, I'm going to roll him. This is our big-game hunt. The blindfold is to keep you safe. You'll just be some kid performing tricks in the bar. I'll be the smart-ass who wants to make bets on you. We don't know each other. Plausible deniability, OK? If this goes wrong, I don't want you on the business end of his jewel-encrusted .357 Magnum."

"What?" I nearly break my neck whipping my head toward him.

"You're going to steal from a guy with anger issues . . . *and a gun?* That seems like, I don't know, *a really bad idea.*"

Bob exhales. "It's a figure of speech, kid. I was just painting an image for you. He probably doesn't really have a gun."

"Maybe we should head back to the mall," I say, feeling my throat starting to close.

"Relax," Bob says. "Just do your stuff and I'll do mine. You won't even notice me. If we reel in this big fish, we're all square. I won't need your help anymore. I'll give you the Baboon's Hand and set you free. No more errands. No more performances." He looks over at me. "Sound good?"

This sounds so far from good that you'd need the Hubble telescope to even see the galaxy that good is located in. But what other choice do I have?

"Sure," I croak, feeling light-headed. "I guess. As long as there isn't"—I gulp—"any actual gunfire."

Bob laughs. "It's going to be fine. This is a straight, basic play. Simple and clean. Do what I say and this all goes off without a hitch."

35

"Run, kid!" Bob shouts as I hear chairs clatter. "He's fingered us!"

A surge of adrenaline spikes through me. I whip off the blindfold and swivel my head left and right, still holding the ESP deck in my hand. There's danger somewhere, but I can't work out which direction it's supposed to be coming from.

The two men on my left—the bank managers hiding tube floats under their sweat-stained dress shirts—simply look perplexed. The heavily made-up ladies to my right seem more bored than concerned.

And then I see him. *P. K. Sweeney*. The full-flanneled, burly, bearded bartender, straight out of a maple syrup commercial. Bob was right, he doesn't have a gun. He's got a hatchet—*A HATCHET!*—which he flails above his head as he leaps over the bar like an enraged lumberjack.

I smile at Steve the Realtor, who's holding my ESP card. "Sorry. Gotta go." I snatch the star symbol from him and run like hell.

I can almost feel the bartender's breath on the back of my neck as I tear through the restaurant. The front entrance seems like it's a football field away and I know, deep in my gut, that I am not going to make it out of P. K. Sweeney's with the same number of appendages I arrived with.

I stare hard at the stained-glass front door, trying to collapse the distance with my mind. *Please. Please. Please let me make it.*

I dart around a table, spin away from a drink-laden waitress, and am stumbling toward the hostess podium when a woman's voice echoes from the restroom hallway, "Wait for me, honey!"

Before I know what's happening, a little blond girl with pigtails and a pink dress blasts out from the hall, giggling and waving a bright yellow P. K. Sweeney's baseball pennant.

Thankfully I'm able to shake-and-bake by the girl without incident.

The angry lumberjack has a more difficult time.

"Oh, *shit!*" I hear him grunt.

I twist around to see the bartender whirling through the air like a plaid-swathed gymnast, safely clearing the little girl but crashing into the wooden umbrella stand in the corner—"*Oof!*"—his hatchet skittering harmlessly across the floor.

There's a part of me that wants to wait to see if he's OK. But it's a small part and it doesn't stop me from blasting through the front door.

"Put on your skates, kid!" Bob shouts, frantically waving to me from his car at the far end of the parking lot.

I drop my head and hurtle by car after parked car, finally darting around the back of Bob's beater and tearing open the passenger-side door. This running-for-my-life business is getting all too familiar.

"What the hell, what the *hell*?" I say, leaping into the car. "He . . . had . . . an . . . ax, Bob." I'm breathing like a dog after the Iditarod. "What happened? Why was he so mad?"

"It's a long story." Bob wrenches his body around to look behind him, slams the car into reverse, and hits the gas.

"How long could it be?" I shout as I'm rocked forward. "We were only in there for fifteen minutes!"

"Hold on to your credentials." Bob hits the brakes hard, skidding the car into a full 180, banging my head into the passenger-side window. "Aaaaand we have liftoff."

He spins the steering wheel, course-corrects, then shoves the gearshift into drive, speeding toward the exit. We sideswipe a shopping cart, ride up on the curb, and almost clip a mailbox, but finally Bob careens the Mercury from the parking lot and onto the road.

"Get ready for a little stealth mode," Bob says, hitting the gas hard, causing the muffler to bark out a loud gunshot.

I keep glancing behind us, again and again, to see if we're being tailed by the millionaire bar owner's Lamborghini or something.

But there's nothing.

Finally I exhale, sink into my seat, and try to stop my lungs from collapsing.

"That was my bad," Bob says, reaching under his seat and finding a crushed pack of Marlboros. "I'm trying to quit." He pulls out a bent cigarette with his cracked lips, opens the half-full ashtray, and pushes the car's cigarette lighter in.

"What happened in there?" I ask, getting a whiff of stale tobacco.

"I moved too fast." The lighter pops out. Bob grabs it and touches it to the tip of his wilting cigarette. He replaces the car lighter and takes a long drag. "Should have taken it slower." Bob releases a giant plume of smoke, then decides he should roll down his window. "I tried to up the stakes too soon. The patience thing always screws me up." He pulls a fleck of something off his tongue, then gestures at me with his cigarette. "He pegged us as soon as I tried to triple the bet. I got greedy. It's the nastiest of the seven deadlies, kid. The others—sloth, gluttony, envy, pride— those can all be done from the safety of your own couch. Not so with greed. I let it get the best of me. My apologies." He takes another drag on his cigarette. "We'll just have to find another big fish."

My heart is finally starting to beat its way back down my throat, returning to my chest. I look at Bob—at the deep lines etched in his face, the almost imperceptible downward turn of his mouth, the gray-blond stubble stippling his cheeks and chin—and I wonder to myself: What the *fuck* happened to this guy? He had it *all*. He was a professional stage magician, doing a professional magic tour. And now it's like he's some kind of has-been TV actor who can't even get a job as a town crier.

"Can I ask you something?" I say.

"As long as it's not for a cut of the proceeds," Bob says, patting his bulging shirt pocket and laughing. "I didn't get it all, but I did get some travel expenses."

"Why did you stop performing magic?" I say. "Professionally."

"Well, if by professionally you mean"—Bob crushes his half-smoked cigarette into the remains of the other half-smoked cigarettes—"my main paid occupation, well, then, I never stopped."

"I mean onstage," I say. "In a theater. In front of an audience."

"A stage is just a floor," Bob says, gesturing with an outstretched hand like a game show model. "A theater just a building. An audience, simply people."

Jesus, can this guy pivot or what? "I just want to know when you stopped being the Dazzling Lazlo and became"—I sweep my hand up and down at him—"Bob, the scam artist."

Bob screws up his face. "Fuck you, kid. You don't know shit about me. Who I am. What I've been through. You think it's easy being a professional magician? Trying to make a living wage? Keep a roof over your head? Support your cheating ex-wives? Your who-the-hell-knows-how-many kids? Watching all your dignity crumble away when you can't book the next gig?"

I look at my feet, my stomach turning to concrete. "I'm sorry," I say. "I had no idea . . . I didn't mean to—"

"Sure you did, kid," Bob says. "You found a shiv and you dug it into my weak spot. Touché. I deserve it. I put you in a tough spot back there." He clears his throat. "However, the more I think about it, the more I realize you're not cut out for this life. You're too soft. I thought I could train it out of you, but I was wrong, so . . . it's probably best for us to terminate our contract. I'm no longer enjoying being under your employ."

"*What?* No. Wait. Come on. I didn't mean anything."

"Whatever," Bob says. "Doesn't matter. Cookie Monster was

right: you're a liability. I've never had so many close calls as I've had in the last week."

"You just said P. K. Sweeney's was *your* fault," I plead, feeling my last hope of salvaging anything from the wreckage that is my life slipping away. But judging by the stink-face Bob's making, disavowing responsibility is clearly not the way to go. "I'll be better next time. I promise. I'm just . . . getting used to everything."

"Forget it, kid. You've got the skills, but you lack the testicular fortitude." He grunts, like the matter is settled. "We both know it's the right thing. Why don't you just pay me my salary for the rest of the week, as severance, and we'll call it a day?"

"Wait, but . . ." I gulp, afraid to ask my next question. "You'll still give me the Monkey's Paw trick? Right?"

Bob laughs. "Uh, correct me if I'm wrong, but the deal was you help me with my errands and *then* I show you the trick. If you're not going to honor your end of the bargain—"

"But you're the one terminating the agreement!"

He shrugs. "Either way, I'm not about to just give away my most prized possession for nothing."

"Yeah, but . . . I *need* that trick," I say. "Otherwise"—I gulp hard—"all of this was a waste of time."

"I don't see how that's my problem." Bob stares at the road ahead, blowing out his cheeks like a puffer fish. A moment later, he exhales loudly. "*Although* . . . on further consideration, I suppose I *could* still teach you that trick." He sucks his lips in. "But it would have to be for a substantial fee. On top of my severance package. To make up for all the money we could have made together this week."

"OK, sure, fine," I say, sitting up like a starving dog being offered a piece of dry kibble.

"It would have to be our final transaction," he says, holding up a hand like I'm already protesting. "After that, I want you out of my life. You're a bad-luck penny, kid."

"Fine. Yes. Deal." I instantly regret the words that slide off my tongue next. "So . . . how much do you want for it?"

36

"*THREE HUNDRED DOLLARS?*" MOM SAYS, LIKE I JUST ASKED for the lead role in their musical.

"That's a mighty large chunk of change, fella," Dad adds, scraping marmalade across his burnt toast in time to "It's the Hard Knock Life," which plays on the HomePod.

"It's just an advance." I try to gnaw off a piece of my bacon jerky in a manly show of confidence, but it just comes off as pathetic. This is one of Dad's "bad" breakfasts. Everything just a little too overcooked. Usually the product of an all-night rehearsal or writing session. "On my allowance."

"Is it for drugs?" Mom asks, her lower lip quivering like she's certain the money's been earmarked for a block of heroin. "You head down that path, mister, and you'll end up naked, facedown, drowned in a lake of your own vomit." Mom looks over at Dad like they've rubbed shoulders with junkies and hopheads.

"Wow," I say, blinking at these strangers who call themselves my parents. "That's pretty dark. Didn't consider maybe I wanted the money for some new clothes? Headphones? Concert tickets?"

"Well," Dad says, nodding his support for Mom's thesis, "we know what can happen to the children of celebrities."

"Right," I say, narrowing my eyes at them. "But . . . you're not celebrities."

"*Mmm.*" Mom scrunches up her face, then slips a piece of crunchy fried egg into her mouth. "We kinda are."

"Uh, *no*." I shake my head. "Unless by celebrity you mean someone who nobody knows."

Dad tilts his head like he feels oh-so-very sorry for me. "Your mother and I get recognized all the time. At the supermarket. At the . . . other places."

"Yeah," I say. "By people you've sold houses to."

"*And* who've seen our shows at the Sage Hollow Dinner Theater," Mom insists, giving me a look. "You may not feel it consciously, but if our celebrity is casting too big a shadow, sending you careening to a life of drugs, we need to get it out in the open. Talk about it."

I sigh so heavily I feel like I might expel my lungs. "Forget it. I'll get the money some other way. Maybe I'll sell one of my drug-weakened kidneys."

I check the clock: 7:13. I have to get to school. The Brawl in the Hall is scheduled for 7:45. I need to be there for Perry, even if he thinks he doesn't need me to be. Just in case things go really south.

I wipe my mouth and set my napkin on the table. "But just so we're clear, it was going to be for my audition. You know, the one that could change the entire course of my life. Not a big deal at all."

"Wait." Mom knits her brow. "What do you mean, your audition? I thought you already got your invitation to try out."

"I did . . ." I say, trying to figure out how to phrase this in the most persuasive light. Sure, I could come clean here. Tell them what the advance is really for. Get a lecture about throwing my money away on yet another trick when I already have so many. Possibly have to sit through a rendition of "If I Were a Rich Man."

"So," Dad says, "what, then? Is there an entry fee?"

Orrrr I could just smack the sweet, juicy ball that Dad's set up on a tee for me.

"Yes," I lie, because that's what Robert Lazlo would want me to do. "There's an . . . entry fee. I just found out about it. They're renting the Beltway. You know, one of those beautiful old theaters everyone is always trying to knock down. They have to pay for the historic restorations somehow."

Dad makes a face. "That's not something they should spring on you last minute."

"They didn't." I shake my head and feign an embarrassed laugh. "It's my fault. It was there the whole time in the acceptance letter. I just didn't read the email closely. I was so excited to get it. But I have to hand the money in tomorrow or they'll give my spot away."

"Well, that's not happening," Mom says, grabbing her purse, pulling out her checkbook. "It's a good thing for you that ticket sales have picked up lately, thanks to Carolyn Smeltzer and her Brazilian Jiu-Jitsu Club." She grabs a pen and clicks it open. "Who do I make it out to?"

"Uhhh," I say, my brain stumbling. "Not sure . . . actually. Maybe just . . . make it out to cash. You know. Just so there's no issues."

"Cash?" Mom furrows her brow like she is not so sure about

this. "OK. Well . . . as long as you don't lose it." She scribbles out the check, tears it from the book, and hands it to me.

"Thank you," I say, taking the money as I swallow the sour taste at the back of my throat. "I'll pay you back. Don't worry."

"Your mother and I believe in you, son," Dad says. "We're more than happy to subsidize your dreams. At a very reasonable rate of three and a half percent interest."

37

"I$_T$'s reckoning day, buddy," Carter says, his left hand clenched in a fist, his right fingers gesturing Perry forward. "Come and get a taste of yours."

Perry scrunches his forehead. "A taste of my *what*?"

"Your *reckoning*," Carter says, sounding slightly exasperated.

"Well, that doesn't even make sense. You can't eat reckoning. It's just a concept."

"You know what I mean," Carter says, practically pleading with Perry not to embarrass him. "It's a metaphor. Now come on. Get over here so I can break you. *Un*-metaphorically."

A huge crowd has gathered in the breezeway. Almost everyone is wearing a dark blue Team Perry T-shirt save for a few scattered yellow Team Carters that look like distant stars in the night sky. I stand on the periphery, wearing my wallflower-gray polo, with an acidic stew of dread and guilt roiling in my gut.

I know Perry keeps saying he has this under control, but it doesn't really seem that way. What if this is the one time his Good Luck Guardian Angel is busy in the can or something? Carter is the swollest kid in school. One wrong punch and Perry could go down, hit his head on the concrete, and never get up again.

I glance around as more and more students stream into the fray. I'm surprised that none of the teachers got wind of this, but since most of them tear into the parking lot at two minutes to first bell, I'm not *that* surprised.

"Can we please just talk this out, Carter?" Perry scans the crowd. "Away from all this. Just the two of us."

"No way," Carter says, clearly distraught, like he doesn't really want to do this but sees no way out now. "I know what you're doing. Trying to be the good one. The righteous one. The peaceful one. Everyone loves you so much"—he points to the sea of Team Perry shirts—"but they don't know what I know. That you're really just a selfish bastard. Pretending to be all love and light when really, you're just out for yourself." He sniffs back a weepy hiccup, like the poor guy is on the verge of a complete meltdown. "It wasn't fair . . . to steal Gwen from me."

"He didn't steal me," Gwen says. "I'm not your possession. We broke up. Remember? It was my choice to go back to Perry."

Carter shakes his head sadly. "That's what he wants you to think. That's how he gets away with everything. He makes you *want* to do things for him. And then . . . you do them, thinking it's what *you* want. It's the worst kind of devious." His eyes harden. He cracks his thick neck, sets his shoulders. "And someone needs to stop it from continuing."

Perry sighs. "Seriously, Carter. This is ridiculous. We're friends. I really think we can work this out."

"This *is* us working it out." Carter raises his fists, all business now. "Cage match–style." He does a little fancy footwork, a few quick jabs, like maybe he's fought professionally.

I drop my head, feeling like a seasick passenger on the *Titanic*. I stare at the concrete. The weeds poking through the cracks. The shoe-smeared beetle who never saw it coming. The empty Twinkies wrapper tumbling with the wind.

This is all my fault.

Well, maybe not *all* of it. Gwen would have broken up with Carter eventually. It was only a matter of time. But I definitely hastened things, and maybe Carter wouldn't have taken it so hard if he'd had more warning.

And let's not forget about Dani, a voice in my head declares. *How much of this is her fault, thanks to whatever she said to Gwen? Did she see something like this happening?*

"Exciting, huh?" A girl materializes beside me, my shoulder gently bumped by hers.

I swivel my head, and Dani smiles at me. For one ridiculous second I wonder if I conjured her. "No, not exciting," I say. Memories of our kiss—Dani's soft lips pressed into mine, the clean, warm-tea scent of her skin—are at war with my anxiety about Perry, making me feel both elated and like I might purge my charred breakfast. "It's horrible. What if they get hurt?"

"Not gonna happen," Dani says. She points at Carter. "Look, right there. Quadzilla's upper lip. The beads of sweat. Outwardly he looks committed. Inwardly he's having doubts."

I try to see what Dani sees, but I just don't. All I see are two nice, decent, sweet people about to kick the snot out of each other because of something thoughtless—and possibly opportunistic—that I did.

Perry sighs and shakes his head. "Can't we just go get a latte, man? You have to know that I never meant to hurt you. Come on, let's go talk in private. Let me make it up to you. Seriously, we've got a big game next week against Westfield. Coach'll kill us if either one of us gets hurt."

"Yeah, well . . . *screw* lacrosse." Carter looks around like he's more surprised than anyone that he's just said this. He takes a hard swing at Perry, who easily dodges it.

"Dude, *really*?" Perry pleads. "We can stop this right now."

"You stop it. With your face." Carter takes another wind-whistling swipe, but again Perry sidesteps it and Carter only gets air.

"I'm not going to fight back," Perry says.

Then, as if he just wants to get this over with, Carter lowers his head and takes a run at Perry. They grab each other. Huge hands grappling at muscled shoulders. Grunting and groaning. Pushing and pulling each other, their feet skittering on the pavement.

"Fight! Fight! Fight!" several asshats in the crowd start to chant.

"Jesus, I really misread that," Dani says, wincing.

"Oh, shit." My hands fly to my mouth. "This is really happening. Crap, crap, crap."

Carter yanks Perry to the right, spinning the two of them in a circle, backing up the crowd that surrounds them.

All of a sudden, Perry's foot catches on the cornerstone of one of the flower beds and he and Carter both hit the ground with a meaty thud.

Dani bites her lower lip. "Should we do something?"

I watch as Carter gets position on Perry, holding him down with his powerful legs, raising a massive fist.

Fuck!

Before I know what's happening, I'm running into the fray.

"Stop!" I shout, waving my arms wildly. "Cut it out! Stop fighting! This is my fault! Don't ruin your lives because of me!"

In the blink of an eye, everyone goes silent and still, like a freeze-frame in a film.

Carter and Perry look up at me, continuing to clutch each other on the ground.

"This is ridiculous. You guys are only fighting because of me. Because I manipulated you both to get what I wanted." I gulp down my shame.

Perry shakes off Carter's slackened grip and stands up. "*What? What* are you talking about, Quinn?"

"Yeah," Carter says, seemingly trying to blink away his confusion. "What do you have to do with any of this?"

"Everything," I confess. I draw in a deep breath and do my best to ignore the massive crowd gathered around, a crowd that includes Dani, the girl I maybe-sort-of had a shot with, but—after she hears all this—no more. Instead, I focus on Perry. "I never actually emailed the MSA. I thought I did, but the message was saved in my drafts folder. I must never have hit send."

"What?" He's shaking his head. "But . . . I don't understand. You told me they wrote back to you, that they said we had to audition separately."

I fight to keep my breakfast down. "Technically I said I'd 'heard from them,' which is true—we both did, when we got our letters—and that they made it 'pretty clear partner acts weren't allowed.' Which I thought at the time was true—I still think it's true, actually. But that doesn't matter. I deliberately misled you so that you would think we had no choice but to audition on our own."

"OK, but . . . *why*?" Perry asks. And his tone isn't even hurt—though I know that'll come soon enough. No, it's simply baffled, like he truly believes that if he gives me the chance, I'll explain this all in a way that does not mean I'm a completely horrible human being.

He couldn't be more wrong.

"No offense or anything," Carter interjects, "but what the hell does any of this have to do with me and Gwen?"

"Yeah!" a few people in the crowd shout. Now that the prospect of a bloodletting seems to be waning, they're growing bored and restless.

I look right into Perry's eyes. "The thing is, I really want to win a spot at the magic fantasy camp. I want it more than anything I've ever wanted." The memory of my kiss with Dani flashes through my mind, because, yeah, I wanted that desperately, too, but I push it away. "And I thought we'd be disqualified if we auditioned together, so I . . . misled you. Lied to you," I correct. "At first I hated the idea of going onstage without you, but then . . . I don't know . . . I thought, this might be my chance to finally step out of your shadow. Not just be the pathetic sidekick." My face flames at the public confession of my feelings of inadequacy—not that it's likely to surprise anyone in attendance. Hell, even Carter pales next to Perry. None of it matters anyway. The only thing I care about now is that my best friend hears what I'm saying. Maybe finds it in his heart to forgive me.

"And even though you specifically told me not to say anything to Gwen about how you've been feeling," I say, my eyes sliding over to Gwen, who's grimacing, "as soon as the opportunity presented itself, I did tell her. I tried to justify it at the time—that you guys getting back together was inevitable. Sorry, Carter." Carter shrugs and nods. "So what was the harm in it happening sooner than later? But it's so painfully obvious to me now that I wanted you to get back together so you'd be too busy and bail on the audition. Just like you did." I shake my head and stare at the ground. "I'm just . . . so sorry."

There is more terrible silence as everyone stands still and stares, seemingly waiting to see what Perry's going to do.

Perry steps forward, his expression unreadable. He opens his mouth to respond—

Just then Carter grabs his throat. He starts heaving and hacking like he's having an asthma attack. "Can't . . . *ruup* . . . can't . . ." His face goes candy-apple red and he crumples to the ground, making terrifying, dying-animal gasps as he falls. "*Ruuup* . . . Can't . . . *ruuup, ruuup.* Can't . . . get . . . air . . ."

"Carter!" Perry rushes to his side. "His lips are swelling. He's got hives. Someone call 911. It's anaphylaxis. This happens to my cousin pretty much every Thanksgiving." Perry looks into Carter's eyes. "Stay with us, buddy. Listen to me. This is important: Do you have any allergies?"

Carter's mouth opens and closes like a dying fish, and Gwen pushes her way to Perry's side. "He's allergic to shellfish," she says.

She leans over Carter and gently holds his face between her hands. "Did your aunt Jenny drop off gumbo for your dad last night, Carter?"

Carter nods weakly.

"Right," Gwen says matter-of-factly. "And did you have some for breakfast, perchance?"

He nods again.

Gwen looks at Perry. "He can't resist his aunt's gumbo—sneaks it even though he knows he's not supposed to. Swears he can eat around the shrimp."

"Shellfish. That's bad." Perry turns to the crowd and shouts, "EpiPen! Does anyone have an EpiPen?"

"Me! I do. I have one!" It's marshmallowy, bespectacled Aaron Hripsack, pushing his way through the onlookers, holding his yellow EpiPen high in the air like it's Excalibur.

In one fluid motion, Perry snatches the injector from Aaron, pulls out the safety release with his teeth, and jabs Carter in the meat of his muscular thigh.

Carter's face instantly slackens, his entire body rag-dolling in Perry's arms, a loud, wheezing rush of air making its way into his lungs.

"Omigod, you saved his life!" Gwen cries, wrapping Perry in a hug. "You're a hero."

"*Team* Perry! *Team* Perry! *Team* Perry!" all the students chant as my heartbreaking confession is completely wiped from everyone's consciousness.

38

"Apparently he went to the hospital with Carter," I say to Dani as I approach the table, my sun-hot mocha cauterizing the loops and whorls off my fingertips. I flip my phone toward Dani and show her Gwen's Instagram story.

I tried to get to Perry after he saved Carter's life, but the crush of the crowd was too much to get through. And anyway, it didn't really seem like the right time to ask him where we stood, if he could forgive me, if he still wanted to be my friend. And so, when Dani asked if I wanted to go for coffee, I was thankful for the excuse.

"Of course he did," Dani says, sipping her black coffee as I take my seat. "The doctors might need him to step in and perform an emergency tracheotomy."

"True," I say, appreciating her attempt at levity. I halfheartedly return the gesture. "Or, you know, donate one of his extra lungs."

Dani smiles, which normally would be all it takes to turn my whole day around. But I'm still reeling from the effects of my public confession, my mind sending me back to the breezeway, standing there in front of Perry, the lost look in his eyes crushing my soul.

We sit there for a minute. Glancing at each other. Forcing smiles. Drinking. Breathing. Listening. The *shoosh* of the milk steamer. The clinking of spoons in mugs. The hum of constant conversation.

It's weird. I know we kissed the other night, but right now, here at this table, it feels like we're on opposite sides of the Grand Canyon.

Dani blows the steam off the surface of her coffee. "You want to talk about it?"

I study her. Are we still talking about the fight, or can she legit read my mind?

"I mean, you guys'll patch things up, right?" she says. "You've been friends forever."

"I have no idea," I say, the words like little barbs. "I mean . . . he'd never do anything like this to me. Never." I clear the phlegm from my throat. "Anyway. I did what I did. I can't take it back now. You'd think I'd be used to it, everything always going wrong for me"—I take a shaky sip of my mocha—"but if you asked me a week ago if I thought my life would be this much of a shit show . . ."

Dani regards me over her cup of coffee. "Maybe it's not all bad," she says, like she's puzzling something out in her head. "I mean, look, you were brutally honest back there. That took major balls. In front of the entire school. I couldn't have done that."

"It took zero balls," I say. "I had to stop it before someone got hurt. I had no choice."

Dani laughs. "Sure you did. You could have created a different kind of distraction. You know, stripped naked and run through the courtyard."

"Now you tell me."

Dani smiles. "Perry was going to get out of that situation unscathed. Deep down you knew that. So you could have just let it go. Like most people do. Stick your head in the sand. Let the lies fester. Let them poison your relationship. But you chose not to. You told the truth. Because you care about him. Which, you know"—she shrugs—"shows who you really are."

"Yeah, well, I don't think I care much for who I really am."

I stare into my drink, the two of us settling into another long stretch of awkward silence, Dani picking at her thumbnail, me mentally flogging myself for all my offenses.

Until Dani finally sighs audibly. "All right, fine. Whatever." She rolls her eyes. "I can't do this anymore."

I look up from my coffee. Her liquid-green eyes filled with a million thoughts, none of which I can get a hook into. "Can't do *what* anymore?"

"This." Dani gestures back and forth between us. "You and me. It's gotten too intense."

"Wait," I say, furrowing my brow, my brain so confused there is actual physical pain. "Are you . . . breaking up with me? Were we . . . were we *dating*?" Leave it to me to be dating the girl of my dreams but *not actually realize it* until it's over.

"Here's the thing," Dani says, looking straight at me, like she really wants me to hear this. "I feel terrible about . . . everything, and . . ." She groans. "What you just did back there. You had the bravery to confess something to someone you care about." Dani looks down at her hands, starts picking at her thumbnail again. She sighs. "I need to confess something, too."

I try to pull in a breath, but my chest feels heavy. Like maybe I don't want to hear what she's going to say. My lips feel as though they might be moving, but no words are coming out.

"As you know," Dani continues, "that kiss was . . . it was really nice but . . . not something I planned on doing. It just sort of . . . happened." She looks up from her fingers, directly into my eyes. "And, in the spirit of honesty, it kind of screwed everything up."

"Uh . . ." I blink at her. "OK, so, I think I'm going to need you to explain *what the hell you're talking about.*"

"It's pretty simple." She clears her throat, starts digging at the cuticle on her thumb once more. "Ever since I saw you and Perry perform at the talent show, I've been trying to sabotage your chances of winning the auditions. I wasn't exactly sure how I was going to do it at first, but my initial thought was to split up your partnership. You guys are way too good together. So, when I read the vague rules of the audition, I thought it was worth a nudge."

My mind flashes to our encounter last week, in which Dani explained how she'd reread the rules and was worried that if Perry and I auditioned as a team, we each might be "throwing away the opportunity of a lifetime." But I'd already reached that same conclusion myself—*hadn't I?*

Dani goes on. "I didn't know if you'd really go for it, but when you did? Well, that was phase one, but then I needed to figure out how to take you out individually. Perry was pretty easy. Once you confirmed how he and Gwen were still in love with each other, it didn't take much to get them back together—and get him out of the way."

My thoughts ping-pong inside my head. Sure, Dani talked to Gwen, but it wasn't until *I* told Gwen how Perry felt that she decided to get back together with him. *Right?* Unless . . . Dani *continued* to talk to Gwen about Perry after I told her how much they loved each other. Dropping subtle suggestions into the conversation like any good magician would. And *that's* why Gwen sought me out at the fair that night.

"And me?" I ask reluctantly. "How did you plan to . . . take me out?"

"Ah yes, well, you were harder," Dani says with what sounds almost like admiration. "But it was clear that you felt inferior next to Perry—which is ridiculous, by the way—and so I figured if I could play on that insecurity, get inside your head a little and get you to question yourself, throw you off your game, then maybe you'd choke during the auditions and I'd sail to a win." Dani exhales heavily. "I don't know. I never expected everything to get so . . . messy. For me to actually . . . start to like you." She looks at me a bit accusingly. "Or for you to detonate a frickin' nuclear bomb in your life."

"So, OK, wait . . . so the whole time you were telling me you were worried you might be influencing me . . . you were *actually* trying to influence me?"

Dani nods, her lips pulled in guiltily. "Li'l bit."

"But . . . why?" I say, trying to piece together everything that's happened since I met her. "I don't understand. You're amazingly talented. You're probably going to win no matter what."

"You underestimate yourself, Quinn Purcell," she says, and I can't stop a little thrill from running up my spine. "Anyway, it's like

I told you before. Same thing you said to Perry." Her eyes drop to her nearly empty coffee cup. "It's something I want more than anything. Enough that I'm willing to do whatever it takes to be sure I win."

We lapse back into an uneasy silence. When Dani speaks again, it seems to surprise us both.

"Look, it's not an excuse, OK," she says, "but do you have any idea how much harder it is for a girl to become a professional magician than it is for a guy? How much more work I have to put in just to get the same basic opportunities?" Dani exhales. "I guess I was just trying to level the playing field." And now she's back to working on her ragged thumbnail. "I am sorry, though. If I could go back in time . . . well, I'd probably do the same exact thing, but that's only because I don't believe in free will. However, I *am* very, very sorry for how this has turned out. You don't . . . deserve that."

I don't even know what to say to this. I'm dizzy from the revelations. I feel like I was trying to recover from having been winged by a Mack truck, when I suddenly got hit head-on . . . *by a second Mack truck*. And is she really telling the truth this time? Or is it just more manipulation? Trying to screw with me? I can't trust anything this girl tells me.

And yet . . .

Despite everything Dani's just told me, despite all she's done, I actually believe she's being sincere about her apology. I don't know how I know. I just do. Call it a "psychic's" intuition. Her body language, her steady breathing, her eye contact, the tone of her voice.

Or is that just wishful thinking—or perhaps even more manipulation?

"I know it fixes nothing, Quinn, but I really am very sorry," she says again. Dani reaches out to take my hand, but I pull back, which makes her bunch her lips to the side. "Right. Of course. I get it. We both did things we regret. And we both feel awful about it. To be honest, it would have been easier if you guys were both pompous assholes. But you're not, so . . ." She takes a deep breath. "Anyway. Not that I can make any of this up to you, but if there's anything I can do to help with Perry, or with your audition, in any way, please let me know. I'd like to *try* to make it up somehow if I can."

I look at her, so many emotions stirred up inside. And the strongest one of all is the desire to lean in and kiss her. It's maddening. I should want to run. Should want to get far, far away from her because she literally told me she could not be trusted.

But instead I just say, "Thank you. For talking with me. For your apology. And the offer. But"—I swallow, wishing I could also swallow the next words I have to say—"we should probably keep our distance. Like you first suggested when we talked at the lockers." I stand and force a smile. "Good luck at the auditions. May the best magician win."

39

"THE MONEY?" BOB ARCHES AN UNRULY EYEBROW, HIS hand pressing a swollen business envelope into the table. Inside are the secrets to the Monkey's Paw—my golden ticket to the magic fantasy camp. "That's how the barter system works, kid."

"Yes, right," I say, blinking myself back to the diner, Dani's confession still glitching my brain. "Three hundred." I reach into my pants pocket and pull out the folded check. I slide it furtively across the table, like we're involved in some kind of drug deal.

"Well, looky here," Bob says, snapping open the check, examining it, then tucking it into his shirt pocket. "A real, live bank account. You've been holding out on me, kiddo."

"I had to borrow it from my parents," I say, hoping to toss a little guilt his way.

Bob laughs. "I know *that* ATM very well. I used to 'borrow' money from my mom's purse all the time."

"*No,*" I say, glaring at him, the smell of burnt bacon making me a little sick. "That's my *mom's* check. From my parents' account. I *actually* borrowed it from them. They're charging me three and a half percent interest."

"Seriously?" Bob wrinkles up his nose like I just pitched a biscuit. "Jesus. And I thought *I* had a shitty childhood."

"Yeah, well, wait till you see the musical." I lean forward and reach for the envelope.

Bob slides it away. "Uh-uh. Not so fast." He swishes it back and forth on the table. "If you don't mind. There are some caveats."

"Caveats?" I say, my eyes darting in rhythm, like a Kit-Cat Klock, to the swooshing envelope. I want it so badly it hurts. If I end up losing Dani, Perry, *and* this trick all within forty-eight hours, I don't know what I'll do. "What sort of caveats?"

"Rules. Clauses. Terms of Service," he says.

I study him, looking for the irony in his flat eyes. "What the fuck are you talking about?"

"Hey, watch your fucking language, kid," Bob deadpans.

"My—" I stab a finger into my chest. "*My* language? You fling out more curses than a witch with an itchy trigger finger."

"I'm an adult," Bob says. "It's too late for me. You still have a chance to clean up your act." He gestures at me. "You can start with the shit that spews from your lips."

"OK. Fine. Whatever." I motion toward the envelope. "What are your caveats?"

"This here—*the trick*." Bob's eyes dart down to the table. "The Simian's Hoof—is my pride and joy. My baby. Even though I'm sending it out into the world, I still need to protect it."

"*Protect it?*"

251

"Yes," Bob says. "All of us only have so many assets to trade upon. This is one of mine. So. First off. I've presented the effect in a way that only you will understand. Which means you'll need to decipher it first." He looks at me knowingly. "Do you get my meaning?"

"You wrote it in code?"

"Yes. Sort of." He nods. "In a way. You'll understand as soon as you open it."

"OK. Great." I make another move to grab the envelope, but he pulls it back again.

"Caveat *número deux*," Bob says. "You have to promise me that you won't open it until you get home. I don't want this getting into anyone else's hands."

"Fine," I say, sighing, tapping my anxious fingers on the table. "Anything else?"

"Yes," Bob says. "Caveat *finalmente*. You will, under no circumstances, perform this trick in public. Ever. For anyone. It's for your eyes, and your eyes only."

"Wait, *what*?" This last condition is like a meat fork to my temple. "*No*. No way. That's not the deal we made. What's the point in having a trick if you can't perform it?"

"Sorry. That's just the way the crapper clogs, kiddo." Bob shrugs and slides the envelope into his lap. "Deal was I'd teach you the method. My apologies if you misunderstood. I can't have you showing this to everyone like it's your first boner. What if I get off my ass one day and want to actually write a book or something?"

"You have to let me perform this," I insist. "It's vital. It's what I was counting on. It's . . . everything."

Bob checks his watch, then turns and stares out of the diner's silt-streaked window.

"I need this for my audition," I plead.

"If wishes were fishes"—he throws up his hands—"there'd be a trout in my britches."

I glare at him, my jaw clenched tight.

"Fine." I hold out my sweating palm, my pulse pounding in my neck. "You win. I agree to your terms of service. I won't perform it for anyone."

Bob tilts his head, regarding me suspiciously. "Ever?"

I dip my chin, glancing away. "Ever."

"I have your solemn word on that?" he asks. "Your eternal oath on all that is holy and sacrilegious?"

"Yes," I say, the lie sitting on my tongue like a snot globule . . . which I force down my throat. "You have my word."

Bob narrows his eyes. His brow folds up. Then he breaks into a proud grin. "*Atta boy!*" He laughs and flings the envelope back onto the table. "I knew you'd do the wrong thing eventually. Goddamn if I don't feel like Willy Wonka after Charlie returns the fucking Gobstopper."

I blink at him, a bitter ooze gurgling in my stomach. "So . . . wait . . . You *wanted* me to lie?"

Bob shrugs, leans forward. "If I could teach you only one thing, it's this: Why tell the truth when a lie will do just as well? Trust me,

it's a skill that will serve you nicely in this shitty sewer of a world."
He lifts his chin. "Go on. Take it. You've earned it."

"And I *can* perform the trick? You won't, like, sue me or something if I do?"

"My lawyer doesn't get out for another twenty years, so"—he swipes his tongue across his teeth—"knock yourself out."

I lean forward. Pick up the envelope. Stare down at the packet in my hands, waiting to feel a rush of elation. But all I get is a sinking feeling. Which should tell me everything I need to know.

"*Well?*" Bob grunts. "What the hell are you still doing here?" He scowls at me. "Our business relationship is over. It's been tolerable. Now get the hell out of my face, kid. I'm bored with you."

40

I'VE BEEN STARING AT IT FOR THE BETTER PART OF A HALF hour. The envelope. The last speck of hope I have to salvage anything from the wreckage of my life. As long as I don't open it—and don't see the take-out menus, or strip-club flyers, or unpaid parking tickets inside—there's still a chance that I haven't flushed three hundred dollars—along with everything dear to me—down the toilet.

I take a deep breath. I can't put this off forever. If it actually is the Monkey's Paw—or Baboon's Foot, or Simian's Hoof, or whatever—I'm going to have to get to work rehearsing it. And if it isn't—

"Screw it." I grab the envelope and tear it open. Folded white pages puff out. At least it's actual paper inside. I sit up and allow myself to get excited.

Then . . . I pull out the stack and riffle through the pages, fanning them out on my desk, their crisp blankness a giant middle finger to my naive trust in humanity.

My body starts to melt into the chair, my chest feeling heavy. I am such a sucker. How could I have not seen this coming? It was right there in front of my face. The guy knows how to check dice to see if they're weighted, for chrissake. The first thing he shows me is three-card monte. He sticks me with his diner tab. He convinces me to steal money from innocent people. He's a con man through and through. I bet he's not even the Dazzling Lazlo. His name probably really is Bob Smith and it was like his game of Bonneteau the whole time. He just let me fool myself.

I grab my face, wishing I could pull it off. I don't deserve to be a magician. Not if I can be so easily duped.

I snatch up the blank pages and am about to tear them into pieces when I hear Bob's words in my head: *I've presented the effect in a way that only you will understand. Which means you'll need to decipher it first.*

Right. Sure. I shuffle through the empty pages. Decipher *what*? There's nothing to decipher. That was just more misdirection. So I wouldn't open it at the diner. All the little bits of nibbles he dropped like bread crumbs for me to gobble up. "This is my pride and joy." "Need to protect it." "Might want to write a book."

Unless . . . what if it wasn't misdirection?

What if he actually did write it out in code?

What kind of code? Imaginary code? Invisible code? The kind you can't see?

I can almost hear the spark of connection in my brain. Omigod. Yes! The kind you can't see! The invisible kind! *Just like in the trick itself.* He wrote it out in invisible ink. The only way the Dazzling Lazlo would. Of course! Just in case I lost the envelope. Or got mugged on the way home. No one else would know what to look for.

No one else but me.

256

I sift through the pages yet again and, for the first time, notice they've been hand-numbered on the bottom right corner. OK. OK. That doesn't mean anything. Nothing to get aflutter over. They're just numbers.

Still.

I quickly sort the papers into the right order, then—

Smoke. I need smoke. I rummage through my desk drawer, find a tiny box of matches buried among a bunch of old key rings, spare change, charger cables, and a spilled bag of rock-hard Tootsie Rolls.

I fumble out a match, light it, and breathe in the vapors. I don't recommend this; it burns like hell and probably causes cancer. But it's a cool effect.

I stare at the top page, silently praying to the universe—*please, please, please let this work, please, please, please let this be what I think it is*—before releasing a billowy plume of smoke from my lips. The fog ripples over the paper, and as the misty gray tendrils wisp away, the faint impression of Bob's handwriting begins to materialize . . . just like the gimmick in the Monkey's Paw.

I start to read the note Bob has written to me, and with each word, a slow, intravenous drip of dread enters my bloodstream, replacing the adrenaline that had so recently been coursing there.

AND FOR MY LAST TRICK: A PREDICTION: I SEE GREAT THINGS FOR YOU, KID. YOU'RE TOO TALENTED TO COPY OTHER PEOPLE'S WORK. CREATE YOUR OWN SHIT. BONNETEAU!

I read the words again.

And again.

And again.

I start to laugh. It's a three-hundred-dollar fortune cookie! The thought makes me howl even louder, until the laughter morphs into heaving sobs.

And *because* I'm a glutton for punishment who never seems to learn his lesson, I waste even more of my precious life-hours blowing smoke on every one of the pages, only to find that they all say the exact same thing.

I crumple the pages in my fist and pound my desk over and over again. *Fuckfuckfuckfuckfuckfuckfuck!* Tears spill from my eyes and I don't even wipe them away. My chest spasms with each blubbing breath.

It's over. That's it. I'm done. There's no point in even auditioning now; nothing in my repertoire would even come close to beating Dani, and I honestly don't have the heart anymore to even try. I've just flushed everything down the drain. All my money, my future as a magician, any scrap of integrity I might have had left, and—absolutely worst of all—my friendship with Perry.

41

I TAKE A SIP OF MY TRIPLE ESPRESSO, HOPING IT WILL WAKE me up, as I wait in the ticket line at the Sage Hollow Dinner Theater. You'd think, being the son of the writers/directors/lead actors, I'd get my seat comped. But "ticket sales are ticket sales," Mom and Dad always say. And so I stand in the queue like I'm Joe Public, excited for an enchanted evening filled with fun, food, and frolicking cave people.

I take a labored breath, the very act of bringing air into my body having become a chore. I feel like I've been drugged. Drugged and beaten with a sock full of grapefruits. I can't remember the last time I had a full night's sleep. My mind simply refuses to shut down. It keeps trying to find solutions. Like a manic rat lost in a maze. Searching for ways I could still audition for the fantasy camp, ways I could make things up to Perry, and—maybe most unsettling of all—ways I could maybe get Dani to kiss me again.

I suck back the last, stomach-wincing dregs of my rocket fuel and step up to the box office booth, where I pass a ten and a five—my own, hard-earned ten and five—to the chalk-white, bored-looking, purple-haired goth girl behind the glass.

"One for *The Hominid's Lament*, please," I say, pulling my hand back from under the window.

"It's twenty-two fifty," the girl says, staring down at my money like it's a fresh turd.

I glance over at the price list, which has been edited with a piece of masking tape and Mom's distinct swooping numbers.

"Used to be fifteen," I say.

"This one's in 3-D," the cashier says, forcing a smile, smacking her gum. "Plus, there's baked Alaska in honor of the Bering Land Bridge." She looks past me at the one other customer waiting behind me. "Do you want a ticket or not? You're holding up my line."

I contemplate telling her that my parents happen to be the creators of *The Hominid's Lament*, but quickly decide that the fewer people who know this, the better.

I get my ticket, hand it to the seven-hundred-year-old usher, whose shrunken-apple head is nearly swallowed up by his ticket-taker fez, and make my way into the lobby. The Sage Hollow Dinner Theater looks like a bridesmaid's dress and smells like roast beef. The crowd tonight—and every night I've ever been here—is fairly geriatric. You need to watch your step so you don't accidentally kick out a cane and cause a domino effect.

I shift this way and that, pushing my way through the fog of old-people smells: carnation, chamomile, and camphor. According to the show program, the hominid is going to be lamenting for three and a half hours, with only one intermission. Which means I better empty my bladder before I take my seat.

The men's room is tight and narrow. There's not a lot of space between sinks and stalls. Especially when the entire audience tries to cram inside. There are white tiles everywhere except where Mom and Dad have placed blown-up "wacky" head shots of themselves: on the walls, the mirrors, and in the frames above the four urinals.

I step up to a black-and-white photo of Mom looking down and making a disappointed face. I don't like the connotation. I look away from her dissatisfaction and notice—for the first time—that I'm standing next to Perry.

Which, of course. Why not?

His eyes dart in my direction but just as quickly slide away.

It's awkward enough standing next to someone at a urinal—holding your most vulnerable of parts—at the best of times. Add a look of disapproval from your mother and your best friend giving you the cold shoulder, and it becomes almost unbearable.

I want to say something to Perry. Thank him for coming . . . despite everything. Tell him my parents will be touched. But he'll just be excruciatingly kind, mumble something about how he loves my parents and wouldn't miss it for the world.

Which would just make me feel even more miserable about myself than I already do. If that's even a possibility.

"Look, Quinn," Perry says, before I complete my slide down the slippery slope of self-loathing, "I just want you to know there are no hard feelings. I realize that I bear equal responsibility here."

Wait. *What?* No. Is he . . . apologizing to me? But why? He did nothing wrong. Oh God, please, someone just shove me into this urinal and flush me away.

"I mean, I'm not going to say I wasn't hurt." Perry sighs. "It's weird. I thought I knew the way things were, between you and me. Like, we always had each other's backs." He shrugs. "I guess . . . I feel like something was taken from me. Something really . . . special." He breathes long and deep. "But then, when I think back, I remember you talking to me about how you were feeling less-than. A few times, actually. And I just dismissed it out of hand, because it made no sense to me. So, for that, I'm very sorry."

"No," I manage to croak out. "You shouldn't . . . You didn't—"

"I did, though," Perry says, looking over at me. "You told me how you were feeling and I didn't listen. How is that being a good friend? In my defense, though, I just don't see what you see. I look at you and I see someone who's talented, creative, smart, and probably the hardest-working person I know."

"Please." I stare down at my feet, each kind word like a tiny sharp cut to my heart. "Don't. I can't . . . You didn't do anything wrong."

"You see," Perry says, "that's who you are—always wanting to shoulder all the blame."

I laugh at the ridiculousness of this statement. "That's not exactly . . . I mean, I *am* to blame. For all of it. So I *should* shoulder the blame."

Perry zips up and turns to look at me. "You're a good person, Quinn. And an even better magician. Which is why I want you to forget about all this. Just put it out of your head, let it go, and slay the audition this weekend. For both of us."

My heart deflates. Even after all this, Perry still has faith in me.

"Except that"—I swallow as I trail Perry to the sinks—"I'm not . . . doing the audition. Just so you know. Because . . . well, it's a long story, but the act I'd been planning to perform didn't . . . materialize. So I'm dropping out."

Perry stops mid-hand-wash and looks over at me, his expression dark and disapproving. "What do you mean you're dropping out? You're not dropping out. You want this more than anything. Those were your very words!"

"Except . . . that I am," I say. "Dropping out. I have to. I don't have an act. I didn't even put anything together. The effect I was planning on using . . . I can't use, so—"

"So you come up with something else." Perry shakes the water off his hands and grabs a single paper towel from the dispenser. "You still have a few days to put something together. You have a million tricks in your head. Or just use the act you designed for me."

"I can't, Perry. My heart's not in it anymore. Not after what I did to you. And after my unbeatable effect fell through. And after"—I hesitate to tell Perry this last part because he did warn me, but I say it anyway—"what happened with Dani."

"Dani?" Perry scrunches up his face "What happened with Dani?"

"Turns out she was working us all along," I say. "Everything you said—all your Spidey tingles—you were right. From the very beginning. She *did* get inside my head. Like you warned. She *did* encourage us to audition separately. Like you thought she had. And she *did* nudge you and Gwen back together. Just like you were worried about. Apparently Dani wants to win as bad as I do. And so she did things just as bad as I did."

Perry regards me. "All right. Fine. So you let yourself get played. You did some things you regret." He shrugs. "Big deal. You don't just give up on yourself. You get over it. Or, better yet, use it as even more motivation to win. Show her you're not just going to tuck tail and scamper away."

"I can't," I choke out. "I just . . . I can't."

"So you're just going to let Dani get away with it?"

"She's not . . ." I sigh. "She's already apologized, so . . . I don't know. I'm probably a sucker for believing her, but whatever, call it my own Spidey tingle. I think she was being genuine." I grab the back of my tensing neck. "Anyway, this isn't about her. I'm the bad guy here. I let her manipulate me. You warned me. I warned myself. Hell, *she* even warned me. But *I'm* the one who did what I did. Dani didn't make me *not* send that email. She didn't make me convince you to audition separately. She didn't make me talk to Gwen. And she's not making me quit the audition. *I* screwed that up. All on my own."

Perry's nodding slowly, like it's all starting to sink in now. What a miserable, disappointing person I really am. What a waste of time it's been being my friend all these years.

"All right, Quinn," he says, blowing out his cheeks. "It's your decision, I guess." He jerks his thumb over his shoulder. "I better get back to Gwen. She's going to be wondering what happened to me in here."

* * *

Dinner at the Sage Hollow is—unsurprisingly—overcooked every-thing. I'm having the Annie Get Your Gumbo (secretly hoping for a quick, anaphylactic death maybe?), but honestly, all the food at the buffet—the Meat Loaf in St. Louis, the Pierogi and Bess, and the West Side Stir-Fry—looked almost identical. Soft and brown. It wouldn't take much vigorous forking to turn this into a shrimp-and-sausage smoothie. Thankfully there's not a grain of salt to be found, so everything tastes like nothing and slides down without even the hint of flavor.

I'm sitting at a table for two, set for one. I don't know how other dinner theaters do it—I've only ever seen my parents' shows here—but the Sage Hollow is a semicircular room with four rows of partitioned tables surrounding the half-moon stage. The plastic checkerboard tablecloths and dusty-satin-roses-in-jam-jars center-pieces really give the place an air of sophistication.

I scan the theater, watching the gray hordes shuffling back and forth from the buffet like skeletal sugar ants. I'm looking for Perry, of course, and find him, mercifully sitting on the other side of the room, pouring some water into Gwen's glass.

Things did not go well at the urinals. That's not a sentence you ever want to have to say to yourself. However, in this case, it's the truth. Somehow I managed to cause Perry to go from forgiving me and wishing me well to being even more disappointed in me than before. If I'd known that was going to be the outcome, I would have kept my blubbering mouth shut.

My rib cage suddenly feels too small for my body. I don't know how I'm going to get through this evening. I want to be supportive of Mom and Dad, but what I *really* want to do is go to bed and crawl under my blankets.

"Last call for the buffet," a raspy woman hawks over the loud-speaker. "*The Hominid's Lament* will begin in ten minutes. Get your Bering Baked Alaska now. The Ice Age won't last forever."

Thank goodness for small favors. At least now I'll be able to hide my shame under the shelter of darkness. I push the mush around my plate until the lights go down and the curtain rises.

The rhythmic thump of a bass guitar fills the theater as a group of nearly naked actors stomp around the fluttering flames of a fabric fire. Thankfully clumps of caveman fur have been strategically applied to all nips, nuts, and cracks because—you know—we're all still eating here.

The Neanderthals begin to shout and hoot in harmony. "*Woof!* Huh! *Woof!* Hah! *Woof!* Hoh!"

Into this cacophonous mix stumbles Dad, wearing what looks like a hair bikini and dragging the severed leg of some prehistoric mammal. He stands center stage, tears a piece of pastrami from the leg with his teeth, chews and swallows, then starts to sing an *actual* hominid's lament. A melancholy tune about living in a small village where there is a distinct shortage of viable Neanderthal partners. "*Life's looking grim, when the pickins are slim. Should I just give in, commit the ultimate sin? Search outside my tribe, for an interspecies bride?*"

The show is absolutely ridiculous and should not work. *At all.* Not as dinner theater. Not as Jean Auel fan fiction. Not even as a children's puppet show.

But it *does* work. Because the songs are good. And the performers are all totally committed to their characters. Everyone is taking it seriously. When it so clearly is just absolutely ludicrous.

I don't know. Maybe I'm biased because I can relate to so many of the things being laid out onstage. *Obviously.* Since my parents stole whole hunks of my life. Not the love story, of course, but many of the more painful details. The best friend who everyone adores. The violent waves of nausea that hit our main character every time he talks to a pretty girl. The cantaloupe masturbation joke. And, let's not forget, the upcoming forest fire. But it's more than that. A quick glance around at all the hanging jaws, wide eyes, and frozen forks, and you can tell the entire audience is hooked. Totally transfixed by the cast's infectious enthusiasm.

I watch as Mom's and Dad's cave lovers are about to kiss for the very first time. And that's when it dawns on me: they love doing this. Mom and Dad are doing this . . . just for fun. Not as a profession; they make their actual livings selling houses. But because they love it. I've always assumed that they were frustrated by their lots in life, but maybe that's not the case. I don't even know if they ever actually wanted to be professional actors. Even if they did, it doesn't seem to faze them, how things have turned out.

Which is where I went completely sideways. I wanted to be a professional magician so desperately, I was willing to take a match to everything. Sure, maybe I'll be one of the lucky few and become a headliner in Las Vegas someday. But if I don't, it doesn't mean I have to stop doing what I love. Or loving the people that I do.

For three and a half hours I'm transported to a forest in Eurasia, watching Finn the Neanderthal stumble and bumble his way through his star-crossed life, making poor choice after poor choice until, in a final act of selfishness, he destroys the one thing that he loved more than anything else.

Now, you'd think watching your pitiful life being exploited for a Stone Age musical might make you want to take a knife to your throat. Or, you know, join a monkery. But I'm on my feet the moment the lights come up and Mom and Dad come out for their curtain call, applauding until my palms sting.

I'm applauding for them. For their success. For the obvious joy on their faces.

But I'm applauding for me, too. For coming to a realization so obvious it kind of hurts a little.

I forgot that performing magic was supposed to be *fun*.

I look over at Perry and Gwen, standing by their table, clapping and cheering. Perry's right. I am giving up on myself. And yeah, maybe I did cause some wreckage along the way.

But I'm lucky.

Because I haven't literally torched everything.

And I still have a chance to fix things.

42

Six cans of Red Bull, three cold showers, and eight hours later, I peel my rug-stippled, drool-soaked cheek from the bedroom floor. I sit up, notice I'm wearing only my boxers, and take in the snowstorm of papers that litter every surface, including several stuck to my sweaty skin.

Bob's words are still echoing around in my head, like they have been all night long. *And for my last trick: a prediction: I see great things for you, kid. You're too talented to copy other people's work. Create your own shit. Bonneteau!*

When I'd first blown the smoke on the pages and read his words, I wanted to crush the papers and shove them down Bob's throat. But when I was racking my brain last night, using his mostly blank pages to jot down ideas, one of Bob's words popped out at me: PREDICTION.

Don't ask me why—I've done a million prediction effects before—but for some reason, seeing that word at that specific time, something clicked.

* * *

"I did it," I say, shaking the sheaf of pages in my fist. "I finally figured it out."

Perry squints at the sunrise, his weary face framed by his partially opened front door. "What are you talking about?" He twists a fist into his red-rimmed eye.

"Here. Look." I uncrumple the papers, showing him my drawings. My jaw quivers and my hands are shaking, which could have as much to do with the Red Bull as the adrenaline coursing through my veins. "After my parents' show, I thought about what you said. About not giving up on myself. And, more importantly, not giving up on us." I push the words past the swell of emotion inside. "I stayed up all night, reread all of Houdini's escape techniques, and nearly sprained my brain, but I think I did it . . ." I flutter the pages at him, hoping he'll take them. "It's the milk-can trick, Perry! I finally figured something out! I'm calling it the Milkman's Revenge, and we can use it for the audition. You and me. Like we should have done from the start."

Perry crosses his arms and stares at the pages. "Was this Dani's idea? For us to get back together? Now that she's apologized she thinks we ought to go on as a team and . . . what? Get disqualified because teams really *aren't* allowed?"

"I haven't even talked to Dani," I say. "Look, I totally get why you don't trust her. Up until last night I still had my doubts about her apology. But then, while I was sweating over these plans, drinking way more caffeine than is FDA recommended and gnawing on my thumb like a rabbit with its foot in a trap, *it hit me.* Dani has a tell."

"A tell?" Perry says, clearly not buying this. "What kind of tell?"

"She picks at her cuticle whenever she's feeling vulnerable. I can't believe I missed it, but it's so obvious now! I saw her do it when she was talking to her parents, and when she was apologizing, and . . . several other times." *Like the time she spontaneously kissed me.* Although now's probably not the time to bring this up. "Anyway, none of that even matters. This has nothing to do with her. Seriously." I hold up my papers. "This is about you and me."

Perry's shoulders sag. "I don't know, Quinn. If you want to do it, you should do it. But I'm just not feeling it anymore." He starts to back out of the doorway.

My lungs are constricting, and I need to get the words out before my air is choked off: "I really am sorry, Perry. I blew it. I took you for granted, and you're the last person in the world I would want to do that to. You're the kindest, most generous, most talented, most amazing person I've ever met. I admire you more than you'll ever know. But sometimes . . . it's like I've told you . . . I just feel . . . low-rent. Standing beside you. Like I'm a ball of cat-clawed yarn and you're this . . . gorgeous cashmere sweater that everyone wants to cuddle with."

"I know I keep saying this to you, but that's not reality." Perry laughs hollowly. "Jeez, Quinn, I mean, come on. You *create* stuff. Make things up out of nothing." He snatches the pages from my hands and riffles through them. "Look at this. It's incredible." He shakes my pages. "Sure, yeah, I can follow these instructions. But *you* wrote them. I could never do that. It's like . . . you're a master chef devising all these incredible creations and . . . I'm a dexterous line cook following someone else's recipes."

"*What?*" I stare at him, trying to find the lie in his eyes. "No. You're just screwing with me. Everything you do, you do amazingly."

"Yeah, everything I practice," Perry says. "Everything I can see someone else do first. I'm a great parrot, for sure. But do you have any idea how many times I wanted to be the one who came to the table with a mind-blowing trick that I just thought up out of the blue?" He exhales heavily and makes a face. "I tried. That's for sure. You should see all the half-filled notebooks I've got hidden under my bed. It's a wonderful collection of magic tricks you've seen a million times before." He looks at me, dead serious. "You're an original, Quinn." He holds up my notes, raises his eyebrows. "*That's* something to be jealous of."

Perry hands me back my papers. I stare at them. "You're serious."

"As serious as a library late fee," he says, which, if you know Perry, is about as serious as it gets.

"Holy crap," I say. "I had no idea."

"That's only because you're not paying attention," Perry says. "How many times have I told you how incredible your tricks are? Why do you think I didn't even want to audition without you?"

"Sheesh," I say, trying to process this shift in the Matrix. "If that's true, then . . . Wow. I really haven't been paying attention. At all."

I look at my friend and smile at him.

Whoa! Speaking of not paying attention, I'm just realizing now that Perry looks like crap—hair disheveled, eyes puffy, cheeks sheet-creased—and Perry *never* looks like crap. You know when you watch a TV show and the actors wake up in full makeup with perfectly coiffed hair and you're like, "Come on, that's just not realistic"? Yeah, well, you stop thinking that after you've slept over at Perry's house.

"Hey, man, don't take this the wrong way," I say, gesturing at him. "But you sort of look like shit."

Perry laughs wearily and pinches the bridge of his nose. "You're not the only one who hasn't slept." He looks at me. "Gwen and I broke up last night."

"What?" I say. "No. Why?"

Perry shrugs. "It was your parents' show, man. It really moved us. Gwen and I talked about it all night long. The ideas, the themes. How you can destroy the things you love with too much love. And we realized that our relationship just burns too bright. We don't want it to burn down everything else in our lives. And so . . . we hugged, we kissed, we wrote each other farewell poems, and"—Perry forces a smile, his eyes filling—"we said goodbye." He clears his throat and runs a hand through his thick, tangled hair. "Anyway, like I said, it was a rough night. I'm actually going to bail on school today. If this doesn't qualify as a legitimate sick day, I don't know what does."

"I'll skip, too," I say. "We'll hang like old times. Play a little *Dawn of Destiny*. Watch some street magic on YouTube. You could teach me how to unicycle." I smile, then shrug awkwardly. "Or, you know, we could just . . . talk about stuff."

"What about your trick?" Perry says. "Don't you need to start prepping it?"

"Screw the trick." I start to fold up the papers. "I was only excited about it because it was something we could do together. That's all I want, is us . . . back together. As friends. Whatever we're doing."

Perry stares at me, shakes his head, then snatches the papers from my hands. "The Milkman's Revenge. *That's* what we're doing." He unfolds the pages and studies the plans. "This is incredible. It's time the world knows how great you are."

Maybe it's the overdose of caffeine, but I suddenly feel my chest getting tight. "How great *we* are. You and me. Quinn and Perry."

He smiles. "You and me. Quinn and Perry."

And with that, my best friend steps to one side and ushers me into his home.

43

THE LIGHTS FLICK ON AND OFF INSIDE THE BELTWAY
Theater, signaling everyone to take their seats. I peer out from the
wings to check the turnout, which is not enormous by any stretch.
Clusters of people here and there. Friends and family of the two
dozen magicians performing today.

There's Mom and Dad, shuffling down the aisles, working the
crowd with Sage Hollow flyers and real estate business cards.

Eight of the seats, front row, center stage, have been reserved
for the judges, who have just started filing in. Six men, two women.
All of them dressed in various shades of starch and charcoal, their
hair identically slicked back with product, eyes cold and distant, like
a group of spellbound cult members. Not the kind of people who
bend the rules lightly.

Normally the sight of such stark authority—judges who could
make or break my magical future—would make my stomach want
to escape its confines. But not today. Today I'm feeling pretty good.
A little anxious, sure, but mostly pretty good. Because everything
has gone smoothly so far. Ed came through lending us his milk can.

He was quite excited when I showed him the Milkman's Revenge, which was a real confidence booster. And now I'm just hanging out with my best friend. Having a good time. About to perform one of the best acts I've ever devised. Sure, it's a little more hastily rehearsed than I would have liked. And maybe performing it as a team means we get disqualified. Doesn't matter anymore. Because Perry and I have never been closer. Have never had more fun putting together a performance. And for that, it's all been worth it.

"You guys are here!" Dani's excited voice startles me. I spin around to see her standing there, smiling at me. "I just saw Perry heading to the bathroom." She's wearing a long blue-and-white Mrs. Claus outfit, complete with fake fur fringe and baby-blue gloves. It's a good call. The sparkly sequins will be distracting; plus, lots of pockets and sagging sleeves to hide things in. She grabs her gloved thumb and starts working on the nail below the fabric. "I'm so glad. I was worried I might have . . . really screwed everything up."

"It's all good," I say. "You go knock 'em dead out there today."

"You, too." Dani darts in and gives me a quick, bashful hug. "I mean it. Break a leg." She pulls back, a worried expression on her face. "But not in, like, the literal sense," she clarifies in a rush. "In the theater sense. You know, for *good luck*." She bites her lip. "Shit. You're not supposed to say that. Sorry. Crap. I didn't mean it. It's not a mess-with-your-head thing. I swear."

I laugh. "It's cool. I'm not superstitious."

"Listen, I really want to fix things between us." She looks at me shyly, her hands back to fiddling. "And . . . I was wondering. Maybe . . . we can be friends—*real* friends—when all this is over.

That is, of course"—she smiles mischievously, puts one hand on her hip, and waggles a finger at me—"once I'm back from the magic fantasy camp."

Before I can say anything, she turns and hurries off, leaving me with a goofy grin on my face.

The lights dim and old-fashioned music begins to crackle over the speakers. A piano playing too fast, like in a silent movie, or an Old West saloon. Just then a firm, sure hand rests on my shoulder.

"Here we go. Let's see what we're up against." It's Perry, standing right by my side. The warmth of his presence like a cup of hot cocoa on a rainy day. He's still hoping we'll win this thing. Even though I've told him it's the last thing on my mind. Having said that, with Perry on your team, you never know what might happen.

The old-timey music starts to fade out and the house lights go dark as Colonel Sanders's withered twin brother shuffles onto the stage, his much-too-large white tuxedo threatening to slide off his stick frame.

"Hello . . ." the ancient emcee croaks, then looks down at the index cards in his shaky hands. "Magicians and magicians' friends and family. Welcome to the Magic Society of America's Masters of Magic Fantasy Camp auditions." He reaches into his pocket, takes out a handkerchief, blows his nose far too close to the microphone, then looks at his cards again and starts to read like a third grader giving an oral book report. "Buckle up. For an afternoon. Of mystery and magic. Let's all give a round. Of applause . . . to our talented contestants." He slowly shoots out an arm, nearly knocking over the mic stand in the process. "Let the show . . . *begin!*"

* * *

Forty-five minutes into the auditions and I am flabbergasted. Seriously, is this the best our great state has to offer? It's sad, really. Do these kids not practice in front of a mirror? Or *ever*? What the hell?

So far we've seen a kid with dreadlocks accidentally light his hair on fire, watched a girl with a giraffe's neck nearly choke on the handcuff key she was hiding in her cheek, and witnessed a guy with the rosiest cheeks I've ever seen fling a Rubik's Cube off the stage, hitting one of the male judges smack in the tackle box.

Onstage now, a tall, bespectacled kid, wearing an actual, star-adorned wizard costume, lets his pointy hat slip from his hands. The hat makes a dull *thud* when it hits the stage. The kid stands frozen for several seconds, staring down in horror at the rounded, motionless, satiny lump lying on the floor.

"Benedict Cumberbunny!" the kid cries, scooping up the hat and its contents and storming off the stage.

Everyone waits, like this might be part of the act. Like there's a punch line coming. But we're left with nothing. Just the horrible memory of that muffled thump and our vivid imaginations.

I can't believe the talent level is so low. We have nearly ten million people living in our state. Surely we can breed better magicians than this.

"Next up," comes the croaky, disembodied voice of Wendell the Astounding, our less-than-masterful master of ceremonies. We haven't seen him in the flesh since his opening remarks, the shuffle onstage apparently the extent of his physical activity for the day. "This should be an interesting . . . performance." The PA system at the Beltway is crackling loudly, but you can make out most of what's being said. "Dani Darling. In a holiday. Mash-up entitled. Um, well"—Wendell clears his throat and reads—"I'll let our performer do the introduction. Ladies. And gentlemen. Dani Darling!"

Perry and I share a look—like, now the real fun starts—as we give her a round of applause from the wings.

Nat King Cole's version of "The Christmas Song" begins playing over the speakers.

"Most of your favorite Christmas songs"—Dani's prerecorded voice intones over the music—"were written by Jews. 'Do You Hear What I Hear?' 'Silver Bells,' 'Winter Wonderland,' 'White Christmas,' 'Let It Snow,' and yes, even *this* most holiday of holiday songs. Written—most ironically—by a Jewish man and sung—most *iconically*—by a Black man. In that spirit I bring you the all-inclusive holiday mash-up *A Very Hannu-Kwanzaa-Christmas!*"

Dani steps out onto the stage in her flowing, shimmering Mrs. Claus outfit, holding a round pedestal table and a large, empty menorah that she wafts around in time to the music.

Perry and I smile at each other. We already know it's going to be good. Simply by the way she's strutting around the stage like she owns it.

Dani places the table down center stage and sets the menorah in the middle of it. A pedestal table is a brave choice. Not a lot of places to stash things. Which is the whole point. It puts the audience at ease.

She marches around the table, motioning at it silently. It looks like Dani is going to perform without any patter. Another brave choice. Now everyone, including the judges, will be hyperfocused on her hands and gestures.

Dani stands beside the table and waves her hands in front of her face, slowly and deliberately. Then, in one swift move, she produces a string of eight unlit mini Christmas lights.

I glance over at the judges and see some subtle, impressed nodding. They *should* be impressed. Dani's the first decent magician they've seen all day.

I turn back to the stage and see her showing the audience that the wires are frayed on both ends of the string. No plug. No source of electricity.

She strolls toward the audience and stops right in front of the judges. Grasping the ragged ends of the cord, Dani pulls her hands outward, tensing the wire, the mini bulbs facing every which way.

She smiles and drops one end of the wire, and all the bulbs light up green. Then they all change to red. Then all to black. And finally to a flickering mixture of green, red, and black—the colors of Kwanzaa and the Pan-African flag.

All of a sudden Nat King Cole is silenced and Ginger Minj's "Christma-Hannu-Kwanzaa-Ka" starts to dance over the PA, the Crossdresser for Christ singing her hilariously inclusive take on the holiday season.

Dani does a little choreographed dance, swinging the string of lights this way and that. She stops dead center stage and drops one end of the lights again, letting them dangle down. She grabs the top of the wire with her other hand and, in one motion, drags her palm down over the mini bulbs, turning each one into a much larger glass version of the Kwanzaa colors.

"Nice," Perry says, nodding like we're back at the magic shop all over again. "How'd she do that?"

"I have an idea," I say, feeling the same awe, wonder, and attraction as the first time I laid eyes on her. "But I'm probably wrong."

Dani smiles at the audience, transfers the string of larger lights to her other hand, gives it a little shake, and all the colors change again. First to all blue. Then all yellow. Then all orange. Then all white.

Then a glorious flickering mix once more.

I actually gasp. It's a fantastic effect and should probably win her the spot at fantasy camp. *Unless . . .*

Unless Perry's right and they don't actually disqualify us. Then, well, maybe we do have a shot. Because, while Dani's performance has been inspired so far, unless she actually turns into a giant, colorful lightbulb herself and flies over the audience, I think ours might be just that much better.

I track Dani onstage as Nat King Cole crashes the party once again, cutting Ginger right off, "The Christmas Song" swelling to a jingly crescendo. And just as Nat is apologizing for saying what's been said so many times, in so many ways, Dani steps over to the empty menorah, waving the string of lights as she goes.

I have no idea how she's going to wrap this up, but I've got a fistful of Pop Rocks in my stomach anticipating what's next. Because what if she literally does turn into a lightbulb onstage? And just like that, I've forgotten Dani is auditioning and I'm just enjoying a professional magician killing it.

Dani swings the string of illuminated lights in back of the table and behind the menorah. She holds up a blue-gloved hand and counts off each long swing of the cord with her fingers.

One.

Two.

Three.

All at once, the bulbs disappear from the wire and the menorah now has nine flames of varying colors—blue, red, green, white, yellow, black, orange—dancing from the nine silver lamp cups.

It's jaw-dropping. Truly magical in every sense.

The audience breaks out in enthusiastic applause.

I turn to the judges, who are frantically scribbling things down in their notebooks as Dani takes her bow. Her act was so good.

Now I just hope Perry and I can give her a run for her money. I mean, I've forgiven her and everything, and yeah, I'm only doing this for fun now, but I wouldn't mind showing Dani up a little. Sure, we might be disqualified, and sure, Dani might win, but if we can actually pull this effect off, even she will have to acknowledge who the best magician really is.

44

IT'S BECOMING INCREASINGLY CLEAR THAT THIS IS GOING to be a two-horse race. Seriously. We haven't even performed yet and that fact alone makes us better than Hoo-Hah the Conjuring Clown; Piper Parasol, the girl with the magic umbrella; and the Amazing "Butterfingers," who is currently being hurried offstage, blood spilling from the side of his head where the tip of his ear used to be.

"Not to worry, folks," Wendell soothes over the PA. "Please remain calm. Mr. Butterfield . . . will be just fine. It's not the whole ear. Just a bit of the lobe. And we've found it. We think." There's some muffled shouting and an agonized groan, followed by Wendell the Astounding clearing his throat into the microphone. "On a . . . *completely different note*, if there happens to be a nurse or . . . an ear surgeon in the audience. We'd love it if you could join us backstage." He exhales and ruffles some papers. "Now. Onto our final. Performer. Hailing from the lovely. Town of Fernwood. With a gritty. Reboot of a Houdini. Classic." Wendell sniffs loudly. "Please welcome. Our next magician. Quinn Purcell."

Perry claps me on the shoulder. "Here we go."

We decided not to tell them in advance that we would be performing as a team. Just in case they wouldn't let us. I take a deep, calming breath and follow Perry out onstage.

There is a murmur from the crowd, some leaning and consulting from the judges, presumably prompted by Perry's unannounced appearance.

I look out into the audience, and there—dead center, third row—are Gwen and Carter, sitting together and waving excitedly, wearing identical TEAM QUINN AND PERRY T-shirts. I flash them a smile. According to their respective social media feeds, they are most definitely not dating again but remain very close friends. We'll see how long that lasts. I'm just happy to see them both happy, and still breathing.

Perry stands up tall, pulls his shoulders back, and approaches the audience, leaping into action before the judges have a chance to throw us off the stage.

"Ladies and gentlemen! Boys and girls! Esteemed judges!" Perry strides around the stage, beaming like a game show host, his arms wide, as though he's embracing the entire Beltway Theater. Which, as we have learned, he would, if he could. "Welcome, everyone"— Perry gestures at the wings, and all eyes turn to watch as the large, gleaming steel milk can is wheeled onstage—"to the wonderful world of mystery and magic."

45

THE WHOLE THING GOES BY IN AN AMAZING BLUR. LIKE A
wonderful dream on fast-forward. I barely have time to register it all.

We use a beach ball to randomly select a large, muttonchopped
volunteer from the audience. Then Perry gets me all tied up and into
a laundry bag, just like with the Drill of Death. This time, though,
Perry jokingly tapes a Sharpie to my forehead. A marker that I will
presumably use to make my prediction, once I am holding my
breath, submerged underwater, and sealed inside the tight quarters
of the milk can.

Perry and I work together like a well-oiled machine. Once the
curtain barrier is pulled in front of the milk can, I escape with ease.
And when Perry pulls the screen aside—allowing me to sneak off
backstage behind it—I grab a new Sharpie and a slightly dampened
laundry bag, write down the volunteer's prediction on the bag
(which Perry so thoughtfully hid inside the curtain screen when he
pulled it aside), and race to the back of the theater.

As soon as Muttonchops and Perry unlock all the padlocks on
the milk can—revealing that there's no one inside—I leap up from

the back of the auditorium with the volunteer's favorite animal—
THE ARCTIC NARWHAL—scrawled on the laundry bag.

There is an enormous amount of applause as I drip water onto the theater floor, holding the laundry bag high above my head, the entire audience, including the judges, twisted around to see me.

I can't tell from here if the judges are pleased or perturbed.

And frankly I don't really care.

That was the best performance Perry and I have ever done in our lives.

We had a complete and total blast.

And I wouldn't trade it for all the magic fantasy camps in the world.

46

"I NEED TO GET MORE LITIGIOUS PARENTS," I SAY AS PERRY, Dani, and I drag our prop bags through the doors of Heritage Acres. "The worst I could threaten the judges with would be an unflattering portrayal in my parents' next musical."

"It's hard to fault them," Perry says. "The Amazing Butterfield really did need the most help of all of us."

"Magically *and* medically," Dani adds, wincing.

I shoot them both a look. "I'm sure Butterfield, Butterfield, and Butterfield will be more than happy to negotiate medical expenses into the settlement."

Once Andrew "Butterfingers" Butterfield was named the winner of the fantasy camp scholarship in what was clearly a desperate attempt to avoid a lawsuit, Dani, Perry, and I ended up laughing so hard and so long, the whole thing turned into a sort of healing balm for all of us.

Besides, it was hard to be upset about the outcome when I'd experienced one of the best nights of magic in my life. The Milkman's Revenge was an unmitigated success, each moment playing out as perfectly as if Perry and I had been practicing it for months rather than days. And the night was made all the sweeter by the fact that Dani seemed as genuinely impressed by our trick as we'd been by hers.

"We have to sign in first," I say as we approach the reception desk.

The lobby is humid with the sweet-waxy stink of lilies, the telltale sign there'll be a portrait sitting on an easel outside the Bistro.

"Personally," Dani says, adjusting her gaucho hat, "I think we dodged a bullet. Or, in Andrew's case, a bowie knife. Seriously. If what we saw yesterday was the caliber of magicians attending their camp, I have to tell you, I like our independent magic fantasy camp"—she gestures at the three of us—"heaps and oodles better."

That was the plan the three of us came up with after the auditions: get together every day, like we really are at camp, perform wherever we can, and dedicate ourselves to becoming better magicians. Teaching one another, practicing together, sharing ideas, all for the fun of it. Con Man Bob would be very disappointed in me.

"Hey, I just had a thought," Dani says, smiling as she signs our names into the ledger. "If we ever go on the road together as a trio, we'd be Perry, Dani, and Quinn. PDQ. How lit would that look on a Las Vegas marquee?"

"I like it," Perry says. "PDQ: The Quickest Hands in the West. It's got a nice ring to it."

"*Orrrrr*," I say, "what about Q-PiD? Magicians of Love. Like Cupid but spelled differently. That way it's *Quinn*, Perry, and Dani. As it should be."

"Do you really want to be known as the Magicians of Love?" Dani asks, her eyes narrowed. "I'm sensing a lot of porn memes."

"Now, now, kids," Perry says. "Let's not bicker over the name of an act that doesn't even exist yet. Let's perform our first show together and see how that goes."

The three of us make our way toward the Bistro, my stomach plummeting as soon as I see the picture on the easel under the words CELEBRATION OF LIFE.

"Oh no," I say, staring at a very handsome photo of a much younger Mrs. Swinick, smiling big and waving at the camera.

"You knew her?" Dani asks.

"Yeah," I say, fighting back emotion. "I did. I liked her. A lot." I peer at the plaque underneath the picture. "Gloria Swinick," I say, learning her given name for the first time. "She was plucky. Spoke her mind. Maybe a little too much sometimes, but still—"

"Oh yeah?" Dani smiles. "I can already tell I would have liked this Gloria Swinick. I wish I could have met her."

"The Bistro's being used," Perry says, regarding the dusty shuffle of residents milling about the cafeteria, each carrying a half glass of watered-down red wine. "The memorial's not over for another hour."

"Must have been sudden," I say, swiping at my sniffly nose. "Let me see if I can find Margie."

I wade into the fray of tottering seniors, buffeted by the waves of odors—cologne, urine, Pine-Sol, cabbage—until I finally find Margie. She's talking to a man wearing a long black coat and carrying a fancy cane. Margie shakes the dapper gentleman's hand and— if my lipreading isn't too rusty—offers her condolences.

The man bows, puts on a bowler hat, turns on his heel, and walks my way. He catches my eye as he passes—

And my heart nearly shoots from my chest.

Holy shit. Holy shit. Holy shit.

Was that—? The crinkles of his eyes. *Was that—?* The mole below his ear. *Could that have been—?*

No. No way. Not a chance.

"Who was that?" I say, charging at poor Margie, who takes a startled step backward. "That man. Who was he?"

"Mrs. Swinick's ex-husband?" she says, her tone bewildered. "Came for the service?"

"Her *ex-husband*?" I twist over my shoulder, watching the man heading toward the lobby. "The magician? Who she despised?"

Margie shrugs. "You explain relationships to me. She may have hated him, but he brought her flowers every week."

Holy crap. If that really *was* her ex-husband, and he really *is* a magician, and it really *was* Bob from the diner . . . then maybe he really was the Dazzling Lazlo after all.

"Did he have a different last name?" I ask, thinking Mrs. Swinick would definitely have ditched the surname after the divorce. "Was it Lazlo? Think. It's important. Was his first name Robert?"

Margie shrugs. "I just called him Mr. Swinick." She sighs. "If it's so important, why don't you go ask him yourself?"

I swivel my head and see he's already out of sight.

"Hey! Wait! Mr. Swinick! Hold up!" I run as fast as I can, ripping around the corner, looking every which way.

I rush into the lobby and watch as the front doors slide shut behind someone: Bob Smith? Bob the Con Man? Bob Swinick? *Robert Lazlo?*

Are they all the same person? Could Con Man Bob really clean up this well? Or is my subconscious just playing tricks on me?

I bolt toward the doors like my life depends on it. The second I'm outside, I scan the area for a blue Mercury. If that boat is here, then at least it's one mystery solved.

I look this way. Look that way. But the parking lot is deserted. Not a soul in sight.

No Mr. Swinick.

No Bob Smith.

No Robert Lazlo.

No Mercury Grand Marquis.

Nothing.

Just a one-legged seagull, standing in the handicapped spot, pecking at a piece of pink sprinkle donut.

"So, seems like our show's been postponed till next week," I say when I rejoin Perry and Dani by the front desk. "What do you guys want to do?"

"You know what I always say?" Dani offers as the three of us make our way back outside. "If you're not performing, you better be practicing to perform."

"Well, my friend"—Perry claps me on the shoulder—"I guess we better get working on making Drill of Death a three-hander."

"*Oh.*" Dani perks up like a meerkat on the scent of dinner. "I like that. What if Perry strapped *both* our heads to the drill press?"

"Yes." Perry points at Dani. "I could stack your heads up like blocks. One on top of the other." He taps his lip, thinking. "Of course, one of you would have to stand on a stepladder to make the physics work."

An excited flutter stirs in my belly, my imagination sparking to life. "We could even amp up the wow factor a bit. Not only chaining both of us to the drill press, *but to each other as well.*"

"Yes!" Dani bellows. "Total fire. I love it! Vegas, look out. Here comes PDQ!"

"Or, you know," I say, shrugging, "Q-PiD: The Magicians of Love."

"Yeah, I think you can probably let that one die," Perry says, laughing.

Just then a car backfires behind us, causing the three of us to jump.

I spin around, expecting to see a flash of the familiar blue Mercury. But the car has already disappeared around the corner.

It can't be him. No way. *Probably just a coincidence.* I check over my shoulder one last time as the three of us cross the street.

Probably.

A cool breeze brushes my hair as we stroll down the sidewalk, side by side. The smell of fresh-cut grass, the start of summer, fills my nostrils. I feel light, invigorated, a bounce in my step as we head home to do the thing that I love most in the world.

Making magic.

Acknowledgments

Every novel poses its own challenges. This one did not disappoint in that area. Be thankful, as I am, that I have an incredible team behind me, doing their best to make sure I don't look any more foolish than I insist on. In this particular case you have been spared a subplot involving a rat-infested backyard; a main character's slow, depressing demise; and a high school football team inexplicably practicing in the spring.

For all that and more, my dearest thanks go to:

My wife for life, Meg, who fills my world with light and joy. Every day she inspires me to be a better writer and, more importantly, a better person.

Kaylan Adair, my tireless and infinitely patient (at least that's how I picture her) editor, whose intelligence and creativity make the marathon of writing a book that much easier.

Jodi Reamer, my phenomenal agent, whose advice, encouragement, and clear head help keep me sane.

Everyone at Candlewick Press. I've said it before, but I absolutely love being a part of the Candlewick family.

Matt Roeser, for creating the most magical of covers.

Maggie Deslaurier and Dan Larsen, my eagle-eyed copyeditors, for making sure this book was published with all its commas, italics, and sports seasons tucked away in the right places.

Chris Conroy and Ron Harner, for all their punny suggestions and for tolerating my frenzied texting in the midst of all my rewrites.

And of course, Mom, Dad, Robert, Camille, Emily, David, Amy Z., Will, Amy F., Ory, Theo, Chris and Darlene Hobbs, Ken Freeman, and everyone else who continues to put up with me and my possibly-sometimes-inappropriate sense of humor. There's just too much inspiration, love, and laughter to detail.